FINAL SERENADE

The Encore Book One

N.N. BRITT

Cover Design by Cat at TRC Designs

Cover Photography by Wander Aguiar

Edited by Shannan Saunders

Copyedited by R.C. Craig

Due to strong language and other adult content, this book is intended for mature audience only.

❀ Created with Vellum

Foreword

Some people come into your life when you expect them the least but need them the most. You may not even know it yet, but as time passes, you start to realize that not a single person you meet during your journey is there just by coincidence. All these people enter your life and stay or leave for a reason.

This book is the sum of what I've learned and what I've gained from those who've made it into my life and left their imprint. There are some of you who may not be listed here by name, but if you're in my life, you are among those who've made a difference in it.

First and foremost, I'd like to thank my mom, my dad, and my sister.

Second, I'd like to thank my editors, Shannan and Renee, who have been so instrumental during the writing process. Cassy and Frankie's story deals with a variety of sensitive topics, including serious health issues, and I couldn't have given those issues justice if not for these ladies.

As always, many thanks to my beta readers, Amanda, Naadira, and Sarah.

Thanks to my assistant Tiffany.

Thanks to those who answered my questions, who provided insightful feedback, who shared my posts on social media, or simply chatted with me in the middle of the night.

Lastly, I'd like to thank my buddy and partner in crime, Chip, for the amazing years we've shared. I'm humbled to be your friend, and I'm forever grateful for all the shows, all the laughs, and all the long late-night drives.

Cassy and Frankie's story is a combination of my own experience, my endless love of music, and countless hours of research. I've tried to be as accurate as possible with certain medical information. Any mistakes are my own.

I hope you fall in love with Cassy and Frankie as much as I have.

Thank you so much and happy reading!

P.S. If you haven't had a chance to read *Adrenaline 1999*, Frankie's story that's available for free, you can snag it here: https://BookHip.com/XJBSSW

XOXO

Prologue

Hall Affinity is an American hard rock band from Los Angeles, California, formed in 2001.

The current lineup consists of vocalist Frankie Blade, guitarist Dante Martinez, bassist Johnny Z, and drummer Carter Valentine. The band has released four studio albums, accumulating sales of more than 50 million records worldwide, including 23 million records in the United States, making them one of the world's best-selling rock bands of all time.

Hall Affinity is known for its diverse rock sound and dramatic imagery on its album covers and for its experimental musical style that pushes the boundaries of modern rock music.

The band secured their first recording deal with Red Eye Records in 2003 and subsequently released their debut album, *Adrenaline Lane,* in 2004, which broke *Billboard's Top 200* in under six months. The band's second album, *Hollow Heart Dream,* (2006) marked a dramatic change in style, incorporating influences from classic '90s grunge sounds. It peaked at number one on *Billboard 200* in December 2006.

Hollow Heart Dream was the last album Hall Affinity released via Red Eye Records. It was also the last album to feature the original band's drummer Quin Kelly, who was replaced by Carter Valentine. In May 2007, the band secured a five-album record deal with KBC Universal and started recording their highly anticipated third studio album. The album release, however, was postponed to mid-2008 due to creative tensions within the band. Blade and Martinez had a temporary falling out, which, after a four-month hiatus, caused the record label to step in and legally pressure both band members to work out their differences and finish the album by March 2008.

Breathe Crimson climbed the charts to number one in under a week after the day of its release. Its lead single, "Ambivalent," the band's most commercially successful single to date, won a Grammy Award for Best Hard Rock Performance. After two years of extensive touring, Hall Affinity returned into the studio to start working on their fourth album *Chasing Memories*, which was released in fall of 2011, earning the band another Grammy.

Hall Affinity was inducted into Rock & Roll Hall of Fame in 2012, the first year of its eligibility.

On July 10, 2012, lead singer Frankie Blade was involved in a serious motorcycle accident, resulting in a temporary disbanding of Hall Affinity. In November 2012, the band's PR representative issued an official statement about Blade's physical condition preventing the singer from continuing as a lead vocalist of Hall Affinity. The record label and Blade's bandmates, under pressure from displeased fans, rejected the possibility of finding a replacement. The band has been on an indefinite hiatus since 2012.

Chapter One

Heart pounding, I stared at the email preview illuminating the screen of my phone as if the devil himself had set it on fire.

My chair felt like it'd been liquefied. With me in it.

Jay Brodie PR PRESS RELEASE. Reunion of the...

The rest of the headline didn't fit in, but my gut told me this was big. And my gut had never wronged me yet. It was one of the main reasons why, out of all the music journalist wannabes who'd interned for Jay Brodie PR seven years ago, I was the only one still going strong in this brain, heart, and morals-corroding sex, drugs, and rock 'n' roll industry.

Jay Brodie just had one band on their roster that was long overdue for a reunion. Hall Affinity.

Gulping past the sudden tightness in my throat, I swiped my index finger over the preview and continued to read.

...Decade: Legendary Rock Band Hall Affinity Returning to the Studio to Work on New Material after a 7-Year Hiatus.

I skimmed over the announcement text, my gaze dropping to the bottom of the email. Jay Brodie was a high-end PR boutique and handled only the cream of the crop, the best and the biggest acts in today's rock music, and they were pretty picky about the outlets they worked with. Getting *Rewired* on their radar had taken us a couple of years.

Linda would make it happen, I assured myself. She'd been good to us when it came to hot exclusives and we'd been good to her when some of her clients needed an extra push. Although most of her clients' names were famous enough to push themselves.

I shook off the doubt and returned to the text.

Lead singer Frankie Blade and guitarist Dante Martinez will make an appearance at the Annual Douglas & Krueger Cancer Benefit that will be held at The Regency on September 28th. Mr. Blade will be available for interviews. Spots are very limited. All applications will be individually reviewed and approved by management. Please fill out the form below to submit the request.

That was six weeks away!

I sucked in a labored breath through my teeth and carefully evaluated every word. They felt rushed and unnatural, almost as if they were doing Frankie a disservice. This benefit show would be the man's first public appearance in years.

Yes, there had been some rumors about new Hall Affinity music, but those rumors had been going around for ages. Dante Martinez had politely ignored all questions regarding a reunion during his last interview.

Shit! I switched to my laptop, my face hot from the sudden surge of adrenaline. My fingers were clammy and stiff as my brain willed them to open the application instead of typing Frankie's name next to *post-accident photo* in the Google search bar. I was frazzled, but I managed to steer my concentration in the right direction, although I had to go up and fix the typo in my own last name twice.

What is wrong with you, Cassy? It's just a job. You've been doing this for seven years. You should know how to spell your own last name by now.

Unfortunately, Frankie Blade had that effect on people. Even I wasn't immune. Back when the band was owning all the charts and radio stations, he'd been titled the sexiest man alive by pretty much every site, magazine, and outlet that practiced grouping men into lists based on their looks and other assets more times than Hollywood had tried to reboot the Spider-Man franchise. Having a crush on someone like Frankie was inevitable. It was childish and silly, but I cherished my love for him and his music as much as I cherished my love for the real people in my life, my mother and my younger brother, Ashton, even though he'd sadly grown up to be a lazy video game-addicted douche.

My phone rang when I was finishing up the application.

"Did you see the email?" Levi yelled, his voice on the line sounding like he'd had a visit from a ghost. Which wasn't far from the truth. Frankie Blade *was* a ghost. No one had seen or heard from the front man of Hall Affinity in over seven years. Rumor was, the injuries caused by his motorcycle accident were too severe and he'd been tied to a bed ever since.

"Yes, I just sent in the application." I hit the enter button enthusiastically and my keyboard squeaked in response.

"This is a big one, Cass. I think it's time you utilize your connections." Levi casually threw it out there, but I knew exactly where he was going with it. It wasn't the first time he'd tried to push me into seeking out Dante Martinez for a favor.

Unlike the mysterious Mr. Blade, Hall Affinity's lead guitarist had always been easy to access. He was a child of the public, a lover of press, and a hopeless womanizer. Six months after Frankie's accident, Dante had announced a solo album and a possible tour. The fans were skeptic. Some got upset over the fact that Dante was moving on. Many didn't believe the guitarist had it in him. Frankie Blade and Dante Martinez were the Toxic Twins 2.0. One didn't work without the other.

In spite of that, the solo album and the tour were a success. Levi and I, still green back then, had pimped the hell out of Dante's venture after the three of us hit it off during the interview my friend Linda Schwab, an administrative assistant who was soon to become

Jay Brodie PR's VP, arranged for *Rewired*. At that time, Levi was still running all magazine operations from his family's garage in Santa Monica. He hadn't met our go-to guys, Stewie and Carlos, yet. And hard rock's bad boy Dante Martinez, who'd finally stepped out from the shadow of Frankie's good looks and charisma, was fame-hungry and took every opportunity tossed his way, even an interview with an overly ambitious three-person operation called *Rewired*. The situation had turned out to be a win-win for all of us.

My interview with Dante had reigned the YouTube charts for months. The *Rewired* Facebook page blew up overnight. Hall Affinity's axman and his side project were on a hot streak, breaking hearts and making cash.

It had felt a lot like we were rewriting rock 'n' roll history. I loved the thrill of the challenge. I loved the people I'd met. Occasionally, I loved the attention. One of those impulsive moments had landed me an invite to a private and very impromptu dinner Linda's friend, who was the guest of honor, was throwing after a charity event Levi and I covered in Studio City. Dante was part of the group when I arrived.

He'd remembered my name. I was smitten. To me, everyone who'd appeared in a music video was a god. Dante, however, wasn't. He was the devil's son, who knew how to make two things melt in his presence—guitars and women. Or a girl, in my case. I was a twenty-one-year-old tomboy with too much drive, a big mouth, minimum makeup, a cute pixie cut, and fresh music-theme tats on my right arm. I fit in. I had the look, and I was smart and professional beyond my years. I smiled, played nice, shook hands, and *never* flirted. My goal was to write memories, real accounts about real people, not some manufactured bullshit.

I knew how to balance the questions—when to ask the right ones and when to back away. Everyone liked me. In some ways, the ability to predict whether the person interviewed would want to open up was my gift and my curse. During the dinner, conversations happened and numbers were exchanged. But nothing ever came of it, because Dante was way past the drinking point of no return when he punched his digits into my phone while complimenting my thoughtful interview questions. Sometime during the evening, he'd even called me a kid. I hadn't argued. He was in his early thirties. He'd lived and seen it all. I was just at the beginning of my career. We were worlds apart.

We'd bumped into each other later that year at a couple of charity events Levi and I were covering. He'd recognized me, despite the fact I'd filled out and dyed my hair. We'd had a short chat, which prompted Levi to think I could simply pick up the phone anytime and call Dante like I would an old friend.

Levi was obviously mistaken. I wouldn't gamble with my professional reputation and my integrity just to see if I could secure an exclusive with Frankie via my private channels.

"You need to drop it, Levi," I said, returning to Google and typing Frankie's name into the search bar. I was itching to see if there'd been any recent photos of him released.

"You know this is fucking big, Cass," he pressed, sounding anxious. "You know we need this interview. You also know there's a good chance *Rewired* won't make the cut."

"We will. We cover the Douglas & Krueger Benefit every year, for God's sake." I tried to calm him down, but I wasn't confident myself.

Chart topping, award-winning bands like Hall Affinity always came with stuck-up management who had no idea how to determine what a respectable publication was. *Rewired* was a small magazine with three contributors and two photographers, but it'd been going strong for over eight years. It was Levi's brainchild. He'd launched it a year before I met him and big things started happening right after we found each other. Helping him run *Rewired* was similar to raising a child. It gave us direction and pushed us to do better and think smarter. Levi's dream was to beat *Rolling Stone*'s ratings. It was somewhat unrealistic, but he loved to entertain the idea from time to time.

I played along.

"This is the reunion of the century, the second most wanted

reunion after Guns N' Roses!" Levi cried out. He was pacing around, the low thuds of his feet against the carpet reverberating against my eardrums like an intricate bass line.

"I'm not going to call, text, or email Dante Martinez. We've never communicated outside official channels." A groan of disappointment met my ear and I drew my phone away, just in case, as my finger hit the refresh button to reload the browser. The photos that littered my screen—blue-eyed, sandy-haired, dressed-to-kill rock star Frankie Blade with a body like sin and the smile of a saint—were all from before the accident.

"Besides, get your facts straight. It's not a reunion. Technically, the band never broke up. They were taking time off." This was my inner fangirl speaking. Frankie Blade was still my idol. Regardless of the fact that he hadn't given me a new song in over seven years.

"Why aren't you like other women, Cass?" Levi asked. His voice was a blend of plea and disappointment. "Why aren't you using what your mother gave you for the greater good of our magazine?"

"Mighty sexist of you, buddy," I retorted, slightly offended but mostly just amused. When I'd decided to stick to music journalism, I'd promised myself not to build my connections with my feminine charms. Of course, my looks were far from those of a Playboy model, but the mere fact that I was a pretty, young girl trying to make a career in a male-dominated industry had its perks.

"You know me. I'm honest to a fault." Levi chuckled.

I could feel his grin over the line. It was impossible to be mad at him for longer than a minute.

"Are you sure you're not adopted?" I laughed.

"My father's convinced I was switched at birth. He's not too fond of my undying love for rock 'n' roll."

"Does your father not know about Kiss?"

"You've met my father. His love of music doesn't extend past singing 'Hava Nagila' at bar mitzvahs."

We laughed at this notion together. How Levi had turned out to be so rock 'n' roll while growing up in such a strict Jewish household had always been a mystery to both him and me. His father had wanted him to take on the family real estate business.

"You need to relax. Linda will make it happen." I actually wasn't so convinced myself. She still had to run all the press requests by the band's management, and those guys were hard to predict.

"She better. All those margarita's I bought her at the Kipling album release party..." Levi never missed an opportunity to complain about the bill he raked up once while trying to make friends with Linda. It was probably the only stereotypically Jewish thing about him.

"No one was forcing you."

"I was trying to show my appreciation."

"You want a tip? One drink is usually more than enough to show your appreciation. Doesn't have to be six. Six means you're trying to get a woman drunk, not thank her."

"She didn't say no."

"Will you take my advice for once?" Levi had no clue what to do when it came to charming women. I didn't remember him ever having a girlfriend. Not that my love life was any better. My last relationship had lasted a whopping two months before it went up in flames like a box of matches doused with gasoline.

My gaze slid down the screen of my laptop. The entire web was buzzing. The news had spread like wildfire, which was both scary and fascinating.

Even after seven years of silence, Frankie Blade made headlines.

"Okay," Levi's voice boomed in my ear. "Text Linda and check on your boy, Dante. I need to post this ASAP, before *Pulse Nation* comes up with a massive write-up on the band's history."

While working on beating *Rolling Stone*'s numbers, Levi was practicing beating the numbers of other competitors. *Pulse Nation* was his guinea pig this year.

"We can do one too," I offered.

"Can you run a poll on our Facebook page? Ten best Hall Affinity songs. Or something along those lines?" Levi's brain was working overtime. He pitched five more engagement post ideas before we finally said our goodbyes.

Heat creeping up my cheeks, I set my phone on my desk near the keyboard and spun in my chair several times. Adrenaline simmered beneath my skin. It'd been ages since I'd been this excited about a press release.

After years of picking the brains of people whose faces decorated everything from coffee mugs to billboards, the excitement had become routine. It was part of the job and it had to be relegated to the background to give way to competence and reliability.

My mind was the definition of a hot mess. It wondered and scrambled, dozens of scenarios playing out inside my head. My gut simply told me to stay put and wait.

Linda would make it happen. The Douglas & Krueger Cancer Benefit was one of the hardest events of the fall to get credentials for. It was a high-end, celebrity-stuffed concert and auction. The tables cost five thousand dollars each. Jay Brodie only approved outlets that had print issues. *Rewired* had a quarterly one, which didn't sell great, but it'd opened up a lot of doors where just a handful of magazines, like *Rolling Stone*, *AP*, and *Pulse Nation,* could get in. *Rewired* was also on the list of Linda's favorites. And that list was very short.

The first post-accident photo of Frankie Blade surfaced on the web the morning after the press release. I woke up at the ass crack of dawn to the maddening rattling of my phone against the nightstand. There was one missed call and two text messages with TMZ links from Levi.

"Crap," I muttered, staring at my phone through the blur in my eyes. At moments like this, I hated this job. Sleep had been secondary for me ever since I met Levi. The blazing headlines were ridiculous. Whoever came up with those must have been doing some hard drugs or had an unhealthy addiction to Mary Shelley's literary work.

"Frankie Blade: Back from the Dead, or is He?"

"Frankenstein of Rock 'N' Roll: Rock Singer Spotted Leaving Beverly Hills Doctor's Office"

I rolled my eyes at the last one and clicked on a photo below it. The image wasn't from the best angle and must have been taken in a rush, because one of the two bodyguards escorting Frankie toward the building was turned toward the camera, his expression mean and menacing, eyes like two rocket launchers. Big guy obviously took his job seriously.

The man in question was wearing a baseball cap that hid his face and a hoodie that disguised his physique. An outfit that, in this particular case, didn't do a stellar job of concealing his celebrity status. I had no doubt it was Frankie. The tips of his sandy locks grazed his cheeks and fell down the back of his neck, just like they did in dozens of other pre-accident photos. His rigid posture gave away his unease, but the way his hands hung loosely at the sides of his body told me he'd been ready for the ambush and didn't care.

A strange flutter tickled my chest as I zoomed in on the photo to study it, trying to make out the face, to no avail.

Frankie Blade was an enigma. A mystery. A man who was worth seven years of scars, and the entire planet wanted to see what those scars looked like.

After checking a couple more websites to get a better idea of what was going on, I texted Levi.

You just made it to number one on my kill list.

Levi: I wasn't already?

Are you upset?

Levi: Very.

A lazy smile stretched across my lips. I dropped my phone next to me on the bed and stared at the ceiling absentmindedly, praying to the universe to make this interview happen.

A text message alert yanked me out of my daze. I fished the phone from the blankets and looked at the screen.

Levi: Who was number one before me?

Laughing, I tapped out a reply.

My alarm.

He responded with an eye-roll emoji.

Unable to go back to sleep, I dragged myself out of bed and resumed working on my summer write-up, but my head felt heavy and my tired brain was scrambled for words.

Levi called around noon when I was on my third cup of coffee.

"Did you see it?" he asked. The tone of his voice could be described as perpetual shock and was accompanied by the sounds of slurping and chewing.

"What are you talking about?" I opened my browser.

"TMZ just released an entire Frankie Blade gallery."

"Any decent photos, at least?" I tried to mask the sudden wave of anxiety with a joke.

"Don't worry. Your teenage crush has still got it," Levi said, a pinch of amusement in his voice.

I pulled up the TMZ page and flipped through a gallery of freshly uploaded photos. There were clear professional shots of Frankie, taken somewhere in Malibu while he was dining. He looked good. There were no scars or any facial deformities, contrary to popular hearsay. I took a moment to study the shots. Frankie wasn't alone. Dante and Johnny Z were with him in half of the photos.

"You think Carter's out?" Levi pondered.

"Why would he be out?"

"I don't know. Maybe they wanted Quin on it. Probably would sell more tickets. The original line-up."

"Nonsense," I countered.

Right now, Frankie could probably sell out an arena on his own and people would pay crazy money to hear him sing a phone book backwards or an instructional manual from Ikea.

Besides, the only two band members that really mattered were Frankie and Dante. They brought the chemistry on stage. Carter and Johnny Z were merely a nice backdrop. Everyone knew that.

Levi didn't pursue the subject further, because this wasn't something *Rewired* would post anyway. TMZ speculated. We created original content.

"Will you have anything ready for me today?" Levi inquired.

"In a couple of hours," I lied. The article wasn't anywhere near done. "I'll upload it when I'm finished. Can you prep the draft?"

"I'm on it... Hey, check this out! They just updated their website."

The iMessage window popped up on my computer's screen with the incoming link from Levi.

I clicked on it and pulled up the band's page, my heart beating a little faster. The signature red and orange flame logo on the homepage had been replaced by an all-black background with a burning butterfly. Nothing else. I stared at the artwork for a good minute, reveling in its intrigue and listening to Levi's speculations about what Frankie had possibly been doing during his long sabbatical.

The imagery was dramatic...and sad. It made my chest twist a little when I tried to imagine what being dragged by a motorcycle across a quarter-mile-long spread of the freeway might feel like.

I remembered the day very clearly. It'd happened a few weeks before I started my internship at Jay Brodie PR. The news had broken early that morning, and I'd spent an entire day staring at my phone and waiting for updates on Frankie's condition. My weak teenage heart barely held it together.

Levi's voice was a muffled noise in my ear as he went on with his theories, slurping some more. He had this stupid habit of eating while talking or doing other things. He was a class-A workaholic. And the condition was contagious as hell.

"Hey, I really need to get this finished, okay?" I interrupted him.

My gaze swept over the digital clock on my laptop screen. I had four hours to put something coherent together. For a second, I thought of using my writer's block as an excuse to bail on dinner at my mother's, but my conscience told me to suck it up and go. I didn't want to be another kid who was a letdown. Ashton was a huge disappointment and I felt obligated to try to change that, although my attempts to talk some sense into him hadn't been successful. He was still undecided on everything. College, job, life. His music.

"Fine. Talk later, Cass," Levi said and hung up.

My mother's apartment was in the heart of Hollywood, a few blocks north of Franklin, which just strengthened my hate toward the family dinner tradition. Looking for parking near her building on Wednesday afternoon was like looking for a needle in a haystack without a flashlight. The blasts of music inside my car muffled the noise of the traffic surrounding me as I circled the block in search of a spot for my Honda. Seeing the photos of Frankie Blade had triggered a wave of nostalgia. I was on Hall Affinity's third album by the time I hit the gridlock near my mother's place, and Frankie's voice was the only thing that managed to keep me sane.

My summer recap had been finished and posted in draft on the website for Levi to review, and I felt good about today.

The apartment smelled like the kitchen of Fig & Olive. My nose picked up the faint scent of cumin and rosemary all the way from the courtyard and my taste buds screamed with delight. Our mother was a great cook. Her hot homemade meals had been a desperate attempt to give our family some sense of normalcy after our father left us, and while it hadn't always worked, I'd appreciated the efforts.

Despite the lack of desire to visit the home that'd harbored so many miserable memories, I still looked forward to our mother's culinary creations.

Ashton's room sounded like a battlefield. I knocked twice before entering. He didn't respond, which added more fuel to my burning irritation.

"Incoming," I warned, peeking inside. The air was stale and the curtains were shut. The place was reminiscent of a bunker.

My brother was sprawled on his twin bed like an amoeba, his eyes staring unblinkingly at the chaos happening on the huge plasma monitor mounted to the wall. The only sign of life was his twitching hands holding the game controller.

"Hey!" I called, surveying the piles of dirty clothes and empty soda cans.

"What's up?" Ashton muttered. His gaze never left the horde of animated people who were dressed in camo and running around with guns on the screen.

Pop, pop, pop! The shots sliced through my head like a hacksaw.

"Could you turn this down?" Wincing, I gestured at the monitor. "Please?"

"Hold up." His hands jerked along with the controller. He wasn't present. The assault on my ears continued.

"Ashton!" I raised my voice. My frustration was about to reach the point of no return. "Come on!"

"I said hold on!" A low growl carried over the noise of the video game.

This, right now, reminded me of the time preceding my father's departure. He'd been withdrawn, lost in his own world. Getting a reaction from him had seemed almost impossible.

One day he'd gone to the store to get cigarettes and never come back.

Rage racing through my blood, I walked over to the monitor and yanked at the cord. The gunfire stopped and the screen went dark.

"What the fuck is your problem?" Ashton cried out, tossing both hands in the air.

Good, I thought triumphantly, *at least that made him move.* But part of me still crumbled. I hated arguing with my brother, but sadly, he didn't understand any other language.

"Since when has 'fuck' become a word in your vocabulary?" I stomped over to the chair and went through the pile of dirty T-shirts, examining them one by one. I wasn't sure what I was looking for. Drugs, maybe, or an explanation why my brother had been ignoring the outside world for the past four years.

"Since whenever I want. Get out of my room." Ashton slid from the bed with the intention of turning the game back on, but I intercepted him before he got to the power cable.

We stood in front of the monitor, his lanky six-two with a messy mop of California sun-kissed curls against my rigid, dainty five-four, staring at each other like two sworn enemies.

"You need to check yourself," I started, trying to keep my voice steady. "If you don't want to go to college, you can't stay here after you graduate."

He laughed in my face. "I'll stay here for as long as I want to. Mom said I can."

"Mom's going to lose her housing assistance the day you turn eighteen, asshole. You need to start looking for a job." My rage grew stronger with every second.

"I'm not moving out." Ashton's lips twitched with irritation. "End of story!" He rolled his eyes for good measure.

Arguing with him was like beating my head against a brick wall.

I blew out a breath, then I lost it. "You can't do this anymore! There comes a point in every person's life when he has to man up and take some responsibility. And your responsibility is to make sure Mom doesn't have to work two jobs to keep this apartment while you're wasting away in your room playing dumb video games and waiting for a miracle to happen. Nothing's going to happen if you don't get your lazy ass out of bed!"

There was a mean side of me that wanted to bring our deadbeat father into the conversation, because Ashton was living proof that the apple didn't fall far from the tree, but something, maybe respect and empathy for our mother, stopped me from saying it out loud.

"You two need to stop!" Her voice drifted at me from the hall. From the corner of my eye, I saw her small figure appear in the doorway.

"She started it, Mom," Ashton whined.

"He hasn't cleaned his room in months." I gestured at the pile of dirty clothes on the floor by my feet and spun around to face our mother.

The air in the room became heavy with invisible threat. "Both of you!" Her finger bounced between me and my brother. She looked ruffled and disproportionate. Her face pale, jaw clenched. "Wash your hands! Dinner's ready." There was a certain level of creativity in the way she ignored obvious problems. Just like she ignored my commentary on the condition of Ashton's room. Sometimes I wondered if my brother's lack of enthusiasm and incapacity to handle simple day-to-day tasks had been inherited from her side of the family.

We gathered in the dining room a few minutes later. The silverware and plates were put out in grim silence that seemed to drag on forever, and sticking around for dinner seemed pointless, but I forced myself to behave.

"I'm not going to tolerate this anymore," our mother said when we finished setting the table. Her arms fell to her hips and she gave us a long, exasperated stare. "You need to stop fighting."

"I'm not even doing anything," Ashton grumbled, dropping into a chair.

"Okay then"—I took my seat across from him—"why don't we talk? Why don't we have an adult conversation?" I tried hard not to sound like a cynic, but it didn't work. My voice was a perfect blend of harsh, mean, and bitter.

"Yeah, why don't you tell us what your problem is, sis?" Ashton tore his gaze from his plate and flashed me a classic go-fuck-yourself smile.

My problem is that you're a lazy douche who doesn't think about anyone but himself.

But I choked back the words and decided to be smarter this time. "Did you hear from Scott?"

No response.

"Honey?" Our mother perked up.

"Not yet." He shook his head.

"Really?" I pressed, "Last time I checked, Scott was still hiring."

"Oh yeah?" Ashton leaned back in his chair, arms folded across his chest. "I guess he didn't like my application." A shoulder shrug.

"I believe you didn't care to fill it out," I countered. "I talked to Scott a couple of days after I picked up the application. He said you never came."

A frown carved into my mother's already distraught face.

"It's not fair!" He looked at her, probably hoping for some sort of support, but none followed. "Why does she get to do whatever she wants and I don't?"

"How the hell did working twenty-four seven turn into doing whatever I want?!" The nerve the little bastard had. I was ready to strangle him right there and then.

"No screaming at the table." Our mother lifted both hands in a placating manner and closed her eyes. The vein in her temple pulsed madly.

"You get to hang out with all the bands and party while I'm supposed to wash dishes in some lame ice cream shop?"

"First of all, I don't *hang out*. Second, I don't party. This is work. We don't have days off, Ashton. I think you're disillusioned about what I do."

"I could help out at an event."

"No. You can't." My palm slapped against the tabletop. I heard my fork rattling, but all of it—the clanking of the silverware, the frustrated gasps of my mother, my brother talking under his breath—was just background noise. "I busted my ass to get where I'm am. For years. I filled out more applications than you can imagine." I stood up from my chair because anger was boiling in my blood. "Not once has anyone granted me anything because I was someone's friend or a relative. I earned it. You need to earn it too. Levi and I aren't going to give you any gigs until you understand what a work ethic is and how to do what we do. And for that, you need experience, and experience doesn't come to those who sit in their room all day."

Blind rage washed over me. I knew what my mother was going to say next. This was the part where she always took Ashton's side because, in her head, he'd suffered the most when our father bailed. He was the youngest and the sensitive one. I was the old, mean sister who blasted rock music all day in her room and worshiped Satan. Even when Ashton picked up a guitar and hit the black emo hair and crappy attitude phase, I was still the bad kid.

"I don't understand why it's so hard for you to let him go with you a couple of times." Mom's voice squeaked to my right.

"Because he has no manners and because he doesn't understand how to behave around the kind of people I work with."

An embarrassing memory blazed through my brain like a torch. Ashton was fourteen. He'd begged me to take him to The Deviant event Levi and I worked. After the show, we all ended up in the VIP area. A treat from Linda. Justice Cross was doing rounds and talking to guests when Ashton asked me to introduce him. We stood, facing each other, shook hands, and briefly exchanged a few words. The entire night was surreal. At that time, Justice Cross was the biggest name on the list of musicians I'd chatted with.

My heart dropped to my stomach when I heard Ashton telling the internationally acclaimed singer I'd interviewed four hours ago that I had his poster up on my wall. And not just any poster. *The kinky one.* That's what my brother called it. I felt humiliation of the worst kind. All the hard work I'd put into making sure rich, famous, arrogant men like Justice Cross took a music journalist my age seriously had been ruined in a matter of seconds.

It stung, even after all this time, and I wasn't going to risk seven years of labor that earned me my respect in the industry to humor my brother.

There were some lines that didn't blur. A very distinct one between them and us. And Ashton crossed that line the moment he tossed me into the fangirl zone.

My appetite disappeared. "I'm not hungry." I was on my way out, fed up, drained, and angry. What started as a promising day had ended in total disaster.

Mind racing, I sat in my car with the music on. Heat burned in my chest as my finger skimmed over the contacts list on my phone. The realization that, despite knowing so many people, I had no real friends I could talk to hit me hard. Like a mallet. Of course, there was always Levi. And that was the number I called, but deep down, I was lonely. Lonelier than I'd ever been.

Once I called him and unloaded my frustration, we fell into a short stretch of silence.

"You want to know what I think?" Levi grunted.

"Sure." I fiddled with the volume control button to hear the music a little better. The song playing was from Hall Affinity's last album, *Chasing Memories*.

"Is that Frankie's voice I'm hearing?" A chuckle.

"I need a refresher on the back catalogue," I deadpanned. "I'm going to rock that interview." I didn't feel like adding "if we get it," because at that moment, I needed the universe to know what I really wanted. *I needed the universe to hear me.*

"You will, Cass," Levi assured. "You're the fucking best. No one else knows how to take all these people apart without them even noticing it."

"Thanks. At least someone has faith in me."

"I have to. You're my locomotive."

"So what was it that you were thinking?"

"You need to get laid."

"Like my list of potential booty calls is very long." There was no list, and that made me sad. I was a pretty, young woman who talked to and occasionally appeared on camera next to celebs, and I had no one to turn to for a round of mindless sex.

"You've got a lot of anger, babe." I heard a stifled laugh on the line.

"Any other suggestions on how to let steam off?"

"Get some ink?" Levi offered.

I let the thought settle in my brain. Tats were my weakness. I'd wanted them as far back as I could remember but waited patiently until I turned eighteen and had enough money to see a good artist.

My first one was a small rose on my left calf. My second one was on my wrist. The third one was slightly bigger and took up a good portion of my right shoulder. I never planned on having too many or getting full sleeves. I liked them sparse and delicate with plenty of skin in between, but the idea of a new tattoo was alluring.

"You know what I think?" I said, glancing at the street. "I'm going to take your advice and go see my buddy Hank."

"Have fun. Use a condom." Levi laughed.

"Thank you for reminding me." I laughed too, then ended the call.

I stood at the counter and absently flipped through the portfolio of a new tattoo artist while the shop attendant scanned my ID and checked my paperwork.

"When did Hank leave?" I was conflicted about letting someone I'd never met touch my skin.

"Hmmm." The attendant handed me my driver's license back. "Let me see." A line on his forehead deepened from concentration. "Six months ago at least."

"That's a bummer. I wish I'd known."

"Jax is great." The attendant leaned closer and whispered conspiratorially, "He was on a TV show last year. Guy's got a huge following. You're going to love his work."

Well, dip me in glue and sprinkle me with glitter.

Frazzled, I nodded slowly. The TV show tidbit didn't impress me as much as the attendant had been aiming for. I sat down with people who entertained stadiums and arenas for a living.

I caught a glimpse of my own reflection in the mirror wall on the opposite side of the shop. That young woman looked nothing like the skinny girl with a pixie cut who'd come here seven years ago wearing platform boots and a band tee. I'd learned how to take care of myself. Physically, financially, spiritually. I'd figured out what clothes worked for my body type, what hair length and color complemented my features, what shadow made my eyes pop, and what gloss made my lips fuller. I tried to go to the gym at least three times a week because keeping in shape was crucial with the workload Levi and I handled. I liked what I saw. Cassy Evans, successful music journalist extraordinaire who had her shit together.

Or did she?

Because I couldn't understand why I felt like a miserable blob of shit every single time after I saw my family.

I also couldn't care less if the new guy had tattooed the president himself. It was my skin and I was going to have his artwork along with his energy on me for the rest of my life, and I didn't want any energy that wasn't real or positive. I'd grown up with enough negativity to last me a lifetime.

Hank was a sweetheart. He'd come highly recommended and had done all my work ever since the needle bit my calf for the first time. Letting some other artist touch me seemed like cheating, and I seriously considered leaving, but my common sense told me Hank wasn't going to fly to L.A. from Miami for a session with me unless I could afford to hire a jet.

"There's a bit of a wait, so just make yourself comfortable," the attendant explained, ushering me toward the lounge area.

The soft leather couch dipped as I descended.

"You already know what you want?" he asked.

"Sort of." I had no clue. "But I'd love to look at some more designs." I smiled as he handed me a few booklets.

The soft hum of the background music and the distant buzzing of a machine started to lull me to sleep. I was beat and sleepy, but my mind still raced wildly after my confrontation with Ashton, and my ego hurt. Fighting a yawn, I peeked at my cell to note the time. It was nearly ten and I was the last client in the shop.

"Hey there," a warm male voice said as I yanked at the poly plastic page of the portfolio.

My gaze skated toward the sound and I saw a full-sleeved arm extended to me.

"You know"—a chuckle rumbled in his chest—"I can make you a copy."

I realized my fingers were pulling the plastic so hard, the page was about to fall off. "Sorry." Blood rose to my cheeks. Depositing the booklets on the table next to the couch, I pushed myself to my feet and shook the artist's hand. His grip was strong but welcoming.

"Jax. How are you?" He flashed me a lighthearted smile that hardly matched his edgy appearance.

"Cassy. I'm great. Thank you for asking." I was lying. Getting a tat on a Wednesday night usually meant the opposite. All I knew was that I'd craved the experience a needle against my skin gave me each time I'd gotten more ink. It was therapeutic.

Jax had a military-style buzz cut to show off the intricate artwork adorning his neck and shoulders. He wore an Ink Master T-shirt, a pair of faded jeans, and sneakers. His deep-set brown eyes ogled my existing tats as I settled in the chair at his workstation. He definitely was droolworthy. I could see why he had the big following.

"So what are we doing today?" he questioned, organizing his tools.

I took a deep breath and glanced up at the ceiling. "I'll be honest with you. This was a rash decision, so I don't know. But I'm open to suggestions."

Jax scanned me from head to toe, his gaze lasering through my light green summer cargo pants and my cotton top. My bra melted around my breasts. Levi was right. I didn't need a new tat. I needed to get laid.

"We can definitely come up with something neat that won't scream rash decision." Jax nodded, a glint in his eyes complementing his smile. "Do you know where you want it?" He looked over the length of my arms, inspecting.

"I don't want anything too obvious—" I stammered at the rise of his brow as soon as I realized I was talking to someone whose skin hardly had any areas that hadn't been touched by the needle. "No offense."

"None taken." He tilted his head and a playful smirk touched the corner of his mouth. "Your skin is great. I wouldn't cover it all if I were you."

"Are you sure you want the job?" I laughed at his selling skills.

"Are you sure you want more ink?" Jax was challenging me and I loved it.

"Just so you know, I like what you have going on." I motioned at the swirls of black, red, and blue ink sweeping across his taut chest muscles that his loose sleeveless tank didn't cover.

We chatted while skimming through more designs. The attendant had already locked up for the day, and Jax and I were the only two people left at the shop. He pitched some interesting ideas, but nothing stuck out to me and I felt bad for not being able to make up my mind.

The new Black Rain Coming single blasting from the speakers somewhere above ended and the intro riff of "Ambivalent" filled the room.

"Can you show me the butterflies again?" I asked meekly, music rush hitting my every nerve. Even after all these years, Frankie's voice still got to me. I took a moment to bathe in its deep, dark sweetness as I flipped through the plastic pages, this time knowing exactly what I was looking for. I missed everything *Breathe Crimson* signified—my last few weeks with my father before he left us. It was a voice of nostalgia, a voice of lost innocence.

It was the album that got me through some very tough times. It was *the* album.

"I'd love something like this on my shoulder blade," I said, showing Jax a small butterfly design.

"Great choice. This is the part where you strip for me." He grinned.

"Can I leave my panties on?" I went along with the joke.

A burst of laughter cut through the music. "You're dangerous, Cassy."

"So are you."

I wasn't sure where our banter was going anymore. Something told me we were dancing a careless dance, but I enjoyed it. Jax had a peculiar sense of humor that I credited to his work on whatever TV show he'd been on. He also had a nice touch and I felt relaxed and safe under the needle once we began.

I lay on the chair, listening to the playlist while Jax hummed along with the music. He had a decent voice. Not arena material, but he could carry a tune ten times better than I could.

I was curious. "Do you play any instruments?"

"I play guitar a little. Do you?"

"No. I wish I did, though."

"How come you never tried?"

I didn't know how to explain that my alcoholic father had spent all our money on booze. We'd lived from paycheck to paycheck. I'd worn one pair of shoes through the entire sixth grade, which had pushed me to be overly creative with homemade footwear accessories because I didn't want other kids to notice. An instrument would have been a luxury. Heck, my iPod was a luxury back then.

"Never got around to it, I guess," I muttered.

"You okay?" Jax switched off the machine to check on me. "We can take a break if you want."

"I'm fine. Not my first rodeo." I turned my head to face him and smiled. His eyes met mine and he did the same.

"I can put on something else. What do you want to listen to?"

"Hall Affinity." It was a reflex. I was obsessed with finding something new in the lyrics, something I'd failed to hear before. I wanted to learn everything there was to know about Frankie Blade so I could pick his brain apart.

"You got it." Jax set the machine aside and wiped down my shoulder blade. "Which album is your favorite?" My new tattoo artist was considerate and my disdain over Hank's absence had subsided.

"*Breathe Crimson*. Yours?"

"I like *Breathe Crimson* too." He took off his gloves and pulled up a Hall Affinity playlist on his phone. "You a fan?"

"I am. How about you?"

"I like them. I'm actually looking forward to hearing their new music. I hope they didn't lose their spark. My baby sister used to spin them for days back in high school." A corner of his mouth curved as he shook his head slightly. "You ever see them live?"

"A few times. My girlfriend won a pair of floor tickets from iHeartRadio right before Frankie's accident. We were in the front. I had so many bruises after. You have no idea."

"You really know how to throw it down, Cassy." His gaze locked on mine for a brief moment and we exchanged invisible smiles. He was light, like a feather, and I enjoyed talking to him. "Was that soon after they got inducted into the Rock & Roll Hall of Fame? 2012?"

"You have a great memory for someone who just *likes* the band."

Jax tapped the side of his head with his index finger. "There's a lot of information stored here that's absolutely useless unless you meet a fan of the band."

"Show off."

"Wanted to impress the lady."

I caught a flash of interest in his eyes. My stomach fluttered involuntarily. It was the weirdest thing ever because I'd never flirted with my tattoo artist before, but then again, Hank was pushing fifty and had a girlfriend. Flirting in general wasn't my strong suit. I just had a big mouth and said stuff that men apparently found attractive. Half of those men also wanted to go out with me in exchange for concert tickets and backstage passes.

"Are you ready to keep going?" Jax asked, retrieving a fresh pair of gloves from the box next to his tools.

"Sure." I shifted in the chair and made myself comfortable.

We chatted some more, mainly about music. By the time he finished, it was well past midnight.

"What do you think?" Jax was cleaning his area and I stood in front of the wall mirror in my bra and cargo pants with my neck twisted and staring at my new tattoo. Even through the plastic, I could tell the butterfly was exquisitely detailed. My skin beneath the ink stung pleasantly.

"I love it. Thank you." I adjusted the strap of my bra to ensure it didn't touch the tat and slipped my top on.

We moved to the counter with the credit card machine and Jax gave me the total.

I handed him my Visa. "I'm sorry I held you up."

"It's not a big deal. We get a lot of late-night clients. Hazard of the job."

I signed the copy of the receipt he gave me along with my card, then returned it to him. "I can understand why."

"You know how to take care of it, right?" Jax grabbed a small brochure from the plastic holder and topped it off with the customer copy of the receipt and his business card, which had something written on it. "Feel free to call me if you have any questions."

He walked me to the door and watched me get in my car. I slid behind the wheel and glanced at the stack of papers in my hand, curious what his business card said.

When I pulled it out and saw *Cell* and a phone number scribbled on it, a rush of excitement rolled through my stomach.

Chapter Two

The interview confirmation came the morning of the fundraiser.

Waiting for it was like waiting for hell to freeze over. Jay Brodie PR hadn't returned either one of our follow-up emails. Linda's response to my text had been a very dry, *haven't heard back yet from management*. She'd even refrained from using emojis, which was so unlike her and could only mean one thing. There was a lot going on behind closed doors and mere mortals weren't privy to the info.

Meanwhile, more photos of Frankie Blade flooded the net. He'd been spotted in Beverly Hills a few times in the company of his body-guards and his bandmates. *Rolling Stone* had teased the public with a Hall Affinity exclusive in their upcoming issue. Frankie's ex-wife had spoken to *Cosmopolitan* about her short-lived marriage to the golden boy of hard rock. The entire planet was holding their breath. The man had returned from the dead. The question was, had his voice returned with him?

The night before our credentials were confirmed, I contemplated whether showing up at the Regency without an invitation would make the Jay Brodie folks scratch us off their preferred outlets list. Despite knowing a number of influential people in the industry, Levi and I had agreed to never lower to the paparazzi's level. *Rewired* produced fresh and original content. We were one of those rare magazines that stayed away from speculative articles. We only showed up where we were officially invited. We worked fast and efficient, and every promoter, bouncer, and artist relation rep in L.A. knew who we were and treated us with respect. There'd been just one case years back when we'd crashed an event. Our credentials hadn't come through due to some stupid administrative mistake. We'd rolled up to the venue, armed with our gear and smiles, and hit up the press table. Ten minutes later, we were backstage interviewing the bass guitarist of the band whose single later that fall would hit number one on every rock station in the US, UK, Australia, and a handful of other countries.

The PR firm that had set up the interview and then dropped the ball wasn't Jay Brodie. Jay Brodie would normally toy with us for a while but would always give their final answer, no matter if it was a yes or a no.

Levi picked me up at two. This wasn't our usual routine, but we'd been swamped with the quarterly issue prep and hadn't had a chance to discuss the interview questions and our course of action. Doing it during the commute made the most sense under the circumstances. To make matters even worse, Kevin, one of our contributors from Orange County, hadn't come through with his "best of" list.

Basically, Levi and I were two stress balls who'd discovered how to compensate the lack of sleep with too many energy drinks and coffee.

The Regency was a flamboyant art deco landmark in the heart of L.A. It sat on a busy, nightlife-filled stretch of Wilshire Boulevard between K-Town and Beverly Hills, and from what I could gather from social media as we battled the Saturday traffic on our way there, the line of Hall Affinity fans had begun to form in front of the venue at dawn.

Levi was rocking the extra hipster look today. Doc Martens, skinny jeans, faded T-shirt with a #hashtag slogan on the front. He hadn't shaved in days and was on his second Red Bull when we finally got off the freeway.

"It's not like he's the president," Levi bickered over the fact we hadn't been informed whether the interview would be on camera. We'd packed our entire gear arsenal—both tripods, both mics, both audio recorders, cameras, LEDs, and an extra pack of batteries, but according to Linda's courtesy text, the chance that Frankie's manager would agree to video was slim.

"Dude's a glorified version of Chad Kroeger," Levi went on, sipping on his drink.

"Oh no, you didn't!" I had nothing against the front man of the Canadian powerhouse, but Frankie Blade was a player of an entirely different league. Comparing him to Kroeger was a blasphemy, and I seriously wanted to kick Levi for even thinking such nonsense.

"I'm just saying. What's wrong with telling us beforehand?" he muttered, his gaze never leaving the road.

"You know how it is." I shrugged, reaching for his phone sitting in the cupholder to change the playlist.

T-shirts with the signature Hall Affinity merch colors, black and orange, swarmed on the sidewalk as we circled the block near The Regency in search of parking. The streets buzzed. Invisible energy charged the warm September air.

"I think we should stick to Ubering from now on," Levi grumbled as the car in front of us came to a stop.

It took us another twenty minutes to get into a lot, park, and make it to the back entrance of the venue, where our bags were thoroughly searched by security before we were ushered toward a media tent on the opposite side of the barricade. The group was small. I recognized Darren from *AP* and Robbie, the owner of *Pulse Nation*. Linda and a couple of girls from Jay Brodie were handing out passes.

We made it in time for the press briefing.

The instructions were very specific.

No questions about the seven-year hiatus. No questions about Frankie's ex-wife. Who cared anyway? They'd been married for two and a half minutes. No questions about his health. No questions about KBC. No questions about motorcycles or any other kinds of extreme sport or adrenaline related activities. Basically, no questions about anything but the upcoming album.

Oh, and no questions about touring since it was still unclear whether Frankie was able to pull off a ninety-minute set.

"And please"—Linda raised both hands in the air and gave everyone in the tent a tense look—"refrain from staring at Mr. Blade's face for prolonged periods of time. It will make him uncomfortable and we don't want that. Understood?"

All heads nodded in unison.

"Great." She flashed us a smile and glanced at her phone. "We'll have a house photographer. You'll be provided images for your editorials. We ask you not to use any other unauthorized images."

We waited a bit longer before security finally escorted us inside to one of the upstairs lounges.

Levi was wired. I could tell from the dark shadows beneath his eyes. He paced around and talked to people to pass the time while I sat in a velvet papasan style chair and stared at my phone.

I had programmed Jax's number into my contacts the morning after he'd decorated my shoulder blade, but my gut was being silent and my brain was too busy to help me decide if I should call him. It'd been too long since a man had actually showed an interest in talking to me on a level that wasn't professional or friendship, and I had no idea how to start this.

"Cassy," someone said to my right. "How's life treating you?"

I lifted my gaze from my phone and swiveled toward the sound. Robbie's doughnut body descended into the chair next to mine. He was wearing a dark blue blazer and his thinning hair looked like it'd been smothered with an entire bottle of gel.

"Life's been treating me well, Robbie." I made it a rule to call people I worked around by their names to ensure they remembered me. Although Robbie and I went way back. I'd done some volunteer work for *Pulse Nation* after my Jay Brodie internship. Sadly, they'd told me the magazine didn't have a budget to hire another staff writer when I brought up money.

"Surprised to see you here," he said, straightening his blazer.

"Why? From what I know, three outlets were approved for an interview with Frankie and the rest can sit down with Dante." I got that info from Linda.

He shrugged. "Did you hear what Smith said?" His voice lowered to a hoarse whisper. "Frankie might not be doing any press today after all."

I wasn't sure whether Robbie was simply pulling my leg or his info was legit, but I didn't like the sound of it. Levi wouldn't either. Especially since he'd brought his backup gear too. "Really?"

Robbie nodded and ran his large palm over his gel-covered head. "I mean...the man's been in hiding for seven years. Could be nervous."

I suppressed my laugh. People like Frankie Blade didn't get nervous. Getting together with the rest of the band to record and tour after everything he'd been through took guts.

A short, round man in his mid-thirties rushed into the lounge, the crackling of the radio attached to his belt following him as he marched over to our group.

"Do we have"—he glanced at the clipboard—"*Rewired*?"

"Here!" Levi called, grabbing the gear.

"You're up. Follow me."

I rose from the chair and gave Robbie a shit-eating grin.

"My name is Smith," the man with the radio introduced himself as we walked down the hall. He turned around and scanned the passes hanging around our necks. "We'll need you to sign a confidentiality agreement first."

Somehow, this didn't surprise me at all.

"Do you know if the interview will be on camera or audio?" Levi asked as we got ushered into a small room at the end of the hallway.

"Corey will get you up to speed," Smith explained, motioning at the man waiting for us inside. He was older, dressed sharply, with streaks of silver in his hair and a deep frown in his forehead, all signs of permanent stress.

The secrecy around the interview format was overwhelming.

"Cassy and Levi with *Rewired*, correct?" Corey shook our hands and led us to the table in the middle of the room. "I'm Frankie's manager." He was reserved and very official, and his smile didn't reach his eyes.

"Yes. That's us." I nodded, setting my bag on the floor next to my chair. My dress pants rode up my thighs and my left bra strap was falling down my shoulder. My clothes suddenly felt like they didn't fit. Was I nervous? I knew all the questions. I knew the band's history and the lyrical content of all their albums like the back of my hand. This was something else, something I couldn't put my finger on.

Corey went over the major points of the confidentiality agreement and left the room.

"This is ridiculous," Levi muttered as he scribbled his name next to the neon pink pointer sticker. "Are we filming or what?"

"Does it matter?"

"Yes, it does. Video will get us more hits." He was obsessed with numbers. Numbers brought us revenue. No numbers meant no money. The face of Hall Affinity's front man would bring lots of traffic.

"You need to slow down with the energy drinks." I tried a joke to release the tension.

Corey returned with two stickers with our names on them. "Frankie likes to know whom he's talking to."

Oh boy!

Levi and I exchanged silent glares. This was a first. We'd never had to wear name tags before.

"We'll go with the video," the manager said, collecting the signed paperwork. "No LEDs," he added. "You get ten minutes to set up and ten minutes with Frankie. You're welcome to stay for the show. Your passes are good."

Music pounded somewhere below. My heart sang inside my

chest. Levi could barely keep from grinning. We were marching through a long hallway filled with enough security to form a baseball team when I saw Dante. He was heading toward us, his entourage consisting of two very young—probably barely legal—blonds, a body-guard, and his manager, Javier, whom I'd met a few times before when *Rewired* was covering Dante's solo album.

Our groups melded, and brief words were exchanged.

Dante wore his usual black silk shirt that wasn't tucked in all the way, faded designer jeans, a leather cowboy hat, and boots. He looked as if he'd just gotten out of bed and thrown together whatever outfit he'd had on before engaging in a nightlong orgy. His flashy style matched his status and his personality. He was a rock star with a capital *R*. Sex, drugs, rock 'n' roll, and then some.

I wasn't sure he'd recognize me, but none of the vices Dante had fooled around with for almost two decades seemed to dull his memory.

His mind was sharp as a razor when he was sober. And he definitely was, because I'd seen a number of videos of him drunk. He was the tabloids' favorite. They probably made as much money on him as he'd made playing lead guitar for one of the best-selling rock bands in the world.

He approached me. "Am I seeing you later?" he asked, ignoring Levi. His smile dazzled like a freshly cut diamond, the white tip of a lollipop stick showing from the corner of his mouth. Last I heard, he was trying to quit smoking.

"Not today." I shook my head.

"Say what?" His voice jumped and heads turned, including Corey's. "You cheating on me, Cassy?" He pouted, plucking the candy from between his lips. A glint of amusement flickered in his eyes.

Dante was the kind of man who liked to touch people. I credited this particular trait to his Hispanic heritage. His free hand slid up my shoulder and he gave me an air kiss. The blonds observed me and snickered.

Dismissing their stares, I returned his smile. They'd be yesterday's news tomorrow morning. "Maybe next time."

"Next time it is, darlin'." Dante topped off his game with a wink.

We disengaged. I buzzed from the collision with his larger than life personality and his aura.

"This little lady is da bomb," he said, jerking his chin at Corey before sticking the lollipop in his mouth again.

A chill raced up my spine.

There was no time for a thank you. Our groups went their separate ways. Levi shook his head and barely bit back his *I-told-you-to-use-your-hookups* grin.

The room Corey took us to was small and intimate. The music disappeared completely when the door behind us slammed shut. There were two security guards outside and an older man with a head full of gray hair sitting inside on a small couch in the corner. He wore a light brown vest, loose jeans, and boots. Faded swirls of ink crept from under the sleeves of his Woodstock-themed shirt.

Billy, I thought to myself. Frankie's father. He wasn't hard to recognize.

The old man gave us a half-smile and a nod.

"You'll have twenty-four hours to send me raw footage and a final cut for approval," Corey said.

There were refreshments set up on a table and I desperately wanted to get a bottle of water for my dry throat, but we didn't have much time. Levi was setting up his tripod and I needed to test both mics.

We worked fast and in tense silence. I wrestled off my jacket and double-checked the batteries. Sweat coated the back of my neck and my hair began sticking to my skin.

I'd interviewed some of the biggest and nastiest names in the business. Anxiety was no longer an option. If the person sensed my hesitation, it always caused a shutdown. Establishing a relationship with a complete stranger in under thirty seconds was a gift. *My gift.*

The one that fed me and paid my bills. Why my mind was suddenly blanking with terror was a brain twister to me.

When we were all set, Levi indulged himself with a free energy drink and I grabbed a water.

Billy kept quiet and I wondered how much say he had in what was going on here today or how big of a role he'd played in his son's decision to return to the music industry.

That Frankie had been adopted by the Wallaces shortly after he'd turned six wasn't a secret. He didn't talk about it much at first, and when his career took off, the topic had become a big no for the press. Of course, his reluctance to discuss the part of his childhood he'd spent in foster care didn't stop gossip-hungry sharks from digging deeper. Fortunately, there was nothing to dig for.

Frankie Blade was an American dream. Living proof that anyone could rise from the ashes. Not once, but twice.

The door swung open and the room suddenly felt like an inferno.

My gaze moved to the people entering. Corey led the group and I saw the bald head of a bodyguard lingering all the way in the back. Frankie was sandwiched between him, his manager, and a voluptuous leggy blond in a bright pink blazer and dress pants. I heard a door slam and my spine stiffened.

Corey asked, "Are you all set?" Then his eyes darted between Levi and me, seeking confirmation.

We both nodded.

The air sparked; the floors rumbled. Frankie's presence was a nuclear explosion, slowly traveling through the room until it hit me full force. My palm that was wrapped around the wireless mic was sweaty as I smiled.

"This is Levi and Cassy from *Rewired*." Corey made the brief introduction and stepped aside. The blond held out her hand for a shake first. "Hi. I'm Brooklyn, Frankie's assistant." She had a throaty, commanding tone and I couldn't tell her age. Too many layers of makeup covered her skin.

When Frankie and his bodyguard reached us, my heart jumped.

The entire afternoon seemed unreal and the memories swept me under. I was a confused fourteen-year-old girl again, who sat in her room, crying through all twelve tracks of *Breathe Crimson* because her father hadn't come home last night.

"Pleasure," Frankie said, his voice deep and thick with emotion. A hand extended to me. "How are you?" No name followed. Not that it was necessary.

I snapped back to the present and slid my damp palm against his, slightly embarrassed. "Great. How are you?" A smile stretched across my lips. The words coming out of my mouth felt stale.

He shook my hand, his stormy gunmetal blue eyes drawing a quick path along the length of my face and upper body. They didn't descend past the sticker with my name, which I appreciated.

Contrary to common belief, Frankie wasn't as tall as the stage and the music videos made him out to be, but his trimmed-to-perfection five-eleven height was a force to be reckoned with against my thin-framed five-four. He was wearing all black. Slim jeans hung low on his hips, leaving very little to the imagination, a satin shirt clung to his chest and abs just enough to show the result of rigorous workout sessions, and sparse ink designs littered his jewelry-clad forearms.

I attempted to follow Linda's advice and refrain from staring at him, but my eyes didn't agree with my brain. They ogled.

Frankie returned my smile and withdrew his hand to shake Levi's. The bodyguard retreated back to the corner to give us space. Corey positioned himself next to the camera.

"If you don't mind"—I grabbed a lav mic from Levi—"audio can get a little messy with this one if things heat up." Heart racing, I shook my wireless Sennheiser. The base was damp from my sweat. I needed a napkin more than anything right now.

"We definitely don't want things to get messy." Frankie laughed softly, moving toward the leather couch. The sound was subtle but infectious. It filtered through me like a sultry heatwave, taunting and soothing.

He motioned for me to join him.

Breathe, Cassy, breathe, I told myself. My lungs were tight and my stomach knotted pleasantly as I neared the couch. Frankie scooted over to one side and I sat on the other. The cool leather squawked under the weight of our shifting bodies as we made ourselves comfortable.

"Could you put this on?" I handed him the lav mic.

"Does it come with instructions?" A hint of a smirk tugged the corner of his mouth. The man was full of silent innuendos. I wasn't sure if they were intentional or force of habit, but I loved it.

"Oh, it's a clip-on," I explained, holding it up.

Frankie's hands didn't move. He tilted his head slightly, then glanced down at his chest. The man had either never secured a microphone on his clothes before or was too lazy to do it himself. Although the latter made more sense since microphones were sort of his specialty.

"Okay, ummm"—I kept smiling as my hands reached for his shirt —"do you have a preference of which side you want it on?" Was there anything about touching Frankie in the confidentiality agreement? My mind drew a blank and I got slightly paranoid. The man's worth was seventy million dollars, and if my memory served me right, his vocal cords and his entire body were insured for double that amount.

Rich people are strange, I thought, leaning toward him to clip on the lav mic. Part of me, the one who'd worked in the industry, under-stood why, but the other part of me, the lower-middle-class-neighbor-hood girl whose family could only afford liability auto insurance, was...disappointed.

"Whatever's going to get us great audio," Frankie said in a low voice as I began to secure the mic. My fingers were clammy and my eyes shamelessly wandered over his sculptured neck and chest. The tip of an unfamiliar tattoo that must have been done after the acci-dent licked a trace across his left collarbone. The shirt hid the rest. I couldn't tell what it was, but I was curious whether he'd talk about it in some other interview. He used to discuss every single tattoo he'd gotten and what had made him do it. His skin was perfect. Maybe even too perfect for a man who'd recently turned thirty-eight. He hardly had any marks or wrinkles on the right side of his face. Had this been the result of plastic surgery? Only faint smile lines fanned out from his left eye.

There was one scar below his chin. Cameras wouldn't be able to pick it up. I'd seen it just because we were inches apart. My gaze lingered on the slim line of skin discoloration longer than necessary. I knew he'd noticed, because his body began to shift.

Heat hit my face. "We're all done here," I said, taking my hands off Frankie's designer shirt that probably cost as much as my entire month of rent. His scent, a blend of expensive cologne, hair product, and pheromones, crept up my nose and coated my lungs.

"Thanks, Cassy." He smiled again and I felt my thighs melt into the couch. "Shall we get started now?"

Ten minutes with Frankie Blade was more like ten seconds. He knew when to laugh and when to be serious. My heart had been beating like a war drum the entire interview.

I had other questions. I wanted to pick his brain about his hiatus, about Billy and Janet, about the lyrical content of "Ambivalent," and about his disagreement with Dante that had caused the delay of *Breathe Crimson*, but I knew all those things weren't allowed and I didn't want to risk it.

Corey hovered like a mother hen, standing next to Levi and staring at the camera with his arms crossed on his chest and a huge frown set above the bridge of his nose. Occasionally, he'd toss us a stifled smile. I didn't know whether he was unhappy with the angles, the light, or me, but I tried not to pay attention to the noticeably tense look on his face.

His job wasn't your typical run-of-the-mill management position. I could only imagine the stress. Or maybe I couldn't.

Our time was up. Frankie rattled off a short message to the band's fans and gave me a nod. "Thank you." His gunmetal gaze held mine as he tried to rid himself of the microphone.

"Thank *you*," I said, taking the device. "We're very happy to have you back." My pants were stuck to the leather upholstery and a scotch-tape-type noise cut through the room when I tried to get up. I hated that sound. It never happened when I wore jeans, but I didn't want to look like a hipster Barbie on camera next to the front man of Hall Affinity.

We all shook hands again. A few more words were exchanged. Mostly further instructions. Corey handed each of us his business card. Despite the air conditioning blasting full force, the room was even hotter than before the interview.

Once Levi packed up his gear, we were escorted out.

"Enjoy the show, guys," Corey said before returning into the room.

"I think that was pretty good." The words tumbled from my lips. I wasn't sure how else to describe what had just transpired. I was still starstruck, my chest filled with raw excitement.

"You looked really good," Levi agreed. The upturned expression on his face told me he wasn't lying.

Radio static and heavy footsteps buzzed through the hallway. Blasts of music came and went somewhere beneath our feet. Soundcheck.

We returned to the lounge and took a small table in the corner to work on the draft. Robbie was still sitting in the same spot, sour-faced. The show wouldn't start for another two hours and I didn't want to waste them. Levi and I had mastered the art of working remotely years ago. Many times, when we weren't sworn to the constraints of the confidentiality agreement, we had our articles up within a couple of hours. All we needed was a laptop and good Wi-Fi.

Not being able to run Frankie's interview annoyed me a little, but I told myself to get over it.

"Will you keep an eye on my bag?" I asked Levi, closing my

laptop. I needed a break. Words didn't flow and I felt blocked. "I'm going to the restroom."

He nodded, his eyes never leaving the screen of his MacBook Pro.

I took a detour and went downstairs to see the soundcheck.

The stage was a hot mess of amps, cables, and microphones and didn't look anywhere near ready for tonight's show. A shiver of warmth rolled down my spine as I watched crew members arrange the VIP donor tables along the perimeter of the main floor. The Douglas & Krueger Benefit was *the* charity event of the season. The general admission tickets sold out in seconds. The concert featured some of the biggest names in the industry and last fall, Paul Krueger auctioned off his Corvette.

I stood next to the soundboard with my phone in my hand, my heart thumping out a wild staccato beat. Linda had been very clear about cells. Jay Brodie PR didn't want any media personnel to take pictures anywhere backstage at any point. Only from the pit during the show. Only approved photographers. No close-ups of Frankie. Although I didn't know how the organizers were going to stop concertgoers from doing that, unless phones would simply not be allowed inside, but there were lines and lines of rabid fans and tele-photo-armed paps milling around the building. They were all here for Frankie and I knew the moment he took the stage, thousands of images and videos would begin to flood the net.

The music stopped. Javier emerged from behind the curtain. There was a brief exchange with Dante's guitar tech, which looked a lot like an argument. I watched them silently from my spot, wondering how hard it must be to work for someone who'd been number ten on the list of Best Modern Guitarists in the World. Dante wasn't merely sex, drugs, and rock 'n' roll. He was also insanely talented. And that talent played a huge role in making Hall Affinity one of the most successful rock bands of the twenty-first century.

My gaze dropped to my phone and I pulled up Jax's contact info. Starting a conversation with a man who wasn't an interviewee or Levi felt beyond weird.

I'm loving my new ink, I typed. Awkward way to begin. I knew it.

From the corner of my eye, I saw Dante. He strapped on his guitar and plucked at the strings, his face tense. The stage crew was busy with their tasks.

My phone pinged with the text message alert.

Jax: I'm glad to hear it.

How are you?

Jax: I'm great. How are you?

I'm great too.

Jax: I didn't think you'd text.

A playful guitar riff pierced the room. I tore my eyes from the phone and surveyed the stage. Dante was messing around with his Fender. There was a hint of seductive charm in the way he played. Raw and powerful. Every note was a work of art. I'd forgotten what I was going to text Jax. Clouds of musical bliss filled my head.

"It's a madhouse outside." Linda's voice drifted over the noise.

I spun to face her. She looked ruffled, and her heels clicked as she neared me. "Do we have any word on the setlist?" I asked. So much secrecy revolved around Frankie's performance that it felt as if we were skydiving without a parachute.

"I'll text it to you"—Linda pulled out her cell—"for your eyes only." Her steely glare bored through me like a drill.

"Of course." I nodded.

"Do you have your passes?" She checked with me before walking off.

I nodded again and returned my attention to the stage. Dante was done. He moved over to the edge and jumped to the floor to greet Linda. They didn't engage in a long conversation. It was a two-second exchange.

The text message with the setlist came in. Frankie and Dante were doing the last two songs—a Doors cover, and "Ambivalent." My heart did a little dance.

"Are you coming to my party after the show?" a voice said.

I looked toward the sound and my eyes caught sight of Dante's lollipop. My chest swelled as he approached. Linda was long gone. The stage crew and the venue employees were concentrating on their chores.

"I'm sorry?" I asked, glancing around to make sure he was indeed talking to me.

"Are you coming to my party?" The candy traveled from one corner of his mouth to the other.

"Ummm..." My mind blanked. I didn't understand what prompted the question. "I wasn't invited."

"I'm inviting you now." Dante laughed softly and handed me a piece of paper that looked a lot like a playing card. It was shiny, black, and had a silver *D* on one side. Nothing else. "The car will be waiting out back after the encore."

"This is random," I shared my skepticism with him.

"Why is it random?" He shook his head and an earring glinted behind the dark strands of his shoulder length hair. "You work your ass off, darlin'. I never see you having a good time. What kind of life is that?"

His words made it sound as if he'd been watching me. It irked me, but the man had a point. I never drank during gigs and never partied after them. The pressure of pushing the material as fast as possible turned me into a mini robot.

"Dante"—I held the card up—"you know I'm the enemy, right? I'm press."

"I'm aware. You'll be off the clock by then." He was playing a dangerous game.

This was bizarre and my brain struggled to understand why I'd been invited. "Can I think about it?"

"You've got"—Dante glanced down at his Rolex—"four hours." He flashed me a wide, toothy smile and I questioned my own sanity when my knees quivered.

No one is immune to the charms of a man who can play a ten-minute guitar solo. Not even you, Cassy, my common sense said.

You've been around testosterone without any physical contact for way too long, missy. It's time to get laid, my ovaries countered.

Dante wasn't necessarily the object of my sexual fantasies. That was territory I never explored. I didn't let my imagination lust after people I worked with. It felt wrong. Instead, my mind was currently playing out a more acceptable rock star party scenario where I drank myself silly and engaged into a hot make-out session with some roadie or someone's assistant in one of the guest bathrooms. That seemed realistic and easy enough to pull off. That seemed like my kind of fun.

I slipped the card in the back pocket of my pants and returned Dante's smile.

"Let me get you a drink," he said, motioning at the bar.

Alcohol during gigs was against my rules, but for some reason, I couldn't tell Dante no. He was charming in an alpha-male-meets-Hello-Kitty kind of way. He bossed people around without being overbearing.

We walked over to the bar and Dante ordered a margarita for me and rum and coke for himself.

"Have a little fun, Cassy." He clinked his glass against mine and checked his watch again. "Gotta go. See you later, darlin'."

Chapter Three

Levi and I watched the show from a small area of the balcony that had been sectioned off specifically for media. The crowd on the floor screamed and pushed against the chain of security in front of the stage when Frankie finally appeared. He wore the same outfit he had on earlier during the interview. His hair shone under a blue spotlight that followed him to the microphone.

My heart galloped inside my chest as I watched him giving a short speech.

A sea of hands thrust into the air. Posters flew up. When the music finally poured, a tangle of gasps and screams filled the venue.

I'd been taking notes on my phone, but my fingers suddenly stopped cooperating. Levi's head nodded along with the drumbeat. The upstairs guests weren't as starstruck as the general admission crowd, but I could hear the whispers of admiration floating around the balcony area.

We'd been given drink tickets and despite my no-alcohol rule— perhaps thanks to Dante's margarita that had loosened me up—I decided to take advantage of their hospitality and ordered myself another cocktail. The pleasant buzz in my head was a blend of highs:

drinks and music. Pure and overwhelming. The best kind of adrenaline.

For two songs, the world stood still. Nothing but Frankie's voice mattered. It was an explosive combination of tenor and baritone and as he climbed through the notes with his typical edgy finesse, I felt him inside my chest, crashing, melting, and burning.

Dante played with his eyes closed, as if he'd gone to some parallel universe where he channeled his magic. He'd taken his Rolex off for the set and his hands were flying across the fretboard and the strings like angel wings.

The two were explosive together. Even seven years of silence hadn't put a dent in their chemistry. If they were planning to tour, they'd be making bank.

There was still an unanswered text message from Jax and an invite to the party in my back pocket, but I didn't want to think about any of those things or the interview while Frankie sang. I wanted to be a fan for ten minutes. I wanted to simply enjoy the music.

After the show, the backstage hummed with raw energy. The house photographer roamed through the VIP crowd. Some of the guest performers socialized and gladly posed for photos. Frankie wasn't present.

"I got invited to a party," I told Levi as we made our way toward the staircase.

He hoisted his camera bag up on his shoulder and gave me a perplexed look.

"Dante's party," I said in a low voice.

Levi needed a few moments to take in the info. "Are you going?"

I shrugged.

"You could use some fun."

"Why is everyone telling me to have fun? Don't I look fun enough?"

Levi laughed. "You and fun don't exist in the same universe, Cass."

"I'm fun," I insisted. My bag felt heavy and my arm needed a rest.

"Okay. Whatever you say."

"Do you think I should go?" I wasn't sure why I needed someone to tell me to go. The line between them and us was thin. They were people with secrets. We were people who wanted those secrets.

"I already told you what I think. I think you need to get drunk and I think you need to get laid."

Levi never beat around the bush. He had no filter whatsoever and his directness was one of the main reasons why girls didn't stick around. Plus the magazine. No one stood a chance against *Rewired*.

My bladder needed relief and when we reached the bottom of the stairs, I handed Levi my bag and asked him to wait for me.

"I'll be outside." He waved, heading for the back entrance. "Don't take too long. Parking's gonna be a nightmare."

I walked down the narrow hall, surveying the signs. The two drinks I'd had weren't doing me any favors. My vision blurred and my legs didn't feel like my own.

"Ma'am?" a throaty voice called out.

I spun on my heels. A tall bald man in a uniform stood in front of me. I always wondered why security guards had to shave their heads, and the question now threatened to leave my mouth.

"Where are you headed?" he asked, hand on his radio.

"Oh... I'm looking for a restroom," I explained, half-expecting him to tell me I wasn't allowed to be here, which happened to me quite often. Not all press passes came with all access ones. Why today had been different was a mystery I didn't care to solve. I'd seen Frankie Blade sing his heart out after seven years of nothing. That was enough.

The security guard's eyes lingered on my name tag hanging from the lanyard around my neck, which I'd forgotten about. "End of the hallway and to your right." He nodded.

"Thank you." Then I was on my way. *Damn margaritas!*

I heard people talking as I neared the turn, but the alcohol in my blood slowed my brain. We collided as I rounded the corner. My nose and mouth pressed against a hard, satin-clad chest. I knew immediately it was Frankie's. His scent, a lush blend of cologne and hair products, made my head spin even faster.

"Umph...sorry." I pulled back, my body swaying. I registered Frankie's palms on my elbows. They felt warm and nice against my skin, and it didn't help my coordination.

"You okay?" he asked, steadying me.

"Yes. Thank you. I'm fine." A nervous laugh of embarrassment escaped from between my lips. I was dizzy, drunk, and apparently clumsy, but I willed myself to stand straight.

Behind Frankie was another security guard with a shaved head. I recognized him from the TMZ photos.

"I'm looking for a restroom," I explained. "I loved what you did with 'L.A. Woman,' by the way." My lips stretched into a grin.

"That was the idea." Frankie released my elbows and took a step away. A smile touched his face.

"I'm sorry"—I motioned at his chest where my glossy mouth had left a pink smudge—"about your shirt."

His gaze slid down to assess the damage, then returned to me. "It's not a big deal."

Electricity zapped through the air. My stomach twisted under his scrutiny. "Well..." I stammered. "Welcome back and have a good night."

"You too, Cassy." He smirked. "Make sure to watch your step."

While I took care of business in the restroom, I cursed myself like a sailor, my cheeks burning and my heart pounding.

Have a good night? Really? You tell a man who's on every the-most-(insert celebrity-relevant adjective and noun here)-in-the-world list to have a good night? Girlfriend. You must not drink anymore. Ever again.

My body was trembling as I positioned myself in front of the mirror to wash my hands. It was all Frankie's fault. His charm was addicting. He was addicting.

I pulled out my phone and absently stared at the iMessage window.

Jax: I didn't think you'd text.

What kind of response would a young, educated woman give to this? That she needed to weigh all the pros and cons. Nah. Too clinical.

Why not?

There. I was going to utilize Levi's favorite answer-a-question-with-another-question strategy.

Outside, Levi was waiting for me as we'd agreed. The rear lot was busy. Trucks roared, equipment rattled. The security guards scanned the perimeter to make sure extra-enthusiastic fans couldn't get past the barricades. Didn't mean they'd stop trying.

"You good?" Levi asked, pushing my bag over to me. My arm hurt and I had no desire to carry anything whatsoever.

A long black limo crawled up to the dock. I noted the barely legal blonds jumping in, along with some faces I'd seen on the covers of magazines and in the tabloids before. The card in my back pocket seemed to burn my ass.

"Are you coming?" a voice asked. Dante.

My brain stalled. God's honest truth, I hadn't taken his invitation seriously.

He was making his way toward the limo in the company of his manager and another woman. No, scratch that. A girl. The man had a weakness. Apparently, he didn't hang out with any females over twenty-five, because I hadn't noticed anyone in his entourage today who looked remotely older than me.

Levi nudged me on the shoulder when I didn't respond.

"Will you take my stuff?" I muttered to him, motioning at my bag.

"Geez." Levi extended his hand. "Hand it over. But you're gonna have to pick it up from my place. I'm not delivering it to you."

"Okay."

"Last chance, darlin'," Dante called. Giggles carried over the evening city noise.

"Can you hold on a second?" I bellowed, fishing my ID, credit card, and pepper spray from the side pocket of my bag. I didn't know why I was going. It was against all my rules and all my beliefs, but my gut told me to.

Have fun, Cassy, it whispered. *Have fun and stop worrying about everything for once in your life. The world will still be here tomorrow.*

"Don't get in trouble," Levi said just before I rushed over to the limo where Dante had been patiently waiting for me.

"Are you ready to rock 'n' roll?" He flashed a crooked smile, ushering me inside.

"I was born to rock 'n' roll."

"That's what I'm talking about, darlin'."

The door shut and we started to move.

I'd been in a limo a few times but never the kind we took to Dante's place, with a stripper pole, disco lights, and built-in fish tank. My favorite part of the ride was when one of the blonds tripped when she attempted to utilize the pole to get Dante's attention.

I certainly wasn't the type to judge other women for showing off their bodies. Athena Angel was one of my favorite female performers, but the naiveté of the youth gathered here tonight made me laugh.

I blamed my cynicism on the alcohol. Every girl sitting in this limo was secretly hoping she'd hit the jackpot and marry a rock star, but every girl would be wrong. Hundreds of twenty-one-year-olds came and went and no one remembered their names the next morning. It was the way the world of the rich and famous worked. That's why I'd never allowed myself to become one of those girls.

Everyone stared at me the entire ride as if I'd been branded, probably because I was the only woman who wasn't wearing a skirt. I didn't care. I was sitting next to Dante and my heart was dancing inside my chest like a drunk cheerleader. Somehow, he managed to maintain a conversation with every single person inside the limo who was still able to produce coherent sentences.

Including me.

The man was a charmer and a terrific multitasker.

Although a spur of words were flying around as various things were discussed, I fully intended to get answers to all my questions the second a good opportunity to pick Dante's brain presented itself.

Was he ever going to record another solo album?

Was he going to try to quit drinking?

Was he drug-free at the moment?

Rumor had it, Dante had written most of the *Hollow Heart Dream* riffs while on coke, and the infamous guitar solo for "Ambivalent" had been born during his short stint with acid. The man was a trip.

I couldn't remember the last time I'd drunk this much and that made me sad. Because margaritas were fun and, apparently, I'd been missing out.

While the limo lazily rolled through the streets of L.A. nightlife, music roared and drinks spilled. It was just as I imagined. Except for Dante's choice of residence.

I'd always thought rock stars favored the beach or the mountains, something away from civilization, somewhere to escape to. Hall Affinity's guitarist settled on neither. He occupied a penthouse in a luxury building a few blocks north of Sunset Boulevard.

We parked near the front entrance and the concierge rushed to help us unload. The elevator was too small to fit everyone, so after Dante and some others went up, I took the next one with the rest of the party. We were crass and insanely loud, and I almost wanted to apologize for such behavior, but I had a feeling this was the norm here and my apology wouldn't make any difference.

My feet were killing me and my head was spinning like a carousel when we finally arrived to the top floor.

I needed a minute—or ten—to fully accept the fact that people indeed lived like kings.

Dante's place was a huge open-concept apartment with wall-to-wall windows overlooking L.A., glittering ceiling lights, and all sorts of freaky artwork. I wandered around the living room with a drink in my hand, ogling the paintings of guitars and talking to people. Surprisingly, not everyone here wanted to climb a stripper pole and undress. The crowd was a colorful mix.

An old rock tune blasted through the main quarters. Pizza and other refreshments were served in the kitchen. Dante took on bartending duties for a while, but as soon as his speech and coordination began to fail him, he resorted to using the blonds as crutches. They didn't seem to mind. On the contrary, they looked ecstatic.

More people arrived. The place was getting wild, indecent, and bred a load of stories TMZ would kill for.

Marilyn Manson's "The Beautiful People" was blasting from the speakers when my bladder started to scream again. I lost count of how many times I'd turned down the offer to "have fun." It was strange that my attempts to actually find someone decent to have sex with at a party this big and raucous hadn't been fruitful. The advances I received didn't feel like fair game. They didn't come from the individuals I could see myself getting it on with. Or the alcohol wasn't working on me. Supposedly, a good amount of liquor made men appear less douchey and more educated, which would normally result in a better "quickie with a stranger" experience.

In my case, the stars simply didn't want to align.

Should have worn a skirt, Cassy.

I refilled my drink purely out of habit and pushed my way through the baked crowd. I needed to pee. Badly.

My shoes tapped against the parquet floor as I continued into a hallway. There was no light here and the first door to my right happened to be locked.

"Shit," I muttered, taking a deep breath. My stomach lurched.

Voices behind me became muffled background noise. My blurry gaze carefully skimmed over the wall and registered another door. I reached for the handle and pushed it open.

The room was dark, but the blinds weren't shut, which gave me a perfect opportunity to witness a potential scandal. The silhouettes of two bodies molded together were drawn against the shimmering backdrop of L.A. nightlife. I wasn't a prude; I watched porn. But I'd never seen two men having sex. The view gave me the best kind of brain freeze. I stood there with my mouth agape and my spine wrapped in pleasant chills, and I watched their beautiful bodies slickly moving together until one of them finally noticed me.

"What the fuck?" His head snapped in my direction.

"Sorry," I mumbled. "Carry on." I pulled the door shut.

My mind was spiraling out of control as I continued along. Then my bladder reminded me why I'd come to this part of Dante's penthouse. The place was huge. I hadn't realized that there was another wing here, quiet and free of the rowdy rock 'n' roll bunch that was trashing the living room and the kitchen.

I floated through the hallway until I saw another door that was ajar. When I pushed it open and walked in, hoping to find a restroom, my leg banged into something hard.

"Fucking hell." I winced as my kneecap wept.

The room was pitch-black, and my drunk eyes couldn't make out anything. My body wobbled as my hands inspected the air. After distancing myself from the piece of furniture that had assaulted me, I set my glass on the floor and bent down to hug my legs because the pain was horrible and that seemed like the best way to make it stop.

"There's a first aid kit in the restroom," someone said from somewhere across from me.

Electricity surged through my chest. My stomach turned over. I'd recognize that voice in my sleep. It was Frankie's.

My common sense told me to return myself to a vertical position, but my knee told me to keep doing what I was doing, stay folded in half with my arms wrapped around my thighs and my mouth pressed against the thin fabric of my pants.

"Thanks," I said meekly. "I just need a minute. Please don't mind me."

"I can call 911," he offered. There was a hint of a smile in his tone. Evidently, my impromptu yoga session amused him.

"That won't be necessary."

53

I heard a click and saw a soft yellow light from the corner of my eye.

You sure know how to impress a man, Cassy.

Drawing a deep breath through my teeth, I released my legs and straightened up. Frankie was sitting in a chair across the room. A drink sat on the table next to him and he looked...tired. Traces of stress and fatigue marred his face.

Beside the table, there was a floor lamp. A large leather couch that apparently had a problem with me separated us.

"We meet again," I said, smoothing my palms over my pants.

"Three times in one night."

"Freaky coincidence."

"I don't believe in coincidences, Cassy."

Frankie Blade remembered my name! His words made me high as a kite. In a good way.

"Well..." I paused to collect myself. "I'm not sure what else to call it." That was the truth.

Warmth filled my stomach when his gunmetal blue eyes caught my gaze.

We stared at each other for a few moments, and I couldn't think of anything to say. My mind was scrambled. I knew everything there was to know about this man, yet I had no idea how to behave in his presence while I was off the clock.

Could it be the alcohol?

"You really need to watch your step." Frankie motioned at my legs, smirking.

"Ha." A stifled laugh came out of my mouth. "I'm actually trying to find a restroom," I explained, surveying the room. Then my journalist's brain took over. "Can I ask you a question?"

His brows knit. "You can try."

"How does it feel to be performing again?"

Frankie kept on looking at me, his face a combination of tense and relaxed. He took a swallow of his drink and finally said, "Different."

I nodded and rounded the couch. "I'm happy to see you back."

Surely, Frankie Blade had heard this many times today, but I had the need to tell him anyway.

"Are you a fan of the band?"

"I am. Yes. I own all your albums." I rubbed my sore knee and sat on the edge of the cushion. Something told me he wasn't opposed to this conversation.

"Which one is your favorite?"

I bit the inside of my cheek and pondered. Frankie Blade wrote beautiful songs that made me feel alive, and perhaps telling him that now, before we went our separate ways, would be okay. "My dad"—I dropped my gaze to the expensive upholstery and ran my index finger against it—"left us a couple of weeks after *Breathe Crimson* came out." Saying it out loud seemed strange. It hurt a little too. "I believe there was a period when I really hated that album because it made me think about my dad and how much of a coward he was to walk out on his wife and kids, but nothing else at the time spoke to me like 'Ambivalent.' I have a very weird relationship with that song," I confessed. "It was the dark comfort I needed to get through my first real heartbreak."

My breathing faded into silence. The room was still and I didn't dare look at Frankie, because I didn't want him to see what was happening in my head right now.

"People we love always hurt us the most," he said after a while. His voice carried over the charged air, which felt hot. I didn't know what the hell it was, but the man elicited this strange energy that made the temperature jump through the roof wherever he went. It was distracting.

Rock stars. Go figure.

"Is that what the song is about?" I asked, glancing back at him.

The lyrics of "Ambivalent" were open to interpretation. Frankie had said it himself during a *Breathe Crimson* tour interview. That was the beauty of art. You chose what worked for you.

"It's what *life* is about," he said cryptically, sipping on his drink.

My blood pounded in my ears and an incredible rush ran through me. Not every woman had an opportunity to discuss her favorite songs with their creator, especially when the creator was surrounded by bodyguards twenty-four seven because he was wanted by the entire female population of the planet. This was the most surreal moment of my life.

Frankie didn't seem to mind my company either. He sat in his chair, unmoving. The light spilled evenly across the left side of his face, leaving the other one in shadow and making him look deliciously mysterious. The two top buttons of his shirt—obviously a different one, because my lip gloss wasn't on it—were unbuttoned, revealing the design of the tattoo I noticed earlier, but I was too far away and too drunk to make it out.

"Is that recent?" I asked, motioning at his chest. "Your tat?"

"Yes." He nodded, dragging the fabric away to show me the rest.

The warmth coating my stomach spread to my legs. My thighs clenched. Oh no. The sight of Frankie's hard, inked chest was turning me on and I hated it. I was breaking my rules once again.

"That's neat." I inched my ass closer to the edge of the couch and leaned forward to try to get a better view of the tat. There were a few feet of empty space between us and the design was a blurry blob, but I didn't know if getting closer was allowed. I'd signed something today that could have been me giving away my firstborn to Frankie. So instead, I narrowed my eyes, willing my vision to work for at least a few seconds, and was finally able to see that a bird was splayed across his pec.

I took a wild guess. "Is that an...eagle?"

"Yes."

"I got one a few weeks ago too," I spouted. My mouth, my brain, and my common sense were in total disagreement. I shed my jacket, spun on my ass, and pulled my top down my shoulder to show him the butterfly.

"Nice detailing." He didn't say anything else.

I heard footsteps approaching.

"Are you two getting along?" Dante's voice entered the room.

"We are." Frankie's eyes smiled along with his mouth and my body shook. I'd fallen for his subtle sex appeal like Alice down the rabbit hole. Every part of me buzzed with tension.

I pulled my top back up and squirmed in my spot. My legs were cramping and my heart drummed a wild beat.

"The party's out there, you know." Dante motioned at the door, then staggered to the couch and sat next to me. When hot alcohol breath skated across my neck, I shivered.

"It's too crowded," Frankie explained, bringing his glass to his lips. The fabric of his shirt stretched tightly over his biceps. His every move was another nail in the coffin of my self-control. The man radiated sex.

"What are you doing, darlin'?" Dante's arm snaked over my shoulder. He was a hugger. He was also drunk, which made me think of the pepper spray in the front pocket of my pants. I wasn't sure why. This get-together we were having was pretty civilized. No foul words were said. Except for the ones that left my mouth when my knee didn't agree with the couch.

"Just showing off our new ink," Frankie said.

"You too?" Dante's face turned to me. He was happily wasted. His eyes were two dark orbs and his hat was missing.

"Yes. I got a new one too." I nodded, my head a vibrating black hole. Blood hit my temples so hard, I could barely hear myself speaking.

"Are you enjoying the party?" he slurred.

"I am."

Everything about this moment was bizarre. I was sitting in a room with two of the most popular rock musicians in the world and despite the strange tension their presence created, I didn't feel intimidated.

Hot and bothered. That's what I was. Which I blamed Levi for. Ever since he'd pitched me the idea of getting laid, it had refused to leave my brain. I couldn't remember the last time I'd slept with someone, let alone gone on a date. Come to think of it, dates didn't even make it on the list of things I needed to experience. My life was currently an endless string of events, write-ups, interviews, and too much caffeine. And I happened to like it.

My crazy schedule didn't give me time to worry about the things I was missing. The things other twenty-five-year-olds were doing while I chased my next big story.

Right now, that story sat in a chair five feet away from me and oozed sex.

It was pure torture and my pheromones couldn't take it anymore.

I pushed myself off the couch and rubbed my screaming knee. "Gentlemen"—my head spun—"it was a pleasure, but unfortunately, nature calls. Will you please tell me where the restroom is?"

I couldn't see Dante, but I felt Frankie's gaze. It lasered up and down my body slowly until our eyes met.

"First door on the left." He jerked his chin toward the hallway.

"Thank you for the company." I smoothed my palms over my pants to iron out the creases and saw my way out.

Sensible Cassy understood he might not take her seriously, but drunk Cassy figured, why not? Ignoring the response to my earlier question, I typed, *Are you busy?*

Then I waited. Levi was always my first choice when I entered a temporary damsel-in-distress state, but today, I didn't feel like calling Levi. I needed a man. Hot, raw, and willing to blow off some steam with me.

Jax seemed to be the right guy for the job.

I hid in the bathroom. My bladder was happy; my ovaries weren't. The aftertaste of Frankie's cologne still ruled my system. In a nutshell, the whole conversation with the golden boy of hard rock messed with my existence and I seriously considered getting myself off.

My phone pinged.

Jax: Finishing up at the shop.

I know this might seem very random, but could you give me a ride home?

I waited some more. The time dragged on like a church sermon.

Jax: Sure. Where are you?

Good question. Based on the grandeur views of the hillside properties Dante's place overlooked, I knew I was somewhere near either West Hollywood or Beverly Hills, but of course, no one had given me the actual address.

I pulled up Google Maps, pinned my current location, and sent it Jax, hoping it was accurate.

My pleasant buzz was turning into a splitting headache and I didn't like it a single bit. I didn't want to feel like a sack of potatoes during my round of sex.

Jax: I'll be there in thirty minutes.

Relief washed over me. Half an hour wasn't too bad. I had every intention to stay in the restroom until Jax got here, but ten minutes later, there came an insistent knock on the door.

"Hey, are you gonna be long?" a puny female voice called. "I really need to pee." She sounded desperate.

"Just a second." I checked myself in the mirror one last time. Not that my looks mattered at this point. Jax probably wouldn't care about my lip gloss or the color of my eyeshadow. Last time I checked, orgasms and makeup didn't go hand in hand.

I had a one-track mind that craved meaningless sex. Oh, the things alcohol did to my brain. No wonder I never drank.

Taking a deep breath, I pulled the bathroom door open. The girl standing in front of me had a scarf wrapped around her body for a dress. She looked familiar. Strawberry blond hair, fake lashes, butterfly lips. I'd seen her earlier at The Regency wearing a different, more conservative outfit. Her shoulder was propped against the wall for support and her eyes stared at me unblinkingly.

I floundered out of the bathroom and offered her a smile. "All yours, sweetie." My vision was crap, so my legs miscalculated and we collided. Her purse slipped and fell, sending lipstick, tampons, and a flash drive rolling across the floor.

"I'm sorry." I kneeled to help.

"Don't worry about it," she purred. "I got it." The scarf slipped off her breast. She wasn't wearing a bra.

"You might want to...umm"—my hand reached for the fabric to place it over her nipple—"fix this."

"Oh..." A giggle left her mouth as she tossed the contents back into her purse. "For sure."

Poor gal. I had to help her get to her feet again. I also thought of offering her a sandwich. I knew I was skinny, but she was something else. "Are you going to be okay?" I double-checked.

"I'm good. Thanks." Clutching her purse to her chest, she stumbled into the bathroom and closed the door.

I stood in the hallway for a bit, listening to the sound of her voice muffled by the noise of running water. The entire building felt as if it was spinning and I desperately needed to get out of here.

In the living room, people were acting like savages and I almost regretted not returning to the room where I'd left Frankie and Dante.

A text from Jax came in shortly after. He was waiting for me downstairs in a black convertible. I slipped into the passenger side and scrambled for the seatbelt. Clouds of heavy fog filled my head.

"Hey, stranger," Jax said, hands resting on the steering wheel.

"Hey." My body ached from being subjected to tons of walking and mean couches. "Thank you for doing this."

"No problem." Jax nodded and reset the GPS app on his phone. "Where am I taking you?"

"Home." I rattled off my address and fastened my seatbelt.

"Looks like you had fun."

"Sorta." I wanted to tell him I'd interviewed Frankie Blade, but then I remembered about the confidentiality agreement.

"You didn't?"

"Yes and no." I tried to imagine us kissing, but my mind didn't want to go there anymore. Jax's lips weren't Frankie's, and the fact that I kept on thinking about the man I could never have while sitting next to another perfectly available inked hottie frustrated the hell out of me.

We drove off in silence that went on for what seemed like forever. My knee cried, then my body was suddenly weak and didn't want sex anymore.

Instead, it wanted a hot shower and a soft bed.

"Why'd you take so long to text me back?" Jax broke the silence first.

We were on the freeway, wind messing up my hair, and an early Soundgarden song pouring from the speakers soothed my wounded heart.

I wasn't sure how to answer the question without hurting Jax's feelings. He wasn't on my priorities list, yet I'd dragged him out to Westside to drive my drunk ass home. And I'd planned on using his body. Although this part of my devious plan was no longer happening. My libido had apparently gone to sleep.

"It's been a busy couple of weeks," I said over the music.

"What exactly kept you busy?" The question itself was blunt, but the way Jax asked it made it sound...polite. He was a genuine guy whom I was using tonight. Which only reinforced my belief that I was a shitty person.

"Weren't you on some TV show?" I changed the subject.

"Yes. *Mad Ink.*"

I'd never heard of the show before. I made a mental note to check it out. "Did you like it?"

"I did, but the network decided not to renew. The show just ran one season."

"That's a bummer."

"It was a great experience, though."

"That's good."

We chatted about Jax's work on TV for the remainder of the drive. He was easy and his simplicity made me like him even more, but it wasn't a lustful pull and that baffled me. By the time the convertible rolled up to my apartment complex, I was fairly sober.

A flash of guilt ran through me. "I really appreciate it," I said, checking my pockets to confirm that my ID and the credit card hadn't fallen out.

"Of course." Jax turned to face me, his eyes locking on mine. "Do you maybe want to get a cup of coffee sometime?"

I needed a second to process his question. Now that I was halfway back to my senses, the events of the entire evening felt different. There had been too many conversations with too many men today and they all started to crash inside my head.

"Sure. I'd love to," I whispered, unfastening the seatbelt. My gut told me to leave. Fast. *Now you're just leading him on, girlfriend.* "I'll text you tomorrow?"

"Sounds good."

"Thanks again for the ride." I stepped out of the car and hurried inside.

Chapter Four

My brain was a war zone. I sat at my desk and stared at the empty page of my Word document. Nothing was coming to me.

"Could you upload it by five?" Levi's voice thundered against my left eardrum as I took a sip of my lukewarm coffee, and I had to draw the phone away from my ear and switch to speaker mode. My mind was a million miles away, flipping through the haze of last night's events. I still couldn't believe I'd embarrassed the crap out of myself by telling Frankie Blade about my father.

What were you thinking, Cassy?

Oh, that's right. You weren't. That's what happens when you drink.

"Yes. I'll have it ready by five," I droned.

You'll be lucky if you get the headline ready by five, my scattered brain countered.

"When are you going to pick up your stuff?"

"A little later." My laptop was still at Levi's, but the thought of getting in a car made me sick to my stomach. Besides, I had my desktop and I didn't plan on leaving my apartment until Wednesday. That was when I had my next event to cover on my calendar.

Carlos and Steph were going to take care of tonight's show at Staples, and Levi had found someone to review the shebang at WeHo.

Besides, my knee needed time to heal.

"Any juicy stories?" he probed.

"Not really." My gaze crept back to TMZ's home page. I carefully looked through the recent posts. Nothing about the party at Dante's last night. Good.

There were, however, a lot of videos of Frankie's performance. People loved him. He was the hottest trend of the day. Facebook, Twitter, Instagram, Yahoo. The planet was celebrating his return.

Even the shitty cell phone videos couldn't dull the power of his magnificent voice.

"Did you at least have fun?" Levi asked. I heard him chewing.

"I'm never drinking again." My laugh sounded more like the scream of a strangled cat. "Any word from Jay Brodie?"

Levi had cut Frankie's interview last night after he got home. Then he sent it, along with the raw footage, over to Corey and Smith as instructed. Now we just had to wait.

"Nope. There haven't been any other interviews released either. I don't get it. Dude looked fine to me."

Frankie Blade looked better than fine. He looked *delicious.* And I was no longer going to deny the fact that the man stimulated me sexually. Turning women on was his job, after all, and he did it well.

"Yes," I agreed. "I don't see why he shouldn't be in video." If Frankie and his management were worried about one barely visible scar, they were all mad.

My Douglas & Krueger Cancer Benefit recap was like a pancake flip fail, sloppy and flat. I re-read the article twice before forwarding it to Levi, but the words still didn't flow.

"Oh... To hell with this." I hit Send and pushed my chair away from the desk. My back ached from sitting all day and I needed to stretch. The idea of not getting out until Wednesday now seemed pretty stupid.

I decided to go to the gym to blow off the steam I hadn't been able to blow off last night.

When I got home at nine, exhausted, my desktop screen was littered with notifications.

I rid myself of my sweat-drenched clothes and parked my ass on the edge of the chair to quickly skim through my emails before my shower. One of the main reasons Levi and I were so good at what we did was because we always stayed on top of everything. Days off didn't exist in our universe. We worked non-stop. We were online, connected, available, and ready to jump into action twenty-four seven.

Our lives didn't belong to us. They belonged to the world of news. That was the price we paid for success.

Non-urgent messages and unimpressive headlines flashed at me from the screen as I scrolled through my inbox, my gaze stalling the moment it reached an unread email from fwallace426364@iCloud.com.

I didn't put two and two together until I clicked on the message.

How about a late-night dinner?

My heart stuttered. I checked the sender's email again, then pulled up Frankie Blade's Wikipedia page.

Frank Wallace (*born June 3, 1981*), *known by his stage name,* **Frankie Blade**, *is an American songwriter, who is co-founder and lead singer of the rock band Hall Affinity.*

I rubbed at my eyes to make sure. This made no sense whatsoever, but my fingers itched to respond. So I did.

FROM: cassyevanswrites@gmail.com

TO: fwallace426364@iCloud.com

Are you serious?

I hit Send and rose to my feet. The shower was calling my name. I wasn't going to sit around in my wet sports bra and panties and wait to find out if the person who was trying to prank me really thought I was this dumb. But an unread email alert stopped me when I was halfway across the living room. I don't know why I returned to my computer to check my inbox. Maybe because this felt a lot like a challenge.

FROM: fwallace426364@iCloud.com

TO: cassyevanswrites@gmail.com

Dead serious.

Was this guy for real? *Game on, asshole,* I thought to myself and typed another response.

FROM: cassyevanswrites@gmail.com

TO: fwallace426364@iCloud.com

I don't dine with strangers.

FROM: fwallace426364@iCloud.com

TO: cassyevanswrites@gmail.com

I wouldn't call myself a stranger. We met last night.

FROM: cassyevanswrites@gmail.com

TO: fwallace426364@iCloud.com

I met a lot of people last night.

FROM: fwallace426364@iCloud.com

TO: cassyevanswrites@gmail.com

So did I. Is that a yes to dinner?

FROM: cassyevanswrites@gmail.com

TO: fwallace426364@iCloud.com

How did you get this email?

FROM: fwallace426364@iCloud.com

TO: cassyevanswrites@gmail.com

Confidentiality agreement.

I didn't believe for a second that this person was the real Frankie Blade. Anyone could have gotten my email from my Facebook page. Of course, not just anyone knew I'd signed a confidentiality agreement yesterday. Bottom line, I needed reassurance.

FROM: cassyevanswrites@gmail.com

TO: fwallace426364@iCloud.com

How do I know you're not some psycho trying to lure me out of my apartment and then kill me and dump my body in the Pacific?

My imagination was going to sick places.

FROM: fwallace426364@iCloud.com

TO: cassyevanswrites@gmail.com

You have a butterfly tat on your left shoulder blade.

Crap. My heart slammed into my chest. I hadn't showed the new ink to anyone except for Frankie.

FROM: cassyevanswrites@gmail.com

TO: fwallace426364@iCloud.com

Why do you want to have dinner with me? Aren't there any Playboy models available?

FROM: fwallace426364@iCloud.com

TO: cassyevanswrites@gmail.com

Been there. Done that. They don't make good conversationalists.

FROM: cassyevanswrites@gmail.com

TO: fwallace426364@iCloud.com

I still think this is a prank.

FROM: fwallace426364@iCloud.com

TO: cassyevanswrites@gmail.com

Only one way to find out, right?

I tore my gaze from my computer and paced around the room in my underwear. Adrenaline ran through my veins. I couldn't determine whether I was excited or terrified. My blood pounded hard in my temples and not because of my trip to the gym. Drawing a deep breath, I returned to my desk and wrote a response.

FROM: cassyevanswrites@gmail.com

TO: fwallace426364@iCloud.com

I'm allergic to wheat, eggs, and soy.

FROM: fwallace426364@iCloud.com

TO: cassyevanswrites@gmail.com

I know just the place. Where do I pick you up?

This wasn't happening. Frankie Blade wasn't taking me to dinner. Or was he? After careful assessment of the situation, I decided to send him the address of the apartment complex across the street.

FROM: fwallace426364@iCloud.com

TO: cassyevanswrites@gmail.com
See you in two hours. Be ready.

My stomach knotted as I crossed the courtyard.

This is insane, Cassy, my common sense whispered. *What if the guy is really a serial killer?*

There was a preview of an unread email from fwallace426364@iCloud.com on the screen of my phone.

Outside, it said.

I stopped in front of the gate and surveyed my surroundings. Of course, it had to be a red Ferrari. The car stuck out like a sore thumb in this neighborhood. It sat in the middle of the street, engine roaring, LED headlights shining blue. *To match his eyes.* The man either didn't know how to blend in or wanted to be caught by TMZ. I know I didn't. Thank God it was late and most people who lived on this block were fast asleep.

My jeans seemed two sizes too small and the red Guess crop top I'd pulled out from the back of my closet felt like a roll of scotch tape wrapped around me. Putting together outfits for interviews had always been easy. I had a system. For small indie bands, jeans and T-shirts were fine. Bigger names usually called for formal with a splash of hip kind of attire. Dinner with a man whose name was on every website and every TV channel? Well, color me blind. Not the slightest clue.

Taking a deep breath, I approached the Ferrari. The tinted passenger side window rolled down and I poked my head inside, cautious. My heart jumped to my throat. This wasn't a prank. Frankie Blade sat behind the wheel.

A soft gasp of surprise left my mouth. Unsettled, I scanned the posh interior of the vehicle.

"There's just one body in the back. Picked her up on the way here," Frankie said.

Who knew the man had jokes?

"Do I need to sign another confidentiality agreement?"

A soft smile curled his lips. He shook his head, his eyes roaming my face. "No. I trust I won't read about our dinner in *Rewired* tomorrow morning."

I was shocked he knew what magazine I wrote for. Most people of his status didn't even go online, let alone keep track of the publications who ran an editorial on them.

"You're funny." I pulled the door open and slid into the passenger seat. My knees were weak and my chest swelled with fearful bliss. I couldn't wrap my head around what was happening and why I'd been asked to dinner.

"Is the air okay?" Frankie checked. His voice filled me with a strange tremor.

"Yes." My gaze captured his and electricity rushed through my veins. I was ashamed and confused because he obviously did something to me, something all good-looking men of power did to women, turned me on. Deep down I understood he was selling an idea. And not knowing whether I was talking to Frankie Blade, the rock star, or Frank Wallace, the real deal, was terrifying.

I matched his heated stare. Linda could go to hell with her instructions. If the man wanted to have dinner with me, he was going to endure the full spectrum of my audacity. This wasn't work-related, and I had the right to do as I pleased. And I pleased to look at him for as long as I wanted or needed to make sure I wasn't in trouble.

Frankie wore a light brown trucker jacket and a white T-shirt that outlined his toned stomach and chest. Thin fabric revealed splashes of ink scattered across his ribs. They must have been recent as well, because he hadn't had any tats on his torso before the accident. Sunglasses perched up on top of his blue Dodgers hat were a nice touch. He checked every box in the useless-items-celebrities-absolutely-must-wear list.

"So, no eggs, no wheat, no soy?" he asked, shifting gears. The car responded with a roar.

"Unless you want to spend your night in the ER."

"That bad?" A chuckle.

"My body just doesn't agree with those three."

"Any music preferences?"

I considered pinching myself to make sure this wasn't some drunk post-party dream.

"Funny you should ask." A nervous laugh escaped my lungs. "What do you have?"

"Everything."

Now I really felt challenged. "Hmmm... What are you in the mood for?"

He jerked the gear lever again and the car moved. The engine was louder than the crowd last night at the Regency.

Frankie answered with a smirk, "Surprise me."

"Well...I have no idea how this works." I motioned at the stereo. "I don't want to break anything."

As the Ferrari drove down the street, he laughed. It was bright, sexy, and infectious. It made my tummy melt.

"Why are we having dinner again?" I asked.

"We didn't get a chance to finish our conversation last night."

I needed a few moments to process what I'd just heard. "I thought we did."

"You walked out."

"Did I?"

"Yes. You totally did, Cassy. You walked out and never came back." He paused for a second, then added, "And I don't like when people walk out on me."

I sensed there was a hidden meaning behind the last words but didn't pursue the opportunity. His voice was a rough caress and I wanted him to keep talking to me until the end of days.

Frankie's gaze never left the road as he fiddled with the stereo to get me started.

"Jeff Buckley?" I noted as the soft tune filled the car.

"*Grace* was the first record I owned."

"Really? How come you never talked about it?"

"I don't know." He gave me a shrug. I saw a hint of a smile on his lips. "I wanted to keep it to myself, I guess."

I could understand why. I imagined always being in the public eye and having the entire planet discuss what you ate, liked, or shit could be overwhelming. What I couldn't understand was the reason behind this invitation.

The music pouring from the speakers was euphoric and I was losing myself in its soothing rhythm. I loved that album. It was my second favorite after *Breathe Crimson* and while the two had absolutely nothing in common, they both tore me apart.

We discussed *Grace* and drove down a quiet Los Feliz neighborhood until we hit the trendy Franklin area. Hollywood was alive and kicking. Sidewalks buzzed. Clubs roared. The city went on as it had been for decades. Every night, fascinating stories happened here, and today, mine was apparently one of those stories.

"I love the new artwork on the band's website," I said as the Ferrari wormed its way through the traffic.

"The butterfly?"

"Yes."

"Let me take a guess? You like butterflies."

"They're interesting creatures."

"They are."

"Is there a hidden meaning behind the artwork I might be missing?"

"Hmm." Frankie's grip on a steering wheel tightened. "It'll be on the album cover."

"I think it's very—" I had to pause to look for the right word. "Recherché."

"Recherché?" He shot me an over-the-shoulder glance. "I didn't know you spoke French, Ms. Evans."

"Sadly, I don't. I took a semester in college. Didn't have a chance to pursue it further, but back to the artwork."

Frankie was quiet for a long moment. "It's a reminder of how delicate the balance in life is, something I didn't really have to consider before—" His voice cracked and the words died on his lips.

"So the concept is yours?"

"Yes. The idea is mine." He nodded. "But obviously, we had a graphic designer develop it further."

"It's beautiful."

"Thank you."

I tried not to freak when the Ferrari finally pulled into the underground parking lot of an old Victorian building off 101, but dread twisted my gut. We were at a hotel and I hadn't brought my pepper spray.

"Frankie," I muttered, unbuckling my seat belt as fast as I could in case I needed to run. "Why are we here?"

He turned to face me, his brow arched. "To eat."

My stomach quivered in panic. "In a hotel?"

"Get a grip, Cassy." He laughed. "There's a restaurant here in the basement."

"Why in the basement?"

"That, you will have to ask the owner."

We stepped out of the car and made a beeline for the hotel entrance. Frankie's hand was on the small of my back as he guided me through the empty lobby, and I could feel warm shivers zipping down my spine.

Black and white artwork decorated the walls. Small planters with flowerbeds lined up both sides of the walkway. The air smelled like citrus, cinnamon, and old money.

The concierge and the security guard greeted us with a nod as we passed the empty front desk area. I felt like a heroine of a David Lynch movie. This was a creepily exciting turn of events.

We reached the end of the hallway and paused in front of a door marked *Tommy's*.

No hours of operation were listed.

"Best steak in town." Frankie grinned wolfishly, ushering me inside. His fingers felt wonderful on my back.

"Let me be the judge of that." I tried to match his lighthearted tone.

He seemed at ease and I understood his choice of establishment but wondered if he'd been worried about the paps at all.

The place was tucked away in the literal underground and from what I could tell, the only point of entry was through the hotel lobby, through the concierge, and then a guard.

We sat in a private booth, casually flipping through the menus. Frankie still wore his jacket, but he took off the sunglasses and set them on the table. The Dodgers hat hid his signature sandy locks, and a thin fringe of stubble shadowed his strong jaw. This was a very-well-thought-out intentionally disheveled look that was obviously created to help him blend in with the rest of the L.A. crowd. It didn't work. I could sense his sex appeal from across the table. The man was a tantalizing enigma, and the heat he elicited was a dark vortex of all-consuming desires.

Everything with him felt almost...criminal.

There wasn't a single question in my head that I didn't want to ask Frankie, but I wasn't certain where to start or if I was allowed.

He'd been gone for seven years. No one had heard or seen him since he crashed into a freeway divider on his motorcycle while going 120 miles per hour. At least that was what they said on the news.

I'd been an impressionable teenage girl. Lost and utterly broken. With a crappy life. I hadn't known Levi back then. Or Linda. I had a minimum wage part-time job and was trying to save up for my own apartment. That day, I'd secretly sobbed for Frankie. I'd never been the kind of person to pray, but I did that too.

And now, he was sitting across the table from me. Magnetic and taunting. A man I wouldn't imagine having dinner with, even in my wildest dreams. It almost drove me to the edge.

My phone buzzed in my purse.

"Sorry," I muttered, setting the menu aside to check the message. Force of habit. I couldn't afford to miss an important press release. "It's work."

"Sure." Frankie rested his forearms on the table and watched me.

The text was from Levi. He wanted to know when I planned to pick up my laptop.

Got held up with some stuff. Will come by tomorrow, I typed and tossed the phone in my purse.

"Sorry, does it bother you when people do other things in your presence, your highness?" I joked, my eyes meeting Frankie's.

He laughed. "No."

"Oh." I brushed the page of the menu with the tip of my index finger. "That's good to know."

"I recommend either meatloaf or steak."

"Can you vouch that neither of those have the stuff that'll turn me into the Green Goblin?"

"I think it's best we ask the waitress," he suggested.

We ordered both dishes and requested extra plates. Frankie hardly ate anything. He was moving a piece of potato and some green beans around his plate with his fork while I was polishing off the meatloaf. The food tasted amazing and for a second there, I didn't care if sauce dripped down my chin, no matter who I was with. Simple things made me happy too. Not just rock stars. We kept our conversation light. Music. Career—mostly mine. And a few Hall Affinity songs came up.

This was by far the most bizarre dinner I'd had in years. And my mother sure knew how to organize reality-TV-show-worthy family nights.

"Okay..." I set my fork down and leaned back in my chair. My stomach was pleasantly full and my brain had received enough fuel. Time to get serious. "I don't want to sit here and pretend you're my neighbor Pete. You can't seriously expect me not to ask you any questions."

"I don't mind being Pete." Frankie's smile shot straight to my heart.

"But you're not."

"What do you want to ask me about?"

"Why now? Why after seven years of silence did you decide to return?"

The intensity of his gaze washed over me like a murky wave. I saw it in his eyes. He didn't want to talk about those seven years. Yet here we were.

"Asking a music journalist to dinner implies sooner or later she'd raise the topic," I tell him, my voice quiet but firm.

"I didn't ask a music journalist to dinner." He leaned closer, his elbows flat on the table. "I asked a woman who was in a room with Frankie Blade and Dante Martinez and walked out."

My breath hitched. The words spiraled through me, unreal and uncanny. I took them as they came and evaluated, letting myself believe the meaning was open for interpretation.

"Soo...let me get this straight." I leaned forward to meet him halfway, our faces inches apart above the table. "Is this Frankie Blade or Frank Wallace talking to me right now?"

He gave me an eerie smile, his eyes darkening under the visor of his hat. "Does it matter?"

"Yes, it matters. Am I having dinner with a man or an idea?"

"It's Frank."

"Pleasure to meet you, Frank." I held up my hand and he shook it. "And no, I will not do the body folding trick for you again. It was a once-in-a-lifetime opportunity. Like a solar eclipse."

His laughter rumbled in my ears, head, and chest. I loved it.

"Can we leave the questions for next time?" he asked.

Heat rushed through me. "Sure." I nodded. "We can. If there *is* a next time."

"There will definitely be a next time, Cassy."

"Is something wrong?" My gaze followed the waitress who'd just left our table.

Frankie...Frank looked up from his phone, then slipped his sunglasses into the pocket of his jacket. "There's press outside."

My stomach dropped. I glanced down at my own phone to note the time. Two forty-five a.m. Sooner or later, we needed to get out of here. "There's press inside too. So you're surrounded." I flashed him a grin.

He shook his head slightly, a playful glint in his eyes.

"Am I amusing you?" I asked.

"You definitely make me laugh."

It felt like a compliment and I took it. They were rare in my line of work. The ones I received from people in the industry weren't always real. This one was.

"What's the plan?" I watched him tapping out a text.

"Roman's here."

I cocked a brow in question.

"My bodyguard. You've met. At The Regency."

"Oh...well." A sigh of relief left my mouth. "That's reassuring. Did he bring SWAT?"

"He doesn't need SWAT."

"Wait..." I was starting to understand what was going on. "You had your bodyguard follow us here?"

"Yes." Frank nodded. "There was no room for him in the Ferrari."

It was my turn to laugh. The man had an amazing sense of humor. I hadn't been this entertained in a very long time.

We waited a bit longer until Roman arrived. He stood in the hallway outside Tommy's wearing a jersey, loose jeans, and a pair of Adidas. I wondered if Frank yanked him out of his bed on his day off or this was his usual non-event attire.

The race through the hallway was like a scene from a James Bond movie. We moved fast, Roman leading the procession. The concierge at the front desk gave us a nod again.

"Here." Frank pulled off his Dodgers hat and gave it to me.

Panic crept over my skin. "Wait. Is there a crowd of reporters?"

He shrugged. "No idea."

"How did they find out you were here?" Assholes worked extra fast. I knew they were sneaky, but I didn't think they were *that* sneaky.

"I'm a wanted man." He gave me a sad smile, glancing at me over his shoulder as we marched through the quiet hallway. Blood pounded in my ears and my knees shook.

I stalled. "Frank, I don't want to be on TMZ." My voice was a whisper. Being seen with a man like Frankie Blade in a hotel parking lot at three in the morning would ruin my professional reputation. It would also reflect badly on *Rewired*. We were the only magazine left that didn't run any gossip. I wasn't about to become the gossip myself.

Sensing my anxiety, Frank stopped, shed his jacket, and put it over my shoulders. "You won't."

I imagined this was what a baby cocooned in a blanket felt like. "Are you sure?"

"Positive. Just keep your head down. As long as they can't get any shots of you they could run through facial recognition software, we're good." Frank reached for his hat and pulled the visor low on my forehead. My hair grazed my cheeks and I couldn't see anything except for his belt buckle and his white T-shirt stretched across his defined abs and muscular chest. His hand swam into my line of vision and I grabbed it.

"Ready?" he asked.

"Facial recognition software?" I squeaked, lifting my head to get one last look at him. We stood near the door to the parking lot and there were no signs of paps, but the tense expression on Roman's face told me someone was waiting for us out there, on the opposite side of the door.

"Relax. It was a joke." Frank's fingers squeezed my palm. "I don't think TMZ would have access to those types of resources."

"What is this world coming to?" I muttered to myself as we exited into the lot.

Frank's hand wrapped around mine felt otherworldly and my skin sizzled where we were connected. I heard a barrage of loud footsteps and a sea of obnoxious voices. The group was small, but they were like sharks. Cameras clicked. Flashes blinded. Questions poured.

"Frankie! How does it feel to be back?"

"Can you tell us how many broken bones you have?

"Frankie! Any plans to tour?"

"How many plastic surgeries have you had since the accident, Frankie?"

Roman strode straight ahead, his massive body protecting me from the reporters. Eyes on the concrete floor, I pushed through the line of microphones. There was a part of me that wanted to bitch slap a woman who kept on asking about broken bones, but my common sense talked me out of it. It wasn't the time or the place.

We reached the Ferrari, and Roman helped me inside. From the corner of my eye, I saw cameras grating against the window when Frankie began to pull out from the spot.

"I'm sorry about that," he said, putting the gear in Drive. The engine screamed and the reporter stepped back.

"Let me know when it's safe," I squealed. My hands covered my face, and my cheeks burned.

"I think we're good now," he said a few moments later.

"Are you sure?"

"Absolutely, Cassy." He was smiling. I could tell by the lilt in his voice.

We spent the rest of the drive to my apartment joking about what had just transpired in the parking lot.

Our farewell was quick. Roman's Escalade was parked right behind the Ferrari and he watched the street like a hawk while we were saying goodnight. We didn't hug or shake hands but exchanged words and smiles and it was nice.

Chapter Five

I woke up to a sea of emails and a dozen distressed messages from Levi and Carlos. Panic rose up my throat as I skimmed through my inbox, fingers mentally crossed.

The dinner with Frankie felt like a dream, an illusion. Something my mind had cooked up after hours and hours of listening to the entire Hall Affinity catalogue.

I'd fallen asleep with my laptop while stalking TMZ's home page. Along with the paranoia, there had been hopelessness. If my name was going to be on that devious site, I needed to be the first to know so that I could take the necessary measures. Like buying a one-way ticket to Siberia or blowing up TMZ headquarters.

I braced myself for the worst and read through the headlines. Acid rose at the back of my throat, and I wasn't sure whether to laugh or cry. Photos of Frankie and me *holding hands* were on every news site and on Facebook, Twitter, and Instagram. I looked like an Easter bunny in his Canada-sized jacket, but if wearing someone else's clothes, no matter how ridiculous, was going to help me keep my identity secret, I was all for it. Hell, I was ready to do cosplay. *Dress me up as Spider-Man if you must.*

The idea of being subjected to endless scrutiny if I was discovered filled me with terror. I didn't want to talk to Levi before I confirmed the assholes hadn't figured out my name.

Thankfully, my face wasn't distinguishable enough in any of the photos or videos. The brunette Frankie Blade had been caught with remained a mystery. The question was, for how long?

It was only after my thorough internet search confirmed that my identity hadn't been cracked that I called Levi.

"Your boy is cheating on you, Cass," he joked.

I played along because an I-had-dinner-with-Frankie-Blade type of greeting would probably freak my partner out. I also wasn't sure I could, or even should, tell anyone about last night. Real Frankie, Frank, was my *Grace*. I wanted to keep him for myself. For as long as the world would allow me. "I saw it. I'm heartbroken."

"Are you going to pick up your stuff today?"

"Yes. I'll be there in a couple of hours. I just woke up."

"Cool. I have something I want you to see. A friend tipped me off."

Levi sounded mysteriously enthusiastic, which usually meant he had a lead on a hot exclusive. Although I didn't think anything was going to beat my secret dinner with a man everyone wanted. At least, not in this lifetime.

"Hey, Carlos texted me, but I haven't had a chance to answer. Do you know what's up with him?"

"He can't shoot tonight. Already found a replacement."

"Who did you find?"

"That kid who photographed for us at The Whiskey a couple of times. Jonah."

"Oh, his stuff is great," I approved.

I had no idea why Carlos had contacted me. Levi was usually the one to handle administrative or outsourcing duties. I was the girl who wrote articles and asked questions in front of the camera.

After we refreshed the list of upcoming events *Rewired* was scheduled to cover this week and ended our call, I moved on to sorting my emails. My smitten side hoped to see a message from Frankie, but rational Cassy knew it was too soon. The concept of time in the world of the rich and famous was defined by the optimal number of business meetings, shows to play, functions to attend, and parties to host. I couldn't possibly expect the "next time" that Frankie had promised me to happen today or even this week.

Patience, Cassy, I told myself on the way to my car.

Santa Monica was a humid and cloudy hell. Traffic jammed every single road in typical Monday fashion. Shuffling through the multiple playlists on my phone, I drove down Wilshire with my windows down and let the cool September breeze bite my skin. The weather was neither too hot nor too cold. Almost perfect.

Levi was in the middle of his afternoon snack when I arrived. Nachos and hummus sat on the coffee table next to his iPad. For a guy who never worked out and lived off junk food and energy drinks, he was abnormally fit. Concern twisted his face when I walked in.

Jay Brodie still hadn't gotten back to us regarding the video interview, and the lack of response began to worry me. *Rewired* needed to be on the list of publications to run Frankie Blade's first post-accident interview. This was our big break. An opportunity to move up, to actually hire staff, to get a real office space.

"You're right on time." Levi motioned at my bag as I sauntered through his man cave. "I was about to sell your shit on eBay."

"I don't think my shit would be worth much."

"You'd be surprised." He shoved a handful of chips into his mouth. "There's a huge market for used laptops."

"You wanted to show me something?" I found a clutter-free spot on the couch across from him and sat down.

Levi's apartment was *the* bachelor pad. Cables, gear, and piles of hard drives took up most of the space.

"My buddy's cousin is friends with this girl." He slid his iPad over to me. "Isabella Solana. Nineteen. She was Equality 18's face of the month last January."

"The LGBTQ nonprofit?" I tried to push my worry to the back of my head and concentrate on the information my partner was sharing.

"Yes. They were working with some indie label in San Francisco to secure her a record deal, but the suits pulled the plug the day after she was in an accident."

"Why?"

"Her girlfriend was drunk. Drove the car into a tree. Isabella was the passenger. She's in a wheelchair now."

A strange mix of dread and adrenaline rushed through me. I reached over to the iPad, clicked play on the YouTube video, and turned the volume up. Seconds into the recording, I knew we were onto a hot story. The song had a mellow, soulful beginning but hit hard after the first chorus when the singer's voice truly opened up. At only nineteen, she sounded fierce. By the end of the song, I stopped noticing the wheelchair. I saw a performer who gave it her all.

"Girl got some pipes, huh?" Levi grinned, his eyes lit.

"Absolutely," I agreed. "Any upcoming live shows?"

"Yes. She and her band are playing The Viper Room in a couple of weeks. I've been talking to her manager—that's her mom, by the way—and I think we can do something really meaningful here. Get an exclusive. Get live footage. Maybe involve some people."

"Yes. We can and we should."

Rewired wasn't just about numbers. Causes mattered to us. Especially when the talent was part of the equation, and Isabella definitely had a special gift. I didn't need to hear her live to determine that. I've heard enough people sing to know gold from a piece of rust. Some voices were powerful enough to get you with a shitty cell phone video. Isabella's did and it gave me goosebumps.

The radio silence pushed me into googling Frankie.

It was nearly one in the morning, too late to stalk a man online. *Don't do it, Cassy. Don't do it,* I reasoned with myself.

Besides, I'd told myself to set my expectations low. Better yet, to not have any expectations at all. But the reality of being one woman among thousands was tormenting. And sad. I wasn't the type to make the first move as far as the man was concerned. Especially if the man was rich and famous. Deep down, I was old-fashioned, but all these strange feelings I didn't want were surging through me like a broken floodgate disaster.

My ears burned when his photos from some red carpet event he'd apparently attended earlier today littered the screen of my laptop. To make matters worse, he wasn't alone. Frankie Blade had shown up in the company of Taylor Rhinehart, two-time Emmy nominee and the most sought after actress under thirty in Hollywood right now.

I didn't want to be upset or disillusioned, because I was mature and educated enough to understand the man led a very complicated life, but my ego screamed and I felt it. I felt it with my heart, my gut, and even my goddamn earlobes. It stunk. It hurt. And it made me want to erase the dinner.

My phone rang.

"Cassy," my mother yelped on the line, her voice broken. "Your brother hasn't come home and he's not picking up his phone!"

Frankie and Little Miss Hollywood plummeted to the bottom of my priorities list. "Calm down, Mom." I tried to sound rational, but anxiety had other plans. "Have you checked in with any of his friends?"

"I talked to Mike."

"Mom, he hasn't hung out with Mike since last summer." Mike was busy with SATs and college applications.

"Well...who else should I call then? What if he's hurt? What if someone took him?" My mother wasn't making any sense. I didn't even know if she had a good handle on what was happening at home anymore. Or if she cared. It enraged me, but at the same time, it saddened me. None of it was her fault. She tried really hard for us.

"Don't panic, Mom," I said, leaping over to my closet. "I'll be there in twenty minutes and we'll see if we can figure out what's going on." My intuition told me Ashton wasn't in trouble. On the contrary, he'd be the one to cause the trouble. "I'm sure he's fine. He's just acting out." Probably to get back at me for grilling him the other day.

"Do you think maybe we should call the police?" she asked.

But the police called us first. I was already at Mom's, rummaging through Ashton's closet and looking for clues. I started to believe that maybe he was on drugs. Because, in my head, no person in his right mind would be able to spend an entire week in front of the screen shooting up virtual reality enemies. Getting law enforcement involved would be the next logical step. My mind was numb with rage and my hands trembled for some reason. I didn't find anything incriminating except for a couple of *Penthouse* issues, which wasn't illegal. My brother was seventeen, after all. I had sex at seventeen left and right. I didn't really enjoy it at that point, but I was curious. It was cool. Everyone was doing it.

In the living room, the phone rang. My mother's gasp drifted through the apartment.

"What's going on?" I rushed out, agitated and worried.

"He's been arrested for public intoxication," my mother muttered. "He's at the police station."

"You gotta be kidding me!" I tossed my head back and covered my eyes with the heels of my hands. *He's exactly like his father.*

"They said I need to come pick him up."

"We can take my car, Mom." I shook off my anger and tried to act normal.

On the way to juvie, she wouldn't stop talking. She didn't seem to understand what was happening and how this little stunt could affect Ashton's future. Public intoxication was a crime. Potentially, my brother could get a record, but I didn't want to get ahead of myself until we received more information.

We sat in the waiting area for what felt like an eternity. I researched Isabella Solana. My mother filled out paperwork. It was almost six in the morning when the officer finally escorted Ashton out.

I didn't speak to him until we left the building, but my patience cracked in the parking lot.

"What the hell were you thinking?" I asked as we neared the car. My blood boiled with resentment and frustration.

"Cassy," my mother said from behind me.

"No, Mom." Tense, I spun to face her, my gaze darting between her and Ashton. "When are you going to stop babying him? He's almost eighteen, for God's sake. I had a job at sixteen!"

"Yeah, like you're so perfect!" Ashton mumbled, reaching for the passenger door of my Honda.

"No one's perfect," I countered, grabbing the sleeve of his sweatshirt. "And you're sitting in the back, buddy. No DJ privileges for you in my car." Everything about my brother's behavior was wrong. I had no words. Or, at least, they weren't coming out the way I wanted them to.

He jerked his arm away irritably. "Get off."

I nudged him in the direction of the back seat. "What on earth were you thinking? Getting drunk in a public place on a school night?"

"It's okay." My mother tried to be a referee, but I wasn't going to let her win this one. She'd been forgiving my not-so-little delinquent brother for everything, and at some point, it had to stop. Preferably before he ended up in jail for longer than eight hours.

"Don't touch me," Ashton grumbled. "Mom? Tell her. This is child abuse."

"If you drink, you're not a child anymore," I snapped, motioning at the door. "Get in or I'll go get the officer and tell him you're creating a public disturbance."

Rolling his eyes, my brother got into the back seat.

We drove home in grim silence. No words, no music. A freaking machete couldn't have cut the tension inside the car. I was too wound up to talk and didn't want to say something I'd later regret.

By the time we got to Mom's, I'd started receiving emails from folks on the East Coast. People across the continent were awake, rested, and ready to seize the day. I was a miserable bundle of nerves wrapped into a whole lot of mixed feelings who hadn't gotten a minute of sleep and who needed to finish three articles before lunch.

Ashton headed straight to his room. Mom didn't care to give him a lecture. Instead, she hid in the bathroom. It was typical behavior in our family during a time of distress. We chose denial over facing our fears. I tried to refocus my energy on something else, something less vile. Then I heard her crying.

"Mom?" I knocked on the bathroom door several times.

She didn't answer.

"Mom. Come on. Can I talk to you for a second?"

The lock snapped and her head peeped through the crack, eyes red and swollen. "I don't know what to do with him anymore. He doesn't listen to me at all." She wrung her hands. "And now this."

"Why don't you get some sleep and I'll see what I can do."

Things needed to change around here, and since begging and yelling didn't work, the situation called for a different, more holistic approach.

"We're going to have a serious talk," I stated as I let myself into my brother's room.

"Don't you know how to knock?" He sat on his bed cross-legged, chewing his lips, index finger exploring the newly formed hole in his jeans. For the first time in months, he wasn't holding a game controller or staring at the TV screen.

I went straight for the Xbox.

"Don't fucking touch anything!" There was genuine panic in his voice. Determined, he slid from the bed. I found it funny that the legal repercussions didn't bother him as much as confiscated video games. My brother was so out of touch with reality, the notion scared me.

"Sit your ass down," I said, ripping the tangled web of cables from the wall.

"Go to hell!"

Our furious gazes clashed like two volcanos. My brother clearly hated me. I had no idea why. I just knew he did from the blank look in his eyes.

"Sit down, Ashton." I stood in the middle of his room, pissed, his Xbox in my hands. My mind was racing a thousand miles a second, trying to latch on to the right words.

"You don't live here anymore. You can't come into my room and take my shit!"

"I can. And I will. Because I'm the one who'll end up paying for your citation. End of story. Now sit down. I'm going to tell you what's going to happen."

Rolling his eyes, Ashton fell to his bed and stared at me vacantly. "So?"

"First of all, you need to stop cursing." I hugged the Xbox harder, secretly hoping the damn thing would break.

"Uh-huh." He nodded and crossed his arms on his chest. "What else?"

"Second, no more video games. You are to delete all the apps from your phone too."

Ashton kept on looking at me as if I were speaking Chinese naked.

"Lose the attitude, buddy." I paused to give us both a moment to absorb all this. "Third, you're going to pack your stuff and come stay with me starting next week."

"Where am I going to sleep?"

"On the couch. This is non-negotiable. I'll drop off the key copy in a couple of days. This is a very busy month for me and I won't have time to babysit you. You'll have to find a way to bring your things over on your own. You'll also have to clean this room before you leave."

Ashton's face was a mixture of expressions, mostly terror.

"Fourth, you're going to listen to all the Iron Maiden albums and sort them from best to worst."

"What?"

"You heard me."

"Why?"

"Because if you want to work for a music magazine, Ashton, you need to know how to sort stuff. Because this is what we do half the time. We listen, we evaluate, we review. Because if you want to interview musicians, you need to know their catalogue from A to Z. You don't get to pick. You get an assignment, and you do it."

Shock and awe flashes in his eyes. "Iron Maiden has like a hundred albums. And I don't even listen to them."

"It's sixteen and I don't care how you do it. YouTube them. Study them. Write down your thoughts. Make a list. That's part of the job."

"Are you for real?"

"Yes. I'm for real. You have two weeks. You're not doing this for me. You're doing this for you and for Mom. She's overworked, stressed, and sick. And we need to take care of her. Not drag her down."

I grabbed the game controller from his desk and left the room.

Chapter Six

My head hurt as I stared at the screen of my desktop. There, in my inbox, was an email from fwallace426364@iCloud.com.

Do you have any plans for tonight?

Tonight was a couple of hours away. My sleep had been messed up badly because of the trip to juvie earlier in the week. I'd spent my entire Tuesday in bed and stayed up all Wednesday night working on the recap of an event *Rewired* had covered.

It was nearly five in the afternoon, and I'd just finished my second coffee.

My phone rang. I felt like ignoring the call, but in the end, stupid habit made me pick up.

"I'm considering doing a mini documentary on Isabella," Levi said.

"What?" My mind was far away in the Frankie Blade universe.

"I believe we can get a few labels interested."

"We haven't even seen her perform live yet," I countered. I knew the girl was a powerhouse and I was going to do the interview. No questions asked. But before committing to a major project like Levi's, I wanted to meet the artist.

"I haven't run this by anyone in her team yet. I'm just sharing my ideas with you."

"This sounds great. Why don't we come back to it after The Viper Room show?"

"You're not very enthusiastic about this." There was a pause. "I can always have Shayne help me."

"I didn't say I didn't want to do it. I merely think that before we jump into it, we need to evaluate everything carefully. This is going to suck up all our time."

Shayne Mason was a sweetheart in person, but she turned into a snobby pushover during interviews.

"Just say it, Cass. You don't care anymore. If you want to stick to contributing whenever you can, let me know."

My heart sank to my stomach. Levi had never accused me of not caring about everything we were doing, and his words stung. "Where did this come from?"

He waited before responding. "You're not present. You missed the deadline on Tuesday."

"I told you I had some family stuff." I didn't feel like telling Levi about my decision to bring Ashton on board, because part of me was convinced my brother wouldn't even finish the assignment he'd been given. Therefore, he wouldn't make it to the intern pool.

"I really think this is *the* story."

"Me too. I simply want to meet Isabella in person. I'm not saying I won't do it. I'm saying I want to make sure she's not some mean bitch trying to get a free ride. You understand we'll be playing the role of the nonprofit, right?"

"I have another call. I'll hit you up later," Levi muttered and hung up.

I tossed the phone on the desk and spun in my chair, contemplating.

Not only did Frankie Blade have a voice of heartbreak. He *was* heartbreak. Sweet, brooding, and unforgettable. My gut told me he was going to wreck me if I responded to his email. Turned out, I wanted to be wrecked. There were three texts from Jax on my phone I'd been conveniently ignoring. He was perfectly available and perfectly hot. Instead, I chose the man who wouldn't even give me his cell number.

FROM: cassyevanswrites@gmail.com

TO: fwallace426364@iCloud.com

Work a little. Watch Game of Thrones. Eat some vanilla ice cream and wheat and gluten-free crackers.

FROM: fwallace426364@iCloud.com

TO: cassyevanswrites@gmail.com

I was going to ask you out, but I don't think I can compete with Jon Snow. I don't own a sword.

FROM: cassyevanswrites@gmail.com

TO: fwallace426364@iCloud.com

Try me. What else do you have you believe I might be interested in?

FROM: fwallace426364@iCloud.com

TO: cassyevanswrites@gmail.com

I can definitely get some gluten-free crackers.

FROM: cassyevanswrites@gmail.com

TO: fwallace426364@iCloud.com

You can do better than that, Frank.

FROM: fwallace426364@iCloud.com

TO: cassyevanswrites@gmail.com

I have a couple of demos I'd love to get some feedback on.

Excitement rolled through me like a tornado through Texas, crashing all my defenses. I felt special. Taylor Rhinehart who?

FROM: cassyevanswrites@gmail.com

TO: fwallace426364@iCloud.com

I suppose I can hang out with Jon Snow tomorrow night.

FROM: fwallace426364@iCloud.com

TO: cassyevanswrites@gmail.com

Pick you up at nine?

FROM: cassyevanswrites@gmail.com

TO: fwallace426364@iCloud.com
Make it nine thirty. I want to finish this episode.

I didn't know what to expect when an email from Frank came in three hours later. He was outside. Instead of the Ferrari, a black Range Rover waited for me downstairs, which was a relief because the car didn't make as much noise, so it attracted less attention. The last thing I needed was for my neighbors to see me getting into a car with the rock star who'd been rumored to date Taylor Rhinehart. Because, obviously, the internet was flooded with speculations after their red carpet appearance. I scanned the street as I climbed into the passenger seat.

"Cassy. Nice to see you again."

I felt his words simmer against my skin as they rolled off his tongue. Then his eyes captured mine.

He wore fewer clothes today. A black T-shirt that clung seductively to his trim body and a pair of faded jeans. I could tell they were tight, but I was willing to wait until he got out of the car to conclude my evaluation. No sunglasses and no hat.

"Nice to see you too," I replied, my gaze totally enthralled by his heart-stopping gunmetal stare. I was melting.

"You look great."

"So do you."

"I hope you had a nice week."

"Could have been better. Yours?"

"It's better now." His smile was like a stray ray of sunshine, burning its way into my heart and I hated it. He was so easy to like. And would probably be hard to forget.

We played a game. We exchanged pleasantries when, in reality, they were merely fillers. Frank didn't ask me out again because he wanted to tell me how nice I looked. There was something else, and I was going to pull it out of him today. I needed to because the unknown terrified me.

"Where are we going?" I asked as the Range Rover began to move.

"Where no one can find us." A hint of a smirk cut through his cheek.

"And the demos? Or were you just playing dirty and they don't exist?"

"They do. We'll get to that later."

Frank drove with one hand on the steering wheel and one on his thigh, his eyes never leaving the road. For a man who was presumed to be an adrenaline junkie, he was extremely cautious. I wasn't sure whether it was because I was in the car or because he truly feared the road. Yet there was something incredibly alluring in how seriously he took driving. Men usually never missed an opportunity to show off. I would have expected someone like Frank to go out of his way to do so, but tonight, that wasn't the case, nor was it the last time I saw him.

He'd given me full control of the stereo, and although it took me a good minute to figure out how the damn thing worked, I thought I made a pretty good DJ. We skimmed through his '90s collection and even listened to some hip hop as the Range Rover crawled over the serpentine road somewhere in the heart of the Hollywood Hills area. It was wide enough to fit one car, with one side still hanging over the bushy cliff.

"Where is this secret establishment where the paparazzi can't find us located?" I questioned, staring out the window. The glittering city lights stretched as far as my eyes could see.

"We're almost there."

I felt his smile. It was in the air and stuck to my skin, making my cheeks burn and my legs weaken. Being next to him was electric.

Ten minutes later, we pulled up to a construction site with a large building on it that overlooked Hollywood and part of the Valley. Frank killed the engine.

"What are we doing here?"

"Dinner." He stepped out of the car and headed toward the trunk.

I followed him. "You always pick the weirdest places. What's it gonna be next time? The space shuttle?"

"I don't know if I can make that happen." His voice drifted through the night, and when I heard another smile in it, my tummy fluttered.

We were up in the mountains. Silence here was almost absolute. Gated properties with million dollar houses with views to die for lined the opposite side of the road. I imagined they belonged to movie executives or people like Frank, people with a lot of money who could afford to be away from the madness of the big city while still being able to watch it.

I heard the trunk open. "I didn't want the ice cream to melt on the way here," Frank said, pulling out a container. "So we'll have to schedule that for next time. But crackers are happening."

I moved closer, my eyes finally adjusting to the darkness.

"Could you grab this?" Something soft was thrust at me.

"As long as it doesn't bite," I whispered, hugging the tangle of fabric. There was a lot of it. A blanket?

Frank shut the trunk and motioned for me to follow him. "Just make sure to watch your step. It's a long way down," he joked.

"Is this even legal? Aren't we trespassing?" I surveyed the crooked outline of the building drawn against the black, starless sky. It looked like the roof hadn't even been started yet and the smell of cement and dust filled the air.

"No. I know the owner of the property," Frank explained, carefully walking through the construction debris scattered across the lot.

He led me to an area hidden behind the building, which was covered with patches of grass and untrimmed bushes and had a great, unobstructed view of the city.

Frank set the container on a lonely bench sitting near the edge of the cliff and I stopped a few steps behind, intimidated by the intimacy of the situation. My eyes lingered on his back at first, then darted over to the shimmering net of lights below. The blanket in my hands felt heavy and my heart hammered in my chest like a kick-drum. Everything about this moment frightened me.

Frank turned to face me. I couldn't see him well, just the lines of his silhouette, but I could still sense his gaze on me. It burned down all my walls and ruined the last of my self-control. I didn't understand, why me? Out of all people, he'd chosen to bring *me* here after seven years of silence.

"Pick any spot you like," he said, moving closer. The warmth of his body was an invisible brush that painted goose bumps across my skin.

"Sure." A shiver zipping down my spine, I tapped the heel of my foot against the ground. It was rock solid. Not very ass-friendly. "Are you positive we can't sit in your car?"

"We can, but we won't be able to see what I was going to show you from there."

"You really know how to trick a girl into a late-night picnic." I let the blanket fall loose and took a few steps to the right to find a grassier patch.

This was romantic and weird and all sorts of wrong. Frank sat next to me with his legs outstretched in front of him and stared at the busy curl of the freeway running between the mountains. He'd brought food and drinks. Water. Sprite. And an assortment of crackers and other exotic snacks I'd never seen before.

I breathed in deep and loud, trying to take as much oxygen into my lungs as they would hold. The air was clearing out now that we weren't disturbing the ground and the Range Rover had been off and still for a while.

"See, right there." Frank raised his hand and pointed at the road down below. "That dark spot between Cahuenga and Barham?"

Acid rose up the back of my throat when I realized we were above 101. "Yes." I nodded.

"That's where I crashed." His voice was abnormally calm, as if he were talking about the weather and doughnuts.

My chest constricted. I didn't want to hear any more, yet I knew I had to.

"I didn't feel anything at first," he went on, "during the collision. There was a delay. It all came at me when I hit the ground."

"Were you still conscious?"

"Honestly..." He paused for a second and his breath hit my cheek as he turned to look at me, but I didn't dare look back. I was afraid to move. "I don't know what I was," he continued. "I remember lying on the ground and hearing the noise of the cars as they were passing by. I felt exactly where I was broken. My legs, my arm. My ribcage. I wondered if that was how it would feel if I ended up in hell. I don't remember anything after that. Not until after I woke up in a hospital days later."

A tremor took over my body. I dropped my hand to my lap, my cracker crumbling against my jeans. I wanted to tell him I was sorry, but *sorry* probably wasn't the word he wanted to hear. I was sure he'd heard it a thousand times.

"Can I ask you something?"

"Shoot."

"Why are you telling me all this? And don't get me wrong, it's not that I don't want to know. I do. In case you haven't figured it out yet, I'm a fan. I've been a fan of the band for a while."

"Oh, I figured it out all right." He laughed softly and plucked a handful of grass. "I can tell when someone is a fan and when someone isn't."

His revelation surprised me. "And it doesn't bother you?"

"It always bothers me on some level, but if we let our insecurities and fears rule our lives, we may never get to live the way we really want or should."

"How do you know I'm not going to write a book about it and make millions off your name?"

"You can. But you won't. I'm eighty percent sure."

"Eighty?" It was my turn to laugh. "Wow. Glad to hear you have that much confidence in me."

"Besides, I haven't really told you anything that's not searchable on the net. You don't have enough for a book. Maybe a short story." A chuckle.

"You're nuts, Frank Wallace. You just picked a fangirl from a crowd of reporters and went all Prince Charming on her without verifying she won't sell you out."

"She won't. And I didn't pick her. It was all the Universe's doing."

"So what is this then?" My hand bounced between us.

"Remember I said that I don't believe in coincidence?"

"How could I forget?"

"Back in my day, people used to meet the old-fashioned way—in person. They chatted a bit, and if sparks flew, they went out to get a drink or a cup of coffee. None of that Tinder crap."

"Oh my god, you sound like you're my grandpa. What are you, sixty-five?"

"No. But trust me, thirteen years is a pretty decent difference, especially when seven of those are a black hole..." He paused to let the words sink in. It hadn't really occurred to me how much older he actually was. In my mind, Frankie Blade had always been a rock 'n' roll stud with blue eyes and the body of a twenty-five-year-old to match his boyish smile. Seven years away had changed him. His features had become sharper, more pronounced. He was a polished-to-perfection man nearing forty who didn't look a day over thirty-two or thirty-three. Traces of youth still graced his beautiful face and I didn't care that a scalpel could be given credit for some of the work.

"...especially when it comes to technology." Frank's voice pulled me back to the real world. "Can you imagine my shock when my publicist told me I was on Instagram?"

"That's right. There was no Instagram before you..." I stammered, "B-before you took a break."

"Right. Everything was about Myspace until Facebook came. Then one day, I woke up from a coma and there it was. Instagram." He leaned back and propped himself up with his elbows. "I'm scared to go to sleep now. Might miss the next big thing."

"And where does coincidence factor in here?"

"Well, that's a different story. I was getting there."

"I'd love to hear it. It's not like I'm in a rush to leave."

"In my line of work it's not easy to remember one person in particular when you meet so many...especially women. They blend in..." He paused to take a breath. "But you...You stood out that night at The Regency. It was like someone kept on putting you in my way so I could remember you."

"I take it you're a third time's a charm kinda guy?"

"Something like that."

"And since we've gone out to *get a drink*"—I raised my water bottle to him—"I'm assuming you thought sparks flew?" I pressed.

"There was definitely some electrical activity."

I took a moment to process everything. I was spending my evening in the company of an international rock star who, for some reason, liked me. The notion seriously blew my mind.

"And you just decided to ask me out because we bumped into each other three times in one night? Or because I wasn't throwing myself at you like the rest of the women? That would have been kinda clichéd, you know."

"There's nothing wrong with clichéd."

"What about Taylor Rhinehart? Rumor has it, you two are a thing."

"That was the idea."

"What do you mean? Like a decoy?"

"Yes. Give the press something else to talk about after our parking lot fiasco."

"Wow. You're sneaky. How did you get her to agree on such short notice?"

"I didn't have to. She's a fan of the band. Like you. Besides, I'm one of her wet teenage fantasies. I simply asked my manager to give her manager a call." His tone was serious and I couldn't tell whether he was messing with me or he really took pride in seducing the poor actress into a public appearance because he knew how she felt about him. I couldn't tell a single thing about Frank Wallace. He was so close yet seemed so far away.

"You're very full of yourself." I shook my head and turned to face him.

"Comes with the territory, Cassy." He shifted on the blanket, his blue eyes sharp and wild against the darkness.

We fell into silence for a few moments, and my brain started working overtime.

"And you think you're my wet fantasy?" I questioned, curious.

"Am I?" There was a whole lot of cockiness in his voice.

"Let's say hypothetically, for the sake of argument, that you are. Doesn't it make you an asshole to go after women who you know already have a preexisting condition?"

"I was born an asshole, Cassy." He slid over to me. "Only assholes and lunatics make it in this business." The faint smell of his cologne crept up my nose. "Just because I mellowed out over the past couple years doesn't mean I won't use my charm to get the girl I want."

"Your charm, huh?" I bit the inside of my cheek. "And do you always get the girl you want?"

"Most of the time."

"So is this like a sport for you?"

"Not in the slightest. I even married one of them. Thought it was forever."

This was a small window of opportunity to pick his brain about Heidi Fox, but I chickened out. Something told me dragging his ex into our conversation now would tip the scale. Instead, I said, "Playboy models aren't cutting it anymore? You're into emo chicks now?"

"You say it as if it's a bad thing."

"It's not."

I didn't have any illusions about who I was. I dyed my hair black, wore bra size 32B, and listened to a whole lot of music that made me cry. I never tried to be someone else. I worked with what I had. I didn't peg a man like Frankie to be interested in a girl like me. But I could totally see an up-and-coming tattoo artist wanting to take me out.

"I think you're..." Frank paused for a second. I wasn't certain if he was looking for the right word or merely wanted to prepare me for what was about to come out of his mouth. "Exquisite."

My stomach tightened.

"You still believe there's some ulterior motive behind my inviting you to dinner?"

I looked up to the sky and scanned the dark, heavy clouds hanging above our heads. The air was still and there was no moon tonight. "Okay"—my gaze returned to his face—"let me get this straight. You, the man who has an entire planet lusting after you, including a number of famous and beautiful women, checked out for seven years and now that you're back and lusted after even more, you want some reporter from Burbank who may or may not sell you out for a big buck."

He nodded.

"Remind me again... Did you hit your head during the accident?" I reached for his hair and ruffled it. My fingers were lost in its silky thickness.

The corners of his lips curled up. "Did anyone ever tell you your empathy levels are incredibly low?"

"No. Did your ego get hurt somehow? I'm sorry about that."

"I like that you don't shy away from cracking jokes about my head after it's pretty much been through a meat grinder."

"Laughter is the best medicine, Frank." Unwillingly, I drew my hand away from his hair.

He pushed himself up to return his upper body to a vertical position. "I need to tell you something, Cassy." This time, his voice was serious. "You and your partner will be getting an email from my publicist tomorrow, but I wanted you to hear it from me."

Panic crept up my spine. I waited.

"Your magazine can't run my video interview."

Bitterness filled me. "Why not?" I asked, disappointed. At that moment, I wasn't a woman on a date—or, at least, I'd thought it was a date—with a man. I was a mother who'd just lost one of her babies.

That interview meant a lot more to me than Frank could have ever imagined.

"This is why." I heard his whisper.

Then it happened. He gently caught my mouth with his, a cool gasp tingling on my lips. Our bodies were close but not touching; our hands didn't dare move. The entire city stood still. My heart was a restless storm in my ribcage. I was drowning. Drowning in the sweet heat of his breath, in the light graze of his stubble against my skin, in the sudden promise of something real.

His mouth, soft yet insistent, slid against mine slowly, teasing. My mind was in shock while my greedy lips took everything he was willing to give. Each and every second of sizzling pleasure.

I heard the box of crackers fall over as he shifted on the blanket, his broad chest pressing to me. Our tongues danced a gentle dance, and holy shit, for a spoiled man, Frank knew how to be generous with a kiss. Electrical currents ran through my body. My blood was thick with desire, and I was ashamed of all the thoughts in my head because I'd finally let myself wander into forbidden territory.

"Now you have enough for a novella," Frank whispered against my mouth before pulling away.

I sat there, motionless, and watched him with my heart drumming a savage beat against my ribcage. My throat tightened. For the first time in my life, I didn't know what to say.

After putting the picnic supplies in the trunk, we climbed into the Range Rover and Frank turned on the music. Mild shock still ruled me. My lips ached for his mouth. I'd forgotten all about the interview.

"Have you ever scuba dived?" he asked matter-of-factly.

"No." I shook my head.

"Would you like to?"

"Sure."

"Pick you up tomorrow around noon?"

Wow, this is moving too fast, I thought, but prior real life commitments reminded me who I was. "I actually have an event to cover tomorrow."

"I guess my charm doesn't work on you, Cassy Evans." He laughed.

"Oh, it works fine. I simply can't drop everything I'm doing for a scuba session with a rock star."

"What are you covering?"

"Umm... It's a small awards show."

"Yeah?"

"At El Capitan. Downtown."

"What kind of awards?"

"You ever heard of KGLT?"

"The radio station?"

"Yeah, they mainly play grunge. So they're the ones hosting the awards. It's the second year they've done it and it's pretty low key so far..."

"Any interesting bands?"

"Oh, there's going to be tons."

I went on to list all the artists. Frank watched me with fascination, his eyes set to my lips.

"Zombie Annihilation?" he repeated the name of the last band I said. "Well, how the hell am I going to compete with that?"

"Maybe some other time?"

"Yes, has to be some other time when the zombies aren't throwing a show."

We stared at each other. The music stopped.

"So...tell me the truth." My gaze roamed his face and body. He was eye candy for sure. Raw and radiant with a pinch of dark. "There are no demos, are there?"

"There are. We have most of the new record tracked. Just hasn't been mastered yet."

My spine stiffened. "So the new album is already written?" I clarified.

"Pretty much."

"The press release said something different."

"To hype up the crowd."

"Will there be a tour?"

His chest rose, and thin fabric stretched across his firm pecs. He was holding a breath and I felt his fear at that moment. I couldn't explain it yet, but it crawled through my veins like a spider.

"Frank?" My gut told me it was time to ask the questions I'd been wanting to ask. He'd opened the door today, and all I needed to do was to walk in and take a look around.

"Yes." I heard his whisper. "We have a few one-off shows booked later this year and a US tour is in the works. The information just hasn't been released to the public yet."

I wanted to ask why because "later this year" was very close. Too close if you looked at it through the lens of a music business insider. Shows and tours for a band like Hall Affinity, especially under the circumstances, were announced many months, sometimes even years in advance. Intuition told me there was a lot more going on behind the scenes than Frank led me to believe.

"Why is the label holding out then?" I asked carefully.

He looked at me with a faint smile. "It's not the label. I'm waiting for the doctors to clear me."

"Oh." My breath came out in a gasp.

"Want to hear something sexy?" He smirked, bringing his face to mine.

"S-sure."

"Right now, there's more metal in my body than in the periodic table, Cassy."

My eyes widened with shock.

"Titanium," he added, pulling back.

I was still. The words I wanted to say had deserted me.

"After the accident, I had to learn everything all over again. How to walk, how to hold a spoon, how to brush my teeth... How to sing."

"But you were magnificent during Douglas & Krueger."

"It's not the singing, Cassy. Singing is the easiest part."

"How many surgeries have you had?"

"Honestly, I lost count." He shrugged. "I have a rod in each leg. I had my ribs realigned. There's a plate in my right shoulder."

Part of me didn't believe him because he looked almost normal to me. Healthy even. "Are you in pain?"

"No, not now, Dr. Evans." Amusement pinched his face, the side of his mouth curling upward.

"Are you often?"

"No."

"Damn... You could give Iron Man a run for his money."

"I sure could."

We laughed.

"Wait! You can scuba dive with all that hardware?"

"With an instructor, yes. Roman is usually around too. Just in case."

I was blown away. The man had almost died because of his addiction to bikes. Now that his body was half-metal, he was trying the underwater activities.

"Remember, this is still a demo," his voice said as he pulled out his cell to connect it to the Range Rover's Bluetooth.

I wasn't prepared for the music. It poured over me like a torrential rain. The song had a haunting beginning. Dante's signature riff came first, followed by a bass line. Frank's voice, layered and soft, joined subtly. His vocals slid into the arrangement with caution, as if he needed reassurance this was still his vocation, his calling. The drums didn't kick in until after the first chorus.

I listened to the song without looking at Frank. I couldn't, because he'd kissed me less than an hour ago. If he wanted to hear my honest opinion, I had to separate the man on the record from the man in this car. And boy, was it difficult.

The music stopped and silence took over.

I expected a question from him, but none came.

"You're going to break my heart all over again," I whispered finally.

"That's not what I was going for."

"It's really good." *Fucking terrific.* "Cassy Evans-approved." I didn't know what else to say. This was a solid Hall Affinity song. Rich, deep, and very powerful. They hadn't lost their touch.

"Thank you." He nodded and put his phone away.

"Does it have a title?"

"Yes. 'Awake.'"

"I love it."

"Are you sure you can't find someone to cover for you tomorrow?"

"No. I'm sorry." I wanted to, but I couldn't do that to Levi. There was Frank and then there was the rest of the world. And I had to make it work with each without sacrificing the other.

Chapter Seven

El Capitan was a hot, messy, screaming hell full of guys in Pearl Jam and Audioslave T-shirts and girls with neon hair and pictures of Kurt Cobain slapped over their clothes. Levi and I had six interviews lined up for the night, and the PR company that handled the event publicity was kind enough to give us a separate room backstage. Which didn't happen often.

Carlos was in the pit, doing what he did best, securing live shots for *Rewired.*

I took a couple of trips to the main floor to get an idea of how big the crowd was. The place was stuffy and was too small to host an event of this caliber. While still low-key compared to major awards like Billboard or Grammy, the KGLT's Best in Alternative had been getting more and more recognition. Tonight, there were quite a few bigger record label artist relations reps and music acts here. There was a better PA system than in the past. A nicer stage setup. According to Levi's projections, next year, this event could very likely be held at a much larger venue, such as the Microsoft Theater. Assuming the organizers kept pushing forward. People who crapped out on their causes in this business weren't rare.

It was around nine when the energy level backstage kicked up. We had just finished our third artist interview. The door to the small dressing room where Levi and I were set up was wide open. I stood on the threshold with my microphone in my hand, staring at the bullet list on my phone. The AC here was shit. I felt like I was wearing a wet towel instead of a tee and a pair of jeans. I regretted the boots too. Their only benefit was the extra couple of inches they added to my height.

Yesterday's late night picnic with Frank and today's official email from Jay Brodie PR had turned me into a high-strung bitch. I didn't like myself, because I couldn't tell Levi anything about why we weren't chosen to run the interview. Although Frank had never said it, I knew why he didn't want a video of him and me circulating on the net. We'd already been seen holding hands. Having more footage out there would eventually have people digging. A rock singer who'd been in hiding for seven years and a reporter. It would make a juicy story. A story I wasn't sure I wanted to be a part of. But sadly, it was too late.

Then there was the kiss.

"Cass?" Levi called out.

"Huh?" I spun on my heels.

He eyed me from behind his camera. "Move a little to the left for the next one. I'm shooting this wide. Your shoulder looks strange."

"Yeah. Okay." I nodded.

Tonight was one of those weird nights where we had to go with the flow because everyone was behind schedule. Our next artist was still on stage. I could hear the music boom through the busy hallway. Then a tangle of agitated voices and radio static traveled in my direction, a crew member rushing past me.

"What's going on?" I questioned the guy.

He shot me a frenzied glance. "Someone just saw Frankie Blade on the red carpet."

The blood drained from my face. The mic in my hand shook.

"What the hell?" Levi leapt over to me, his head doing a one-eighty around the hallway. "Is this dude for real? First, he shoots down our video. Now he's stalking us."

Levi obviously meant it as a joke. A sarcastic one, judging by his tone. But I wasn't so sure he was wrong. My cheeks burned and my stomach heaved.

We'd posted the transcribed version of the interview this morning. It'd gotten a lot of hits. Tens of thousands. Probably more. I hadn't looked at the stats for a couple of hours, but I knew *Rewired* numbers were flying high tonight. My Twitter wouldn't shut up, and my Instagram followers were ticking in too.

I heard my heart beating inside my chest despite all the hum. The air was full of anticipation; the security guards were alert.

I didn't see him behind the wall of his entourage, but I knew it was him. *I felt him.* A couple of unfamiliar faces led the group. Corey marched in next, his body blocking my view of Frankie. Roman's head bobbed in the very back. Some fans trailed after.

The entire hallway lit up. Necks twisting, eyes wide. There was some handshaking involved. Casual conversations took place. Frankie was in his element. He didn't look like a man who'd been cut open countless times and had a dozen metal plates inside his body to keep him from falling apart. He looked like a rich, spoiled, and entitled ass. He moved slowly, displaying a killer smile until the group finally stopped by our dressing room.

Our gazes met. The hum swelled as the people in the crowd fought for a spot closer to Frankie. A few cell phone flashes assaulted my eyes. Thankfully, Roman quickly intervened, hustling people away.

"Cassy? Right?" Frankie's voice carried over the noise, his brows twisted in concentration. "Didn't we chat a couple of days ago?" He extended his hand.

I placed my palm in his and shook it. "Yes. We did." My skin tingled where we connected. Electricity surged through my wrist and up my arm. This was an incredibly dangerous game, and I loved it.

"The Regency?"

"Yes." I nodded. "The Regency." My eyes ogled his outfit. He wore a simple burgundy shirt and black jeans and looked fantastic.

His grasp on my hand tightened for a brief moment before he let go and switched his attention to Levi. They started talking, but I only heard bits and pieces of the conversation because the crowd had grown so big that people began to slip into the dressing room. Soon, we were surrounded by dozens of screaming fans. I wasn't sure if some of them sneaked in from the main floor or if they were all working backstage tonight. I couldn't tell, because my mind was struggling to stay alert.

I saw Roman moving through the chaos. He pushed his way in and started hustling people into the hallway. The glimmer of the fluorescent overheads slid across his shiny bald head.

"Thank you," I said appreciatively.

"No problem, ma'am." A crooked smile touched his hard face. He stepped closer, his voice dropping a couple of octaves. "Boss wanted to know if you're available for a drink after the event."

I peeked around. Levi was busy talking to Frankie's manager. Frankie was signing someone's T-shirt. People didn't care about me and the rock star's bodyguard. Right now, we were muddy background noise.

My stomach fluttered. "We should be done at eleven. Eleven thirty at the latest," I mouthed, hoping Roman could read lips.

He could.

"Copy that." A chin jerk.

I wondered how many times he'd done this, performed the duties of a messenger when his employer crashed a new flame's workplace. I wondered about many things and couldn't help but compare myself to the women Frankie Blade had been rumored to date.

"Cassy! Very nice to see you again," Frankie said on his way out. Roman hurried to make room.

"Nice to see you too." I waved my mic at him.

He shot me a heated glance before leaving, and my legs went numb.

Frankie Blade was going to be my downfall.

The man was demolishing me slowly but surely.

———————

My prediction was incorrect. Levi and I didn't stop filming until midnight. The last band took forever. They were tired and drunk and asked me to repeat almost every question. Interviewing artists after their set was like pulling teeth, with me being the dentist.

An email from Frank had come in around eleven, but I didn't see it until we were packed up.

I'll be outside, it said. *Lose your partner.*

I wasn't sure if he was going to wait in the loading zone or in the front. I wasn't even sure what vehicle to look for. Maybe a Lamborghini? My racing mind scrambled for plausible ways to get rid of Levi as we left the dressing room. The organizers had given us press passes and our cars were next to each other at the rear of the building. I didn't want to be a weirdo who sat behind the wheel, waiting. Especially when Levi had way more gear. Besides, my partner was too smart. An intricate plan was in order.

"Hey, are you okay?" I asked as we rounded the corner on the way out. My bag dangled against my hip. "I've been feeling a little funny last couple of hours. I think maybe the tacos were bad."

If you're in a pickle, always blame everything on Mexican food. It's too spicy to take offense. Sound advice someone had once given me.

"I'm fine." Levi slowed his pace to match mine. "Do you need to throw up?"

I stopped. My heart pounded so hard, I felt the vibrations in my entire body. I hated lying. "I definitely need to use the restroom." I decided to be vague about my "problem."

"Sure."

"Don't wait up. It's okay." I shook my head and attempted a pained smile.

Apparently, it worked.

"All right." Levi scratched the back of his neck and scanned the hallway. He always checked our surroundings for creeps when we ended up leaving separately. Although I doubted there were any creeps here at the moment. "But call me if you're really sick or need anything."

"I will. Thank you. Have a good night."

"Good night, Cass. You killed it today."

I didn't know if I'd killed it. The last three interviews didn't flow, but I trusted Levi's instincts. I trusted his skills even more. He knew how to cut footage down to just a couple of minutes and still keep all the important info. It was a gift. And his was a perfect addition to mine.

We made a great team and we were going to do great things together.

I locked myself in the nearest bathroom and checked my inbox again. No more messages had come in. *Maybe he got tired and left?* There were still people working inside, but the chaos had subsided. The madness had gone away, along with the bands and the crowds.

The venue was calm and in spite of the sticky floors, the trash everywhere, and the lingering scent of sweat in the air, being here without the crowd felt perversely sublime.

I waited a good ten minutes before responding to Frank's email.
Just finished.
Then I waited some more.
Come out, he replied.
My stomach flipped.

Outside, the loading crew rolled the last of the equipment into the truck. The air was chilled.

Two sets of bright, shimmering lights moved toward me from across the lot. A limo. For some reason, it didn't surprise me at all. Frank was a man of grand gestures. My bag in my hand seemed heavy. The car came to a stop, back door swinging open. I searched the area to make sure no one was filming or taking photos.

"Cassy?" Frank's voice drifted at me from the vehicle. I caught a glimpse of impatience. He didn't want to be seen. Or he didn't want me to be seen with him.

Come what may, I thought and slid inside. My bag thumped against my legs.

The limo was huge but unlike Dante's, it didn't have any party props. The lights weren't disco and the stripper pole was missing. Glass, leather, and wood completed the sophisticated interior.

The divider was up.

"Where's Roman?" I asked, pulling the door closed.

"Wow." Frank's face screwed up with fake shock. "You broke my heart faster than I broke yours. We've only been seeing each other for a week and you're already after my bodyguard."

I couldn't help but laugh. The witty comebacks to my jokes made me like him even more. He was hot and recklessly irresistible. "I'm sorry. Roman has better hair than you."

Frank looked directly into my eyes. He scooted closer, and everything happened so fast, I didn't have enough time to react. His lips collided with mine, gluttonous. Neither my heart nor my ovaries were prepared for that kind of greeting. Raw heat pulsed between my thighs. My lungs were out of air and the hollow organ pumping my blood was a wicked animal wanting to jump from the confines of my chest.

He sucked hard until I gave up control. Then his mouth let up on its assault and he pulled my bottom lip between his teeth. Gently, his bite delicate. I responded with a strained moan. My hands sought his face, and I palmed his cheeks and drew him closer, wanting to feel him. Our knees banged together when the limo started to move.

"You totally ambushed me," I whispered after I broke the kiss to get some oxygen.

"Guilty as charged." His voice was a soft quiver against my heavy breath. He slipped his hand to the back of my neck and returned his mouth to my burning lips. This was a different kiss. Wet, hungry, and downright scandalous. His skillful tongue chased mine. Long fingers tangled in my hair. I was disoriented and didn't care that my clothes smelled like perspiration and weed.

Mad desire for more had taken reign over my brain.

We gasped for air and paused, our cheeks brushing. Mine, hot. His, stubbly. I didn't know where the limo was taking us and I didn't care to ask.

"Hi," Frank said, his mouth near my ear.

"Hi," I whispered and trailed my lips down his neck and kissed his scar. "How was scuba?"

"Ah." He tossed his head back. "Challenging." I heard a sigh.

"So you decided to crash the grunge show instead?"

"Something like that."

I had no idea what was going on between us. We'd known each other less than a week. Correction—he'd known me less than a week. And I still didn't believe I knew much about him. He told me so little.

"Frank?" I ran my fingers down to his jaw, my eyes seeking his. "This is moving too fast."

He licked his lips, his tongue teasing and devious. "Tell me to slow down then, and I will."

My breathing grew deeper as he returned his mouth to my cheek.

"Tell me," his whiskey voice said.

I couldn't. I didn't want to. My mind raced. It took me to strange places every woman's mind probably took her whenever she was on a really hot date and felt a connection to a certain man. I wasn't one hundred percent sure since it'd never happened to me before. But tonight, with Frank, it did. It went like this. Sex. Marriage. Children. I was convinced the sequence was programmed into every woman's brain from birth, because I couldn't explain the reason behind my thinking.

Stop, Cassy. Don't go there. Not with him.

Frank's lips skimmed across my neck and down to my collarbone, dragging me back to real life. To the limo.

"I thought you were asking me out for a drink," I whimpered, fisting his hair. It smelled like sandalwood and tangerine and felt wonderful to the touch.

"We'll get to that in a little bit," Frank husked, moving to my mouth again. He deepened the kiss. My entire body shook. This was insanity. *We* were insanity.

I heard the sirens approach. The limo swerved to the curb and halted. The red and blue flashed behind the tinted glass. One of the biggest cities in the world, L.A. never ceased to be on high alert. Someone somewhere always made trouble.

We parted under the siege of the outside noise and illumination, our hands still on each other.

"I could really use that drink right now," I said, my throat catching. My voice was shot from the numerous interviews.

Frank slid over to the mini bar, filled two glasses with ice, and poured champagne in one and water in the other.

The sirens had passed and the midnight calm took back the street.

Frank handed me the glass with the bubbly.

"Are you trying to get me drunk?" I motioned at his water.

"No." He reclined against the leather cushion, his body relaxed. "Doctor's orders."

"Oh." A meek smile stretched across my lips.

"Have you ever had an affair with a rock star?" Frank asked. His voice, dark and salty, hummed in my head.

I sucked in a loud breath through my teeth. My gaze shifted to his chest and drew a path along the firm outline of his stomach and groin, evaluating. He was well equipped from what I could tell. I'd seen him a thousand times before—in music videos, photos, on stage, but he wasn't hot and bothered in any of those instances. He was now. With me. And it looked promising. "No." My mouth went dry, my thighs clenched.

"Really?" Frank seemed surprised.

I brought the glass to my lips and took a sip of my drink. *A very big sip.* "Really."

"Well, you know what they say, Cassy." A cocky smirk touched his cheek. "There's always a first time for everything."

The limo was moving again. Frank motioned for me to scoot closer. I obliged. He reached for my hair and ran his fingers through the messy flock of black. His eyes roamed my face. "You're attracted to me."

I took another swallow from my glass. "Frankie Blade always gets the girl, right?"

"He does."

"Even if the girl is high risk?"

"Life is a risk, Cassy."

For someone whose motto used to be *all's fair in the world of sex, drugs, and rock 'n' roll,* he was quite the philosopher.

"Are you taking me somewhere where the paparazzi won't find us again?" I teased.

"No, I'm taking you home. But we can go anyplace you want. Just say the word."

The offer was tempting, but I had too much work to do. I couldn't afford to lose an entire day and I knew I would if I chose to spend the rest of the night driving around town in a limo and doing God knows what with Frank.

"I'd love that, but I have a deadline."

"Screw the deadline." Frank laughed.

"I wish."

"You're too responsible."

"Says the hottest man on the planet, who's drinking water because the doctor told him so."

"You got me there."

He leaned in for a kiss. Our lips brushed.

"You're a beautiful young woman, Cassy," Frank said against my mouth. "I want to keep seeing you."

He rendered me speechless. The offer was so simple yet so complicated.

"Do you mind refilling this?" I handed him my glass.

"Absolutely, but don't blame me for the mean hangover."

When the limo finally pulled into my apartment complex, I was pleasantly buzzed. Frank and I had been discussing the Zombie Annihilation set. Apparently, he'd watched several bands perform before leaving the venue and had been thoroughly impressed with some.

"I don't believe the name does their music justice." He took the empty glass from me.

"Speaking of music. I've been thinking about your demo..." my voice trailed off. My head felt like it was floating through a cottony heaven.

"Oh yeah?" Curiosity flashed in his eyes.

"I think 'Awake' would sound great as an acoustic version."

Frank stared at me intensely.

"I'm sorry. I don't mean to step on your turf. I'm not a songwriter. This is just my honest opinion as a fan." My tongue didn't seem to follow the commands of my brain. A mix of champagne and sexual tension had turned me into a blabbering mess.

"Fans' opinions are important." He motioned at the interior of the limo, adding, "As a matter of fact, those opinions are paying for all this. I'd hate to disappoint people who've been waiting for new music from us for over seven years."

"You won't. It's going to be a hit no matter what you and your bandmates decide to do."

"I'm glad you think so."

I reached for my bag. Saying goodbye to Frank was going to be harder than I thought.

He leaned in for a kiss, and our mouths met. It was enough for me to lose what remained of my mind. "Do you want to come...in?" I asked.

He drew back, blue eyes studying me for a brief second. Then his hand grabbed a hold of mine and placed it against the erection straining under his tight jeans. "Yes. I believe I *need* to come in, Cassy." The husk of his voice made the flesh on my arms and neck break out with goosebumps.

My head spun and my heart thundered. I thought about the insurance rumor. It made me wonder if the man was conceited enough to insure his cock. *You're drunk, missy. It's not like he's Ron Jeremy.*

I withdrew my palm from his bulge to pick up my bag and pushed the door of the limo open. The air was warm against my skin. The street was quiet.

I heard the faint squeak of leather as he slid across the seat and stepped outside. The heat of his body engulfed me. His long fingers laced with mine.

"You gave me the wrong address?" Frank noted the building numbers as I quickly led him through the empty courtyard of my apartment complex.

"I'm careful," I explained. "You could have been a psycho."

"Who said I'm not?" He surveyed the property as we ran up the stairs to the second floor. "Who are your neighbors?"

"What do you mean?"

"Any chance they listen to my band?"

"I think a few people in this building might. The couple next door is retired. They're more The Stones and Roger Waters fans. I did hear them listen to some Judas Priest once."

We reached my apartment and I dropped my bag on the ground to unlock the door. Frank steered me to the wall. My back pressed against the rough concrete, keys still in the curl of my palm. Ravenous, he captured my mouth, his groin meeting mine. His rock solid chest brushed my breasts. My nipples hardened against the padded fabric of my Victoria's Secret bra. There was nothing gentle about this kiss and I loved it. I loved the adrenaline rush and the thrill of the danger of being caught. My tongue responded to the wild strokes of his with drunk, unrestrained ferocity.

"My apartment only has one bedroom," I slurred, running my hand up his muscular arm.

"Number of bedrooms or their size won't dictate the quality of our sex. I perform just as well in small spaces."

His wet lips stretched into a smile against mine. He weakened his grasp to give me a chance to unlock the door, then pulled me back into the kiss. Our feet shuffled across the threshold. Our bodies were burning. On edge. I still couldn't believe I'd had enough guts to ask Frank to come in. My place was a mess, full of useless stuff like posters and band merch. Plus, I'd been reorganizing the living room to prepare for Ashton's arrival.

Sliding my bag inside, I shut the door. Heavy breathing swam through the darkness. Warm palms encircled the curve of my waist and glided down to cup my ass. He squeezed carefully, thrusting his erection against my middle. The pressure was perfect. *Wow, that felt good.* The man knew what he was doing. My knees weakened. Unable to stand still, I fell against the door. My hand patted the wall to my right in search of the switch. I rolled my hips to prolong the pleasure the friction of his cock against my sex gave me. The clothes needed to go.

Then came the noise.

I heard a shuffle. Frank's hands froze. My fingers finally hit the switch and light filled the room.

A wave of dread washed down my spine. Heart in my throat, I shoved Frank aside. My brother was on my couch, his blond hair a bedroom mess. A large backpack lay on the floor next to the coffee table.

"Holy shit." A grin spread across his face. He rubbed his eyes and jumped to his feet. "You're Frankie Blade!"

Anger and shock rolled through me. "What the hell are you doing here, Ashton? Didn't I say next week?" My chest swelled with primal rage. I scanned the living room. The Xbox was in my closet and I was ready to use all my artillery if the evidence confirmed that Ashton had gone into my bedroom to retrieve it.

Frank was being quiet when I glanced at him. One hand covered his erection. I was pretty sure it wasn't because he wanted to hide it. At first, there was a flash of genuine terror in his eyes, but it didn't last long. What I read was mostly a mix of disappointment and amusement.

"Shit!" A shriek rumbled through the living room. "You're screwing my sister! Holy shit! That's so gangsta." Ignoring my questions, Ashton leapt over to us and held out his hand for a greeting. "You're like my hero, dude."

Unfazed, Frank shook it, then turned to look at me. "You never told me you had a brother." A smile appeared on his face.

"Yeah, she's like the worst sister ever." Ashton kept on grinning. His tone wasn't mean. Still, the fact that he ran his mouth in front of Frank grated on my nerves. Immediately, I questioned my sanity. Then I questioned genetics. Lastly, I questioned my decision to consider giving my brother a chance.

"Really?" Frank knitted his brows. "I happen to like your sister."

He actually said the words in front of Ashton. The revelation startled me.

My legs shook. I didn't have a response. Instead, I turned around and checked the locks on the door.

"Well..." Ashton drawled, raking his hand through his mop of hair. "She's not that bad, actually. Only sometimes. When she tries to boss me around."

A chuckle. "Boss you around, huh?" Frank shot me a sideways glance. I noted his amusement.

"What are you doing here?" I pressed.

Ashton's gaze jumped to me. "I couldn't find anyone to give me a ride next week."

"There's always the bus. Where's your stuff?"

"At home."

A groan of frustration left my mouth. "Do you even understand English or do I have to speak Cantonese?" Snapping my eyes shut, I pinched the bridge of my nose. Levi and I had massive editorial to work on this weekend. For this reason alone, I didn't want Ashton here.

My brother switched his attention to Frank. "Can you sign my T-shirt, dude?" His voice boomed in my head, high and excited. I'd never seen him this enthusiastic about anything before.

"Sure."

My eyes fluttered open. I gave Frank an apologetic smile.

He responded with a wink and neared the couch, where Ashton was digging through his backpack. My brother pulled out the Hall Affinity T-shirt I gave him on his fifteenth birthday and laid it out on the coffee table. "Hey, dude, do you think I can take a selfie with you too?"

"I'm afraid not." Frank shook his head and settled on a chair, his forearms on his knees. He looked at ease. "It's Ashton, right?"

My brother nodded. "Are you two like having a secret relationship?"

Frank ignored the question. "Do you have a Sharpie?"

I gave him one.

Watching them interact was like watching a scene from Pineapple Express. I didn't understand a word they said. Suddenly, it was all men's language. Ashton used to play some of the older Hall Affinity songs on a guitar. Obviously, before the video games came into the picture and destroyed his entire brain. My brother didn't like *Breathe Crimson* as much as I did, but he could do a decent cover of almost any song from *Hollow Heart Dream*. I never understood why he stopped being interested in music altogether. Seeing him pick Frank's brain about the band's old material was refreshing.

"Can you put *all's fair in the world of sex, drugs, and rock 'n' roll*?" Ashton asked as Frank evaluated the T-shirt sitting in front of him.

"Just so you know, he's seventeen." I needed to mention this fact in case my brother asked for some other dirtier words. "He's going to have to wait a couple of months before he can wear that T-shirt." The Hall Affinity catalogue didn't have a whole lot of explicit vocabulary, but there were a few songs. My brother had enough loose screws to request those lyrics, and I wasn't about to let him walk around L.A. with a T-shirt that read, *stroke me.*

I had no idea what the hell Frankie had been thinking when he wrote those lines. Was he high? Did Dante help him?

"You're a buzz killer, sis." Groaning, Ashton leaned forward and slammed his forehead against the tabletop to ensure I knew how upset he was.

"Quit it already," I snarled back.

"All's fair in the world of sex, drugs, and rock 'n' roll it is then." Frank laughed softly and scribbled the words on the fabric with the pen.

"Ashton?" I called. My brother looked up at me, unusually happy. "You can't tell anyone about me and Frank or how you got your T-shirt signed. If anyone asks you, it was my present."

"Okay. I won't."

"I'm not kidding. This is serious. If someone finds out, it's going to create a lot of problems for you, me, and especially Mom."

"Why?"

Frank cleared his throat and set the Sharpie on the table. "Because people are assholes, Ashton. They'll twist things and all the press attention will make your life very unpleasant. Trust me." His smile was warm and genuine. It melted my heart. "If you promise to keep it to yourself, I promise to get you a backstage pass for our L.A. show."

"Are you for real?" My brother's expression lightened.

"I always keep my word."

"Sick."

"Can I count on you?" Frank held up his fist.

Ashton bumped it with his. "Yeah. Totally, dude."

"Then it's a deal. I'll tell my manager tomorrow to get you guys all sorted out."

"When's the show?"

"Can't tell you yet. But soon."

They chatted like old friends. The hum of their banter moving through my apartment was oddly comforting. I couldn't remember a time my brother had been so normal.

It was almost three when fatigue finally kicked Ashton's butt. He passed out right in front of us, hugging a pillow.

I walked Frank into the hallway and shut the door.

"I'm really sorry about this. He wasn't supposed to be here tonight."

"Don't worry about it. He's a nice kid. He was fun to hang out with."

"He's evil," I countered.

"You're too hard on him."

"How the hell do you know? You met him two hours ago." I slapped his chest playfully.

"Maybe instead of him, you can boss *me* around." A wicked smirk curved the corner of his mouth.

"We can certainly discuss it." My hand slid down his torso, his abs taut beneath the spread of my palm.

Frank leaned forward and pressed his lips to mine. Clouds of bliss filled my head. And my stomach. The ache between my legs came back. I was a woman unsatisfied and now I couldn't even service myself, because my little brother was sleeping on my couch. Life was definitely unfair.

"I'd like that," he husked. "Looking forward to it."

"Me too."

Our lips lingered. We didn't want to part, but he needed to leave before someone saw him, and I was tired and wanted to get some sleep.

Frank pulled his phone from his pocket and handed it to me. "I believe it'll be easier to communicate if I have your number."

Eager, I punched in my digits and returned it to him.

"How's your schedule the next few days?" he asked, his finger tracing down my cheek.

"My weekend is kinda stuffed. Levi and I have a lot to do. My

Tuesday looks pretty light. Wednesday and Thursday I have events to cover."

"Sounds like you don't have time for me, Cassy Evans. My charm must be shit. I better come up with some new tricks." His voice was a sexy tease. His finger moved beneath my jaw and he captured my chin.

"Are you expecting me to drop everything?"

"No. Never. That's part of why I want you so much." He kissed me on the lips. "I'll call you in a couple of days. Think of something fun you'd like to do that you haven't done yet. Just not the space shuttle."

I caught the innuendo. My panties were a wet mess. *I* was a mess. Emotional. Physical. Spiritual. The damage had already been done.

Chapter Eight

Frank didn't call. Not a couple of days later. Not a week later.

With Ashton staying with me, my life was crazy enough without having to worry about an arrogant ass of a rock star who apparently had dropped off the face of the earth again. His last public appearance was at El Capitan. Jay Brodie still sent updates on the upcoming Hall Affinity album. The new single release was slated for late November. Yet the internet hadn't seen a new photo of Frankie since he crashed the KGLT event.

No emails from fwallace426364@iCloud.com popped up in my inbox either.

All this only strengthened my belief that men were indeed a different species, rich men even more so, from a faraway galaxy who spoke a language all their own. In my world, if we said we'd call, we usually did. Or at least texted. Apparently, in theirs, it meant something else.

Still, the silence stung. In my rare moments of weakness when my sexual frustration and genuine worry assumed control of my brain, I wanted to email him, but my pride told me to suck it up and be a strong, independent woman. And my pride, like my gut, was my guide. My compass. I wasn't going to let Frank, or whoever he thought he was, break my stride.

Instead, I threw myself into work. *Rewired* was on a hot streak this month. Our numbers skyrocketed each time we posted Hall Affinity updates. Levi took advantage of the high traffic and tossed Isabella's name onto the homepage to promote The Viper Room event.

He was very skeptical about my decision to bring Ashton to her show, but now that my brother knew my secret, I felt responsible for keeping it contained. Although something told me I didn't have to worry about it since Frank was behaving like a brat.

Rock stars. Go figure.

We left Burbank early because Levi was supposed to meet us in West Hollywood at six and Friday traffic was heavy.

Ashton sat next to me and listened to my crash course on how to behave around people who worked in the industry.

"Rule number one." I paused and glanced over at him to make sure he wasn't on his phone. "You're not a fan when you're talking to an artist. You're a professional. An artist doesn't need to hear how much you admire his or her work when you're establishing communication. Especially if you've never met each other before. They're human beings and should be treated accordingly. Not like a crystal vase. Not like a god or a creature from outer space. You are not to ask them to sign anything, you are not to ask to take a selfie."

"But you have," he countered.

"I've been doing this long enough to have established a relationship with some of these people. That's the key. Once you have a relationship established, you can take advantage of your connections, but you can't expect people to accept you after one gig. You need to work your way up. It's all about professional integrity."

Ashton was quiet, and I had no clue if he understood what I was talking about.

"Look." I sighed deeply and turned down the music. We rolled up to an intersection and came to a stop at the light. "Everyone who works in the industry is a fan. Each person was inspired by another artist. Art is what drives us, but you can't let your feelings and your mouth be your guide if you want to make it. Your admiration needs to take a step back. You can't show your weaknesses to other people. This is a cutthroat industry. There's a lot of money involved. Millions. There are a lot of things you can't talk about. You'll be signing papers and you could get sued for breach of confidentiality. One wrong word and you're out. Then you won't ever be able to get a gig."

"So I have to pretend?"

"Sometimes."

"Do you pretend?"

"Yes, Ashton. Sometimes I do. It's for the greater good."

"Is it hard? Pretending when you're screwing Frankie Blade?"

My brother had no clue his hero had disappeared from my life indefinitely. Poor fella still thought he was getting a backstage pass for a Hall Affinity show and I didn't want to burst his little bubble of happiness.

"Watch your mouth. Frank...Frankie is off limits. We're not discussing him."

"Why not?"

Ashton's question annoyed me. "Because this is my private business." My voice reached a crescendo pitch.

"Fine. Whatever." Arms folded, Ashton slumped in his seat.

He was quiet again and I was bitter. Bitter because of Frank.

For a while, we drove in silence. I doubted myself. A lot more lately. The idea of putting a piece of duct tape on my brother's mouth crossed my mind more than once, but then again...if he was determined to fuck up his internship, I wasn't going to prevent him from doing so. My patience had its limits. And he'd been pushing those limits for years.

A small line snaked around the corner of The Viper Room. There were people of all ages—teens, adults, old timers. Honestly, I didn't expect to see a crowd this size, considering there was very little info about tonight's show on social media. The block buzzed with energy, and the traffic on Sunset Boulevard had hit its peak. A honking hell of exhaust clouds, it was a typical West Hollywood evening. Loud and filled with bursts of irrational anger.

We pulled up to the lot behind the venue and I debriefed Ashton on what was going on.

"The artist we're meeting today is disabled. Her name is Isabella. You are not to ask her about the accident. If she feels like talking about it, she'll be the one to start that conversation. Actually, you're not to ask her anything, because your job is to watch me and Levi. If I see you open your mouth to say anything besides 'hi,' you'll be sleeping under a bridge. I'm not kidding."

Ashton rolled his eyes, which didn't surprise me at all.

"Understood?" I pressed.

"Yes, ma'am." He nodded.

"Great. You're carrying my bag."

"What? Why?"

"Because that's part of the job, Ashton. Carrying shit around." *God help me. I should have grabbed that duct tape.*

The doors were still closed to the public, but the bouncers knew who I was. They let me and my brother in without asking questions. Inside, the girl in charge of the tickets gave me two passes.

"Put this on." I handed one to Ashton. "That's your permission to be here. You lose it, you're going to be escorted out."

Levi and Isabella's mother/manager waited for us in the downstairs lounge. The empty room was like a box. Small, dark, and eerie. The air was stale and a song from *Blizzard of Ozz* played in the background.

Ashton hung back while we chatted. After the introductions, we headed to the upstairs dressing room to meet the band. I wasn't sure what to expect, because the YouTube video Levi showed me was a couple of months old. Instead of the scrawny teenager with dreadlocks I'd seen on the recording, we were meeting a young woman with spiky blue hair.

The room was so tiny and there was so much gear and people swarming around Isabella. that I didn't notice the wheelchair at first. Nor was it the element I wanted to concentrate on.

"Hi, I'm Isabella." Smiling, the girl extended her hand for a shake. She had a sweet round face and glowing olive skin. Her makeup was heavy, but it matched the bold outfit she'd chosen to wear tonight and the dark, edgy vibe of the club. She beamed confidence and I felt her grit in the grip of her handshake.

"Nice to finally meet you, Isabella. I'm Cassy with *Rewired*. I've heard a lot about you. I'm excited to see your show."

"Thank you so much for coming. You won't be disappointed. Me and the boys rehearsed the hell out of this set." She laughed. It was deep and throaty and filled the entire room with simmering waves.

"I love the new hair," I said.

"I'm told blue is my color."

Levi had mentioned that the drummer and the guitarist were family. The bassist was new, freshly recruited out of the Musicians Institute. He hadn't played any live shows with Isabella's band yet. Tonight was his christening. They were all insanely young, hopeful, and broken down by hungry-for-money suits who'd wanted to snatch bank by showcasing a pretty girl in a short skirt.

We kept our conversation light at first. Isabella didn't bring up the accident until after some of the people left the room to give us more space.

Ashton sat in the corner and watched my bag. Levi hovered. His sneaky I-told-you-so glances didn't escape my sight. Asshole knew all along Isabella was my kind of people. I felt guilty for doubting his instincts. It was all Frank's fault. Hard rock's golden boy had messed up my mojo.

"Thank you for doing this," Isabella's mother said. "It's been really hard to get her music out ever since the deal fell through."

"It's a damn shame," I agreed.

"The music business isn't about music anymore." There was a

hint of bitterness in Isabella's voice, but there was also something else I picked up. Determination. Drive.

"If they want me to lose my clothes to sell more tickets, I'm up for it. I ain't saving this for anybody. It's mine. I do whatever I want with it." She motioned at her body, smiling. "But when they want some girl who can't tell a C from a G instead because the crowd has a better view of her ass, then we're doomed."

Isabella had a point. She didn't shy away from speaking her mind, even if some of the words that came out were harsh. I loved her realness. It was refreshing after interviewing the elite. Bigger names were prone to hold back, though it was usually through no fault of their own, because publicists, managers, labels...or fear dictated the words.

We decided to record the interview in the dressing room to keep the edgy vibe of the conversation. Isabella was great in front of the camera.

The smell of alcohol, history, and rotting wood reigned in The Viper Room by the time we wrapped up. The bar was busy. Music was loud. Lights were sparse. I could feel the clouds of anticipation in the stifling air of the club as I pushed through the barrage of people, looking for a good spot to watch from.

A couple of local acts were slated to play before Isabella's band. Ten minutes before her set, Levi decided to put Ashton to use.

He dragged me downstairs where the noise level wasn't as bad to fill me in on his brilliant idea. "Can your brother operate a simple video camera? I brought my backup DSLR. I want him to film from a different angle. Maria said he can sit at their table. All he has to do is make sure the camera is still and the image is in focus."

"I don't know. Ashton's never held a video camera in his life." Yeah, my brother was good at games, but handling a DSLR was a lot of responsibility.

"Come on. You brought him here to carry your bag around? If he wants in, then it's in all the way, babe."

"I don't want you to complain if he fucks up something," I warned.

"How about this? You won't hear a word from me if he fucks *this* one up."

"Okay, deal."

We shook on it and ran back upstairs to where my brother was guarding our gear.

Levi took him to the dressing room and explained what exactly he wanted. I stayed in the crowd to take notes. The band that had just finished up wasn't bad. They were also young and very enthusiastic on stage. Maybe even too enthusiastic for a venue this small and an audience this tame. Nevertheless, they went onto my list of acts to check out later.

My phone buzzed in my pocket. It was a text from Levi with the list of songs Isabella was going to perform tonight. I opened the attachment and skimmed through the titles, my eyes zeroing in on the word "Ambivalent."

I hadn't listened to a single Hall Affinity song since our infamous late night rendezvous with my brother over a week ago. And I sure as hell didn't want to hear the song that reminded me of the biggest heartbreak of my life. Especially tonight, when I was trying to forget my two dates with Frank Wallace. In the back of my mind, I hoped that Isabella was singing another song with the same title, but unfortunately, it *was* a Hall Affinity cover. I saw the text scribbled in small print next to the title when I zoomed in on the picture.

My heart shrank in my chest and my legs shook. I wanted the bitterness to fall away badly, but the bitch held my feelings hostage. Even when the lights flickered and the crowd shifted toward the stage, my body refused to react. I stood in my spot, motionless, staring at the heavy black curtain, my throat tight with anger and my eyes welling. Getting emotional over a man who I truly didn't know was dumb. I understood that, yet I couldn't stop thinking about him no matter what I did. I'd even sent a text message to Jax to apologize for my disappearance because I knew how much disappearance hurt firsthand.

Isabella kicked off the set with one of her originals. It was an energetic, jazzy song. The drums were infectious, the guitars impressive. The wheelchair didn't seem to limit her eagerness to please the crowd. Her upper body moved to the beat and the audience clapped along. I heard whistling and cheers. It was a solid start to the set. Thrilling and radiant. The promise of a fun night.

As always, I took detailed notes on my phone, but my insubordinate mind kept betraying me and going to what I knew was coming up.

By the time the band reached "Ambivalent," my heart was sprinting. I couldn't control my own body. I had to ride this insanity out with panic lodged deep in my chest. My legs quivered and my blood pounded against my eardrums.

Notes weren't the priority anymore. I put my phone away and tried to concentrate on the music. Isabella's voice was nothing like Frank's, but not only did her rendition measure up, it stood tall. Tall and proud. This cover had a rather soulful feel. She added a few pitches here and there. A few quirky notes. A sprinkle of color. The new level of depth blew me away. Everything the song had made me feel before tonight, anger and disappointment, ebbed away, giving way to something new. Something that didn't have a name yet.

"Crap!" Ashton smacked the back of his head against the headrest of my Honda and drew something from his pocket. "I forgot to give this to Levi."

And here I thought my brother was going to be on his best behavior tonight. "What's that?" I examined the SD card in his palm.

"It's the first fifteen minutes of Izzy's set."

"*Izzy*, huh?" Irked, I grabbed the card and slid it into the pocket of my jacket.

After the show, Isabella's mother took us to Saddle Ranch for supper. I hadn't felt like going, mainly because Ashton was with me and censoring him in a public place wasn't part of my babysitting duties. But I knew it would be the perfect opportunity to get to know the entire band, so we accepted the invitation.

Levi had left before dessert. He wanted to start on the interview as soon as possible. Surprisingly, Ashton wasn't a total dud. I only counted three embarrassing things that came from his mouth that I was going to discuss at a later date. Isabella liked him, though. I had a suspicion they'd exchanged phone numbers too, but I didn't bring it up at the table. I didn't want to embarrass him in front of everyone.

"Why didn't you give it to him?" I questioned my brother as I started the car. "He's probably looking for it."

"I told you. I forgot."

"You know Izzy isn't into guys, right? You flirted with her all night."

"I know."

"Okay, I just wanted to make sure you don't get your hopes up."

"You think I'm so dumb I can't tell gay from straight?"

"No, I don't think you're so dumb, Ashton." I paused and listened to the engine purr. Thin fog spilled into the parking lot from the tops of the hills. "Actually, sometimes I do. Because you behave like a ten-year-old."

"No, I don't. I wasn't flirting with her, and I did everything you said today. I carried your bag all night."

"Could you put your seatbelt on, please?"

"Come on. Say it. I didn't fuck up. You're going to see Levi tomorrow anyway. You can give him the card."

I didn't know why telling my brother he hadn't disappointed me tonight was difficult. Maybe because I couldn't remember the last time I'd actually said that to him. At the same time, I understood encouragement had to be a part of his rehabilitation. He needed to hear the praise. He needed to hear he was doing a good job.

"Look"—I leaned back in my seat in an attempt to gather my thoughts—"you were a lot of help today, Ashton. Next time, try to be more attentive. Always check all the gear before you leave. Bags, pockets. You want to make sure you don't lose anything important like an SD card, okay?"

"Okay." He buckled up and connected the aux cord to his phone. "Any special requests?" A proud smile flashed across his lips, but he hid it from me.

"No." I shook my head. "I'll tell you if I don't dig it."

We had a very strange push-pull relationship, which exhausted the hell out of me lately. I wanted my solitude. I wanted my living room empty. I wanted my bathroom free of clutter. But I wanted Mom to have at least a few weeks of rest too.

She deserved it.

In a sick way, I liked the fact that Ashton was always in my face. His company made me forget about my short-lived almost-affair with Frankie Blade.

"That's not how it works," my brother gritted out. "You lose the right to pick songs when you give up the aux cord."

"Oh yeah?" I threw him a sideways glance. "You wanna walk back to Burbank?"

He rolled his eyes.

We stared at each other for a good minute. Obviously, communication for the Evans siblings was lacking.

"Alrighty then." I checked the mirrors and pulled out of the parking spot. "Looks like everyone's on board."

Ashton started off with shuffling through some Blink 182 and Limp Bizkit songs. They weren't my preferred bands to listen to, but I was too tired to shame my brother's strange music choices. My state of mind was perpetual chaos. After tonight's meeting with Isabella, there was no doubt Levi would be moving forward with his crazy documentary idea, and the upcoming workload scared the shit out of me. Sleepless nights and double the coffee. Like the good old days when it was only the two of us.

A Korn song took over the speakers when we were near Los Feliz. Our windows were down and Ashton stuck his arm out to catch the wind while he jerked his head to the beat. I laughed. We truly didn't have moments like this anymore. Or ever. I envied his age. He was still on the brink of adulthood, full of hopes and dreams. He hadn't been broken down and taken apart by life yet. And although he'd never shared any of his aspirations with me, I was certain he had some. Everyone did. I just wished I could make him act on his instincts, make him take responsibility, make him believe in himself.

"This shit never gets old," he squealed as "Freak on a Leash" came to an end.

He skipped a few songs before settling on one of the earlier Hall Affinity singles. Frank's voice was like a knife to my heart.

"Can you play something else?"

"Why?"

"Can you please play something else?" I squeezed my hands around the steering wheel.

"Fine." He changed the song.

I was silent, then Ashton's voice crawled into my head. "We're still getting backstage passes, right?"

"I don't know."

He didn't say a word.

When I finally rolled my Honda into the parking garage of my apartment complex fifteen minutes later, Ashton was snoring. A Linkin Park song blared from the speakers.

"Hey." I nudged him on the shoulder and pulled the aux cord from the jack. "Wake up. We're home."

He stirred and his head rose. "Do I have to carry the bag?"

My patience was wearing thin. I responded with a long stare.

"Fine." Ashton stumbled out of the car and grabbed the gear from the trunk.

Once we got inside, we were both so tired that we went to sleep immediately.

A call from a number that hadn't been programmed into my phone woke me in the middle of the night. I couldn't tell exactly what time it was, but it was pin-drop quiet. I heard my blood pulse against my eardrums and my blanket rustle beneath my body. Every noise in that moment felt amplified. I wasn't certain why I'd left the ringer on. Maybe because I'd forgotten or maybe because a sadistic side of me had been waiting for this call.

"Cassy?" His voice on the line was abnormally small with a hint of rasp, but not the sexy bedroom rasp. It was the kind a person developed after straining their vocal cords.

Excitement and shock filled my chest. I could barely speak. "Frank?"

"I'm sorry I haven't called."

And just like that, the man was back in my good graces. A fraction of me still fought, but deep down, I knew I'd already lost this battle.

My mind scrambled for words. I was mad yet relieved, and putting them into a coherent sentence after two hours of sleep proved to be difficult.

"Cassy?" he called my name again to make sure I was still listening.

"I assumed you didn't have time for me anymore." I was blunt. I needed to tell him that.

Apparently, Frank Wallace wasn't a man of many words when it came to explanations. "I had to leave for a few days. Family emergency," he said.

"Is everything okay?"

His breath caught. He didn't answer my question, and his silence only fueled my curiosity. He'd disappeared for almost two weeks and now he wanted me to be a part of this weird one-sided conversation.

"Frank? Are you still there?" I checked.

"Do you have to be up early tomorrow?"

"I mean"—I skimmed through my agenda—"I have someplace to be in the evening." Plus, there was the write-up of Isabella's set, which I had planned to start first thing in the morning, but something about the way Frank spoke made me believe that I could probably knock out the editorial during lunch too.

There was more of the eerie silence on the line. Then he said, "Do you want to go for a ride with me?"

"Now?"

"Yes."

"You know it's the middle of the night, right?"

"I'm aware. Can't do it during the daytime, Cassy."

"Okay." My mouth did all the thinking. My brain didn't agree, but it was too late.

"I'll see you in an hour. Wear a jacket," he said and ended the call.

I was frazzled during my phone conversation with Frank and hadn't put too much thought into it when he'd called it a *ride*.

The text alert came in at around four thirty. An hour after the call, as he'd promised.

Outside, the message read.

What are you doing, Cassy? my voice said as I rushed through the courtyard, my heart drumming out a wicked war beat.

Thick fog crawled through the quiet tree-lined street. There was no car waiting for me, but I heard the rumble of an engine and noticed the headlights long before the bike came into view.

The tightness inside my chest grew. My breath hitched. I had no idea why I'd forgiven him so fast and why I'd agreed to this madness. My irrational behavior went against all my rules.

Gloved hands on the grips, he sat on a black Harley in the middle of the street, looking unfazed. A matching black helmet hid his face, but I knew it was Frank. *I felt him.* I felt his anxiety blending with mine.

The man was psycho to get on a bike again after what happened to him. Along with his sanity, I questioned my own, but it wasn't the time or the place to demand an explanation. He had his reasons. Whether he was going to share them with me didn't matter at the moment.

If we let our insecurities and fears rule our lives, we may never get to live the way we really want or should.

I zipped up my jacket and neared the bike. A charge of electricity crackled through the foggy air between us. My nerve endings prickled, my limbs tingled with anticipation. I shamelessly dragged my gaze along the length of Frank's body. Drinking him in. Savoring each and every detail of the clothes he wore. Fitted black leather jacket. Stretch denim jeans. Army boots. *And, boy, did he own this look.* The man screamed danger.

No words were said. Not that I needed any.

Frank grabbed an extra helmet from the back of the seat and handed it to me. Worry swarmed in my stomach as I slipped it over my head. The glass darkened the street and it seemed as if I'd become part of a different reality. *His reality.* My pulse raced and my heart banged against my ribcage so hard it hurt. Frank threw the kickstand up with the tip of his boot and motioned for me to get on the bike.

I grabbed a hold of his shoulder and climbed behind him. My arms encircled his thin waist, palms splayed over his tight abs. He was hot, his every muscle tense.

I breathed in deep, inhaling his scent. Sandalwood. Oil. Fear. Adrenaline. The man was my dirty secret. My drug. My ruin. Although my head was spinning, being with him made my panic subside and my worries fall away.

The bike roared to life and I felt the jolt. My body jerked as we started to move, and I dug my fingers into the leather of Frank's jacket. His gloved hand covered mine to readjust my grip as we rode through a foggy tunnel. Yellow pole lights flashed in the corners of my eyes when he sped up. I scooted closer and pressed my chest to his back, needing to feel his solid presence. My skin buzzed where our thighs connected, and I wanted to lose the helmet and ride with my lips on the nape of his neck and his hair in my face, but I knew that probably wasn't a good idea.

We cruised through the quiet streets for a while, then jumped on the freeway. I had no idea where Frank was taking me. All I knew was that we were going north on 5 until we hit 18. Cold wind danced in my sleeves and under my collar. After Porter Ranch, Frank took the narrow, serpentine mountain road that weaved through the Malibu canyons.

We rode for what seemed like forever. My body trembled. I held on to Frank as if he was my lifeline, and in a way, he was. And maybe I was his. I couldn't tell, but I felt his fear becoming mine. I felt his confusion. I didn't know what had caused them, but they were under my skin and in my blood, and we were whole while we rode on that bike. I was him and he was me, and it was the scariest and the wildest adventure of my entire life.

He slowed down near a scenic overlook and pulled over to the shoulder on the edge of the cliff. Swirls of dust greeted us as we got off the bike. A lonely pole light illuminated the road sign.

My legs shook and my clothes clung to my body uncomfortably.

I assumed that if it were daytime, we'd be looking at the side of the mountain. But right now, we were looking at a whole lot of pitch-black.

Frank was quiet. Without offering any explanation as to why we'd come here, he walked over to the wooden rail and slid off his helmet. The soft breeze tousled his thick sandy hair.

As I approached him, my gaze swept over his back, studying the outline of his body. Then we stood mute for a few minutes, facing the darkness. I waited. I didn't want to disturb the moment of stillness that had settled between us.

Frank broke the silence first. "I'm sorry I disappeared." He spun to face me, helmet still in his hand, and his eyes sought mine. They were infinite storms and I couldn't read his expression. It wasn't one I'd seen before.

I drew a deep breath, expecting him to elaborate. When he

didn't, I spoke my mind, "Well, you know what? It fucking sucked. You made me feel like I was merely another plaything who didn't even get a rejection letter."

Rock star or not, he deserved to hear the truth.

"I didn't mean to." He stepped toward me, his eyes lowering to my mouth.

"Look... I don't have any illusions about what we are or who you are." I rolled my shoulders. My body ached after the ride. "If you have other things to do or other women to see and you don't intend to keep this"—I waved my hand at the shrinking space between us —"going anymore, I need you to be honest about it. You can just say 'Cassy, it's over. Can you please delete my phone number?' I won't take it personally. And I won't get upset. I swear. I'm a big girl and I can assure you that my panties will not be in a wad."

"I won't ask you to delete my phone number." He shook his head lightly and took another step in my direction. "Now about the panties..." A smirk tugged at the corner of his mouth. His face lit up. What was it about underwear? One mention of it and men entered puberty again.

"I know you lead a very decadent lifestyle, so I really won't be offended if you decide to call it quits." Although I wasn't certain what exactly he and I were. An almost fling?

His brow arched. "Decadent? You're throwing some big words at me, smarty pants."

"What can I say? Rock stars come and go. A thesaurus will forever be my one and only loyal booty call."

Then I heard it. His laugh. It was soft and quiet, but it was back and I loved how it filled me with bliss. How it made my chest swell and my stomach flutter.

Damn this man.

"I won't ever do that again," Frank said. I felt his hot breath on my cheeks as his body moved closer.

"You promise?" I bit my lip. The tip of my boot was tapping a wild beat against the dirt.

"I do. If I have an emergency and need to leave town for a while, I *will* call or text you."

I didn't believe what I'd just heard. "You promise me?"

"I do."

"And when you go on tour?"

"We'll figure it out when we get there." He leaned in, his voice a ragged whisper. "I've had a rough couple of days. Can you cut me some slack, doll?" His mouth captured my lips as his free hand snaked around my body to pull me to him. The kiss was vicious fire. It tasted of anger and desperation. Our tongues clashed while fighting for dominance. I heard a low rumble in his chest and the squeak of leather on leather as our jackets caught. My legs were wobbly, my head buzzed. I needed leverage and I needed air. But most of all, I needed him. It was the strangest kind of craving. Something that hadn't happened to me before. I'd never wanted to be with a man as much as I wanted to be with Frank. I didn't care about how many award-winning songs he'd written or how many followers his Twitter account had. I didn't care about the words people usually said to each other. Or labels they liked to put on their relationship. I simply wanted reassurance he was mine when he was with me, when he was off duty, when he wasn't playing the role of megastar Frankie Blade. No matter how short this thing between us, the half-affair, might turn out to be.

My hand that wasn't occupied with the helmet sifted through his disheveled locks and I gave them a little tug.

He responded with a soft growl, and pleasant chills ran down my spine. I was burning up and I wanted his damn jacket off so I could lick him all over.

Frank broke the kiss. His hand rose to my face and when he cupped my flushed cheek, his glove felt cool against my skin. "Are you hungry?"

I wasn't sure which hunger he was referring to. In any case, the answer to both was the same. "Very." I nodded.

"Do you want to have breakfast with me?"

"Yes."

"My place is just up the hill." He jerked his chin toward the road.

"Your place?"

"Can't really show up at IHOP like this." A chuckle.

"Right. Your place it is."

Chapter Nine

We raced against the approaching daybreak with clouds of dust kicking up behind us and the dew-scented air coating our clothes. The hum of the engine, loud and powerful, made the perfect sound-track. When the bike reached a fork in the road, Frank took a sharp right.

I saw it then. The gray shimmer of the Pacific blanketed by the morning fog. My heart jumped in my throat and a blast of excitement shot through me. The breeze, crisp against my skin, was ruthless and the first rays of light glittered across the mountains like little fires.

The view was breathtaking and I couldn't understand how in all of my twenty-five years I'd never been here. I'd never seen any of this.

The road began to curve, taking us back to the mountain range. We crawled up the hill and entered a long driveway that led to the property. Frank stopped his bike at the entrance and punched in a code. I heard a creak as the gate slid open to let us in. My arms were still wrapped around his body while he drove through the front yard.

We didn't speak when Frank was helping me off the bike. He unbuckled his helmet and I got rid of mine.

The house sat on a cliffside that overlooked the water. I couldn't tell how big it was or how many floors it had, but the slick, clean lines, the abundance of white tones, and the expansive windows told me Frank was a minimalist. There were hardly any flowers. A three-tier stone fountain sat in the middle of a large grassy lawn.

He threaded our fingers together and lead me toward the house.

The time around us stilled. The ocean roared. We stood on the terrace, speechless, staring at each other. The streaks of fresh morning light danced along the side of his face. He was transcendent.

"Do you want to talk about it?" I asked carefully.

"Not right now," he told me, shaking his head. He got rid of his gloves and cupped my face with his needy hands, scorching hot on my cheeks. The air around was all electricity. The light tremble of the ride still ruled my body, making my nerve endings vibrate. Our mouths met again. I parted my lips, offering him whatever he wanted. His tongue swept over mine eagerly, and I was more than happy to reciprocate.

We kissed long and hard, then our feet started shuffling across the terrace. The new sun beamed above our heads as the wind tangled our hair. I'd never done drugs before, but I imagined this was how it would feel to be high. In a way, I *was* high. High on him.

Hands never leaving each other, we moved inside. He turned me so that his chest was against my back, and steered us across the large room toward the dining area. His palms teased me as they slid down my waist to my hips.

I took a moment to process the fact that I was inside Frank's home. The space was atmospheric with an open concept layout. A true manifestation of modern luxury. There were plenty of windows, exposed beams, and a skylight. This was where he'd been hiding for over seven years. Or at least I hoped this was where he'd been. He'd probably had to spend a good fraction of that time away in a hospital.

"You won't need this." He unzipped my jacket and deposited it on one of the chairs next to the massive airfield-sized dining room table, which sat in front of a glass wall overlooking the ocean. The drop was impressive. Not for the faint of heart. And the sun-kissed view of the Pacific that stretched beneath our feet was stunning. The subtle luxury of his place was overwhelming and I wasn't sure how I fit in here.

"Coffee?" Frank asked, his fingers stroking my neck before he pressed a soft kiss to my temple.

I felt his erection against my lower back, and when I leaned into him, his body grew tight. Heat simmered between us, and the air buzzed.

"Cream and five sugars." I turned in his arms to face him.

Frank's gaze drifted over my features, ending at my lips. "I can arrange that." The side of his mouth curved and the smile gave me shivers. He spun us around and walked us backward until my ass hit the edge of the dining table.

I knew there and then that the coffee was going to have to wait.

His lips captured mine in another passionate kiss, and the need that pulsed between my legs was driving me crazy. I was out of breath, and my jeans and bra seemed two sizes too small. I ran my palms over the trim outline of his shoulders. He was all lean muscle and warmth, his broad chest rising with each loud inhale.

Frank nudged me on top of the table, one hand gripping the edge while the other cupped my ass. His hips parted my thighs and we burned raw where our bodies connected, his erection rubbing against my center, reckless and dirty. We were about to fuck right there in his dining room, and I loved every second of it before it even happened.

The man lived up to his wild reputation.

We didn't speak as Frank pulled off my boots and rid me of my jeans. The glass was cold against my ass, but we were a wild fever, a chaos of loud moans and ragged breaths. His mouth found my ear and he nibbled the lobe before his insatiable lips kissed down my chin and neck. Chests heaving, we hurried through the foreplay like teenagers.

He dug out something from his pocket. A condom?

"Oh my god," I whispered against his cheek, a little surprised. "You prepared."

"I didn't know if you'd want this," he confessed, tearing the package. "According to my calculations, it was a fifty-fifty chance. A chance I wasn't willing to take."

Laughing, I unbuckled his belt. My panties dropped to the floor as his jeans fell to his knees, then he slipped on the condom in a rush. Back flat against the table, I parted my legs to welcome the intrusion, and he drove into me fast and deep, working through my tightness. A delicious ache coiled my stomach—I hadn't been with a man in a long while. Not because I didn't want to but because there was never time or never a man worth my time.

And this...this felt nice. In a debauched way.

Frank was a savage and I briefly wondered how long it'd been since the last time he'd had sex. His hands gripped my thighs and he pushed into me harder. In and out, over and over. My breath caught, and my heart hammered so hard that I could feel it inside my head.

I watched Frank through the flutter of my lashes. Every flex and every roll of his muscles under the fabric of his long-sleeved T-shirt rattled my core. The view drove me to the edge, figuratively and literally. The table scooted under the weight of our rocking bodies. Frank was like a wild animal, ferocious and unrestrained. My hips bucked to meet his thrusts. My walls stretched to meet the demands of his size. I was like warm chocolate, dripping and melting around his cock. My whimpers matched the roughness of his strokes as a wave of sounds—skin slapping, uneven panting, and furniture grating against the floor—washed through the empty room.

It was an angry fuck. Frank was upset and I was a conduit for letting it out. Yet, strangely, I didn't mind it at all. Part of me loved the fact that he'd chosen me.

The release was agonizing. The perfect torture. My calves cramped, and my shoulders ached. Fire burned my airless lungs and my dry throat. Eyes shut, I tossed my head back to chase the filthy nirvana. Frank's hand locked over my knee to help him keep his tempo and his breaths shuddered. He was losing focus. I wrapped my legs around his ass and we rode the final lap of the race together. Our bodies rocked fast with broken, unsteady beats. I came first, my mind exploding as I fell into a state of temporary shutdown. Frank came seconds later. His taut body went limp, one hand still on my thigh and the other splayed over the table. Then he slid out of me carefully.

The surface beneath me was slick with our fluids, and I lay there with my eyes half-closed, looking at him and breathing through my euphoria. He seemed wrecked. His face hard. The air was hot, and beads of sweat glimmered across his forehead.

"Frank?" I called, my voice shot to shit. I needed water and he still had to get rid of the condom.

Without speaking, he reached for my shoulder in an attempt to lift me, but his fingers lost their grip. So I pushed myself up and scooted closer to the edge, pressing my breasts to his chest. My bra was still on and my nipples ached from straining beneath the fabric. My swollen sex throbbed against his skin. Snaking my arm around his neck, I brushed his disheveled hair out of his face and kissed his stubbly cheek.

"I just need a minute, doll," he husked, pulling me into a hug.

He palmed the back of my head and his lips caressed my temple in a way that was comforting. It wasn't a lover's embrace. It was almost...paternal. And twisted. Frank wasn't old enough to be my sugar daddy and he wasn't young enough to be my friend with benefits. It was an in-between affair.

We stayed like that as the minutes went by. I didn't dare move, because he felt so fragile in my arms.

"Five sugars, huh?" His brow rose in question.

"What can I say? I like sweets," I murmured against his soft mouth, and our heated lips lingered in a barely-there kiss. Nothing resembling the barbaric act of sex we'd just engaged in. This was a delicate exchange of breaths, a fine mixture of afterglow gasps. My needy hands wanted to explore his body. Curious, they slipped under the fabric of his T-shirt. I'd never touched him there before and my heart stuttered.

I felt it then. His secrets. The patches of inked skin across his ribs were scarred. Rough and contorted beneath my fingertips. Frank didn't react, but I noticed how the subtle line above the bridge of his nose tensed.

"I'm glad you're here," he said after a while. "Stay a few more hours?"

"You owe me breakfast."

"And five sugars."

"And five sugars. That's right."

Finally, Frank disposed of the condom. I slipped on my panties and cleaned up the table while he handled getting the coffee.

The dining area alone was bigger than my mother's entire apartment and I took a moment to soak in its luxury. The house itself was the perfect hideaway. It was cut off from civilization by an intricate scenic drive and an eight-foot stone fence.

"Is there a pool?" I asked, wandering over to the kitchen. My eyes stalled on the artwork decorating the south-side wall. They were large abstract paintings, hung side-by-side.

"Yes. In the back. You're welcome to try it out after breakfast." He shot me a naughty glance over his shoulder.

"I didn't exactly pack for a day at the beach."

"Swimsuits aren't allowed in my house, Cassy."

He said it with a poker face, but the glint of amusement in his blue eyes didn't escape my notice. "I'll consider it."

"You do that." I heard the slam of the cabinets and the clink of silverware.

"Can I help?" I offered.

"I'm capable of making coffee, Cassy." His soft laughter carried over the noise of the water. "I'm rich, not handicapped." *Said the man who'd refused to secure his own microphone when we met.* There was a pause. "Or at least, I don't think I am."

My throat tightened. There was sarcasm and something else in his voice. Bitterness? I couldn't tell.

"And the doctors? What do they say?"

Frank set the carafe on the base and turned to face me. "They

147

believe as long as I don't lift, walk, or breathe, I'll be fine. Thing is, I doubt twenty thousand people will be willing to pay money to see me stand still in front of the microphone and lip-sync for an hour and a half."

I had questions. Tons of them. I wanted to know where he'd been these past few days and why they'd been rough and what I could do to make him feel better, but he was like a flower. He opened up only when he felt like doing so, and while the anticipation killed me, I was willing to wait for the bloom.

We moved to the corner sofa in the middle of the living room. Plates with food and mugs with coffee sat in front of us. The fridge was fully stocked and organized and while Frank had turned out to be pretty decent in the kitchen, I had a feeling he had someone taking care of the property on a daily basis. There was no dust anywhere, and nothing was out of place. Things looked extra tidy.

He'd given me one of his shirts and I cuddled against his warmth as we sipped our fuel. I couldn't remember the last time I'd gone this long without looking at my phone. My brain was a hot mess of sleep and caffeine. The latter lost its battle eventually, and I drifted off with my cheek against Frank's chest and the taste of waffles and strawberries on my lips.

It was his voice that woke me up sometime later.

"Cassy?" He shifted, his hands rearranging my body carefully.

I lifted my head, and my eyes fluttered open. Frank rolled his right shoulder slowly. His face was tense.

"What's wrong?" I pushed my hair away from my cheeks.

"Just sore." He shook his head, smiling.

Our legs were in a tangle, the shirt I wore riding up my thighs. He'd changed into a fresh pair of sweatpants, but his upper body was on display and I had a perfect view of the eagle tat across his pec. It was detailed and looked a lot like a pencil drawing. More fresh ink covered his ribs. There were swirls of flowers and vines and my fingers wanted to touch them again. To feel the scars. To feel the blend of pain and artwork.

"Care for a massage?" I offered.

"Sounds very tempting." He brushed his lips against mine. "Maybe next time?"

"Okay."

My anxiety was coming back. I didn't know what time it was, but it felt a lot like noon. I had things to do and I had an event to cover in less than eight hours.

"My mother's dying," Frank said. It was random. Like everything else with him.

Heaviness filled my chest. I waited, but he stayed quiet.

"Janet?" I clarified. I didn't remember seeing her at The Regency.

"No, my real mother."

My mind went blank for a second. "I thought you didn't know your real mother."

"I have vague memories of her. Social services took me away when I was three. It's all mostly a blur." A pause. "But after the crash, I decided to look her up."

"Why?"

"Honestly, I'm not sure." He shrugged, and his eyes looked tired. So did his face. "I guess maybe I wanted to find out why she had me if she'd never wanted me in the first place. Or maybe I wanted to rub my success in her face."

My chest was tight, my throat closed up. The words in my head were all wrong. There was nothing I could do or say to change the way he felt at that moment. I understood him. I knew first-hand what being unwanted by one, or both, of your parents meant.

Frank and I were equally different yet the same.

"Either way, she's past the point where my Grammys can impress her."

I sighed. "How come?"

"She had a stroke a couple of years ago. Drugs. She's in a convalescent home back in Arizona, but I don't think she has much time left."

"I'm sorry."

"Don't be. It's not your fault. It's no one's but hers. She wasn't exactly a paragon of healthy living. She had traces of twelve different drugs in her system when she was brought into the ER. I'm glad Billy and Janet were the ones who raised me. I wouldn't have known music if not for them."

I didn't know what to do except hug him. Then we sat there quietly for a little while longer.

"I have a few things I need to take care of," he said. "Roman will take you home."

"I can Uber."

He shook his head, and his tone was firm. "This is non-negotiable. It's safer that way. Trust me."

"Okay." I waited for him to say more.

"The next few days will be very busy for me and the guys," Frank went on, his hand tangled in my hair. "We need to finalize some stuff. We're playing three shows at the Forum at the end of November."

"And you haven't announced anything yet?"

"Press release will go out on Monday morning."

That, right there, made me feel special.

"See, that's what you get when you sleep with the front man." Frank smirked as if he had just read my mind. "All the inside info before the rest of the world."

I laughed. He pulled me into a kiss. This, the insanity of us, was startling and breathtaking and I dreaded the day it would end.

Roman drove me home in the Range Rover. He was polite but quiet. Pleasantly exhausted after spending all morning with Frank, I sat in the back and skimmed through my emails and angry messages from Levi, who apparently had been waiting for my write-up from yesterday's show since nine this morning. Isabella's set was muddled, like a foggy haze, and I blamed Frank for it. Obviously, the dining room table sex had impressed me that much. And then some.

There was a missed call from Mom and two texts from Ashton. Little brother wanted to know if he could borrow twenty bucks.

The first thing I did was message one of our guys, Stewie, to ask him if he wanted to cover tonight's show instead of me. He did.

It hurt almost physically when the vehicle finally reached the busy suburbs. Leaving the calm of Frank's home felt a lot like withdrawal. A small part of me was scared he'd disappear again, and I was tempted to call him just to hear his voice. To make sure he was real and last night hadn't been a dream.

My apartment welcomed me with a stack of dirty dishes and a rent increase notice but no Ashton. I dragged my feet to my room, changed into my PJs, and turned on my computer. The plan was to make more coffee and knock out the editorial on Isabella. But lying down on the couch while waiting for said coffee to be done was a mistake. I passed out and slept until dark.

It was the muffled buzzing of my cell somewhere in the apartment that woke me up. My head felt heavy and full of cotton. Ashton was still out and messages from Levi still needed to be answered.

"You posted the interview?" I drawled with my eyes glued to the home page of the *Rewired* site.

"You didn't pick up your damn phone," Levi raged on the line.

I hated lying, but at the same time, I understood I'd put my partner in a very uncomfortable situation. He promised Isabella's mother a fast turnaround. We were the next-morning folks and we hadn't delivered.

Guilt twisted my stomach. "I'm sorry. I wasn't feeling well."

"I came by your apartment today to pick up the SD card from Ashton. He said you were gone when he woke up this morning."

Shit. Duct tape it is for my little brother.

I closed my eyes and tried to think. Levi wasn't stupid. Denying the obvious would be useless. "I'm having an affair."

"A what?"

"An affair...with a man."

"Is that what you call a late night booty call these days?"

"Yes, it is."

"Who's the guy?"

"You don't know him."

"He better have a really big dick if you're skipping out on your commitments."

"He has an okay dick."

Lie. Frank's was great, but I wasn't going to tell that to Levi. I was going to make up a mystery man. For the sake of us all.

"Honestly, you kinda disappointed me, Cass," he said.

"I'm aware and I'm sorry. It was a really weird couple of weeks and I needed to unwind. It won't happen again. I'm going to finish the write-up before midnight and I want to help you with the documentary. I believe Isabella has a shot. She's sweet, outspoken, honest, and she has a killer voice. We just need to give her a little push. The girl deserves to be heard."

"Why do I always forgive you?"

"Because I'm awesome." I grinned to myself.

"That you are. No wonder *Pulse Nation* keeps trying to steal you."

"They should have seen my potential all those years ago when I asked to be put on their roster officially. Robbie's a tool."

"Too late now."

After we wrapped up the call, I dumped the cold coffee and made a fresh pot. My phone rang at eleven thirty. I had forgotten to program Frank's number into it, but I knew it was him. My heart sprinted. My chest wasn't big enough to fit the hurricane-like flutter.

"I thought you were busy the next couple of days," I said, spinning in my chair. My gaze slid to my door to make sure it was shut, because Ashton was back. He was hanging out in the living room, working on his new assignment. The ten best live performances of the Red Hot Chili Peppers.

"I am. I'm in a meeting, as a matter of fact," Frank said softly. I heard voices in the background and one of them sounded like it belonged to Dante.

"Are you now?" I teased him. "What's on the agenda?"

"Band stuff."

I waited. No explanation followed. I didn't press.

"Hey." He switched to a whisper. "Do you have any plans for next weekend?"

"I have to check my calendar. I might have a couple of places to go to."

"Can you move some stuff around? Saturday and Sunday?"

"It depends. What do you have in mind?"

"How about we go to Aspen? Have you ever been?"

"Colorado? No."

"That's the one. Unless you know of some other Aspen?"

"Well"—I pulled up Google—"there are also locations in Sweden, Kenya, and Germany, according to the internet."

"That trip would probably require at least a week of vacation time. Maybe after the tour if you really have your heart set on one of those."

"Why a week?"

"I'm pretty sure getting to Kenya will require at least a couple of changeovers."

"Don't you own a plane? Blade Airlines. Direct flight."

"Contrary to popular belief, no. I don't own a plane or an airline. I can rent one, though."

"Rent? What kind of a rock star are you? I'm dumping your ass for Bruce Dickinson."

He laughed hard. Then I heard someone calling his name over the chords. It was an intro riff of "Awake."

"I have to go. Hey, I'm serious about Aspen—it'll be another first. I'll call you soon."

"Have fun at the meeting."

When he hung up, I needed a minute to absorb the fact that we were developing a relationship. It didn't feel like an affair to me. It felt like something else.

Because he was making plans. For us.

Chapter Ten

The entire next week was chaotic. Ashton studied for SATs and Levi and I started working on Isabella's project. We met up with her and Maria on Wednesday night to discuss a plan of action.

One good thing amongst all this madness was that Mom got a raise at work.

Rewired numbers grew steadily. The interview, though transcribed, still drew in a lot of viewers. At this point, only five other publications had run exclusives with Frankie Blade. *Rolling Stone* was one of them.

Hall Affinity dominated the internet because of three surprise shows and a tour announcement, along with a thirty-second teaser of an upcoming November single. The public went crazy when the news broke. The tickets were sold out in under a minute.

Frank called me almost every night at random hours. Sometimes he was alone and we could squeeze in a session of naughty talk. Other times, there were people around, so those conversations were short and a little more tame.

We left L.A. Friday evening.

Roman picked me up from my apartment around nine. I was

meeting Frank at the airport. Arriving there separately was just a precaution, but with the paparazzi sniffing around Malibu, we wanted to cover all the bases. The anonymity gave me freedom to lead a normal life and I wanted to keep it that way. At least while Levi and I were working on Isabella's documentary. The shitstorm in the press that always followed people like Frankie when their affairs became public oftentimes got out of hand. Overly enthusiastic fans, jealous exes, hate mail, Twitter campaigns. Justice Cross and his second wife could probably write a book about it.

No, thank you. I wanted my name to stay off TMZ's radar.

My heart drummed wildly in my chest as we drove through the streets. Despite my crazy schedule, the week had dragged on. I even gave myself a pedicure to try to fill the time when my mind wasn't consumed by work.

I couldn't wait to see Frank, to hug him, to hear his voice. It was sick how much I missed him. I didn't know how else to describe this strange feeling that had lodged itself deep in my veins. It was *longing*. The worst kind of withdrawal.

Roman was a bit more talkative this time. We exchanged short versions of our life stories. His was obviously more interesting. He'd served in the Navy and traveled the world before his private security gig. I could bet my entire month of rent that his tales were as wild as his current employer's.

I almost couldn't believe I was going on a romantic trip with a man who was the talk of the planet this year. Flying to Aspen with my teenage celebrity crush was beyond surreal.

Frank had already boarded when we arrived. It *was* a private charter jet, which didn't surprise me at all. He probably couldn't take a breath without some sleazeball snapping a candid photo or some online blog posting a new rumor. A regular flight would be a bad idea. People like Frankie Blade didn't blend in well, even in business class.

There was a small crew to cater to all our needs. Apart from Roman, who had a separate cabin, Frank and I were the only two passengers. Leather couches, a huge plasma TV, and a bar greeted me as I entered the plane. The interior colors were predominantly walnut and soft caramel.

"This is a lot of stuff for two days." Frank laughed at the size of my bag as Roman escorted me in.

"Isn't Aspen cold? Unless you're taking me to Kenya?" That earned me another chuckle.

I wanted to jump the man the second I saw him, but my common sense talked me out of it. He was dressed casually. Jeans, sweatshirt, sneakers, and his hair a bit of a mess. He looked like any other guy you'd see on the streets of Encino or Studio City. Except he was Frankie Blade. He was worth seventy million dollars and according to recent polls, he'd made it on the list of one of the most eligible bachelors in the world. *And he belonged to only me for the next two days.*

"Thank you." Frank gave his bodyguard a slight chin jerk, which I figured was a polite version of "get lost," because Roman was quick to retreat.

We were alone at last and I needed a moment to drink him in, but most of all, I needed a moment to catch my breath.

Frank wrapped his arms around my waist and pulled me closer. His mouth neared my ear. "You won't need any of your clothes there, Cassy."

"No?" I pressed my palms to his chest and my eyes met his.

"We're not going to Aspen to ski."

"Really? So the extra pair of socks I packed won't be necessary?"

"None of these will be necessary as soon as we're in the air, doll." His hands slid to my ass and slapped it playfully, then gave my denim a light tug.

I was immediately turned on.

"Your mile-high club membership package comes with unlimited champagne and your own personal rock star." He gave me a smirk. "Unlimited usage as well."

The anticipation was driving me nuts. I was a happy woman. My stomach coiled and my panties were soaking wet.

He said it then. The same words that were on the tip of my tongue. "I missed you." His fingers sifted through my hair and he cupped the back of my head. His touch was serene. Despite the storm surrounding him, he was calmness in its purest form. "Did you miss me?"

A knot tied my stomach. I nodded.

"Good." He drew a ragged breath through his teeth, chest rising beneath my palms. The thump-thump of his heart was strong and loud.

Someone knocked. A stewardess came in to let us know the plane was about to take off. We moved to our seats. Frank held my hand until we finally reached flight altitude.

I'd told Levi I was going away for the weekend to see Mom's family in Oregon and instructed Ashton to tell the same story to anyone who inquired about my whereabouts.

Once we were on our way, Frank poured himself some water and me some champagne. Legs tangled, we sat on the couch and exchanged our weekly recaps. I told him about Levi's documentary idea and expressed my concern about Ashton accidentally burning my apartment down.

"You don't give your brother enough credit." Frank shook his head.

"He's seventeen. He's never house-sat before. What if he throws a party and I return to a pile of ashes and a lawsuit?"

"We'll get you another apartment, doll."

The "we" factor startled me. I didn't know if he meant he and the people who worked for him or he and I as a whole.

"I like my apartment."

"It's definitely cozy."

"Cozy?"

"You worry for no reason."

"Of course, I do. Do you have any idea how much of a headache younger siblings can be?"

"No, but I'm in a band with three other guys. It's kinda like marriage with a small harem. You have to make sure every wife is happy, and you divide your love and attention among them equally."

"Right." I sipped on my drink, getting lightheaded. "I can see how that could be challenging."

"Yeah. You can't simply quit when you feel like it. We all depend on each other. Our careers depend on each other."

"And now you have a mistress. Must be hard to cover up the cheating, huh?" My glass was empty and my ovaries needed attention.

"Very." Frank's voice was a sweet whisper with dirty intentions. His hand slipped to the back of my head to pull me into a kiss.

Heart pounding, I set the glass aside and straddled his thigh. "I want to take advantage of my unlimited usage of my personal rock star before we land."

He laughed softly against my mouth. "I'm all yours, doll." Then his fingers reached for the zipper on my jeans.

Our eyes met and I took a moment to bask in the color of his irises, an exquisite and rare blend of blue and gray. Frustrated by our often-heated late night calls, my sex ached for action and I rocked my hips against his leg. The pressure was just right.

"I take it this is yet another first?" Frank clarified.

"Me humping you?"

"No, the plane sex."

"Yes. So you better make it good."

"Never had an affair with a rock star. Never been to Aspen, Colorado. Never had sex on a plane. Where did you live, Cassy Evans? Under a rock?" A self-serving smirk flashed at me.

"Rock stars with planes don't come around often." I pressed my lips to his cheek and dragged them across his silky skin. He'd shaved and his scent was my new addiction.

"Well, looks like I'm a lot of your firsts, doll."

"And here I thought I'd experienced it all." A drunk laughter bubbled up my throat. The childish happiness in my chest was overwhelming.

Restless, I slid over to the side and got rid of my jeans and panties. Patience wasn't my strong suit with him. The man was too hot and too available for foreplay. We got right down to it. Hopping back onto his lap, I freed his cock from the confines of his designer jeans and skimmed my hands over its impressive length. He was hard and beautiful and begged to be fucked for endless hours.

I spread my legs and stroked him lightly, savoring every inch. Then my gaze flicked up to his face.

Frank's head was tossed back, eyes closed, a cascade of dark lashes resting against his cheeks as he reveled in the heat of this moment.

"Frank?" I murmured, looking down at him, his cock at my entrance.

"Hmmm?" A hint of a smile touched his mouth.

"Do you have a condom?"

His lids fluttered open. "Yes." He reached for a small compartment in the armrest, retrieved a foil pack, and handed it to me.

Sheathing him, I asked, "Can you talk dirty to me?"

He cupped my ass. "I've been waiting for you to start bossing me around, doll."

"Oh yeah?" I grabbed a hold of his shoulders and lowered myself onto him. Slowly. There was something incredibly sensual about the way he made me feel when his body invaded mine, when he delved into me. The press of him against my walls from this angle created a sinfully elegant sensation. For a moment, I wondered what it would be like without a condom between us, without any barriers.

A ragged hiss left his mouth. His fingers dug into my skin. "Fuck."

"Is that all you've got? The man who writes songs for a living? Is that your dirty word?"

"My songs aren't usually about fucking, Cassy." He laughed deeply.

I sank lower, taking him all the way in with my knees against the leather upholstery of the couch. "Do you like that, Frank?"

"Yes. I do." He nodded. His eyes roamed my face, then dropped to my breasts. I still had my top and my bra on. "Keep going, baby."

I lifted my hips and slid down his cock again, this time a little faster. "Like this?"

"Yes. Deeper. Fill it up, baby."

"I'm the one who's in charge." I moaned, rocking against him.

"And I'm the one who made you this wet." He pulled down my top and reached for my breasts, taking them into his mouth one by one. His tongue swirled around my nipples, teasing me, as feverish whispers skated across my puckered skin.

We were a lustful mayhem. An exchange of filthy words and requests. Our bodies and breaths in synch, our lips scorched and bruised. I was floating, my sex raw and swollen, welcoming each thrust with eagerness.

Frank found my sweet spot and worked it until I came. Once. Twice. The ride was magnificent. I fell on his chest, my throat sandpaper dry and my lungs out of air.

"Cassy," his ragged voice called.

"I'm not done yet," I mumbled deliriously, pushing myself up. My insides throbbed with want and needed more. Needed another orgasm.

His fingers locked around my wrist.

"Oh... I'm sorry. Is it sore?"

"Yes." He removed my hand from his right shoulder and placed it on the arm of the chair. "You're going to fuck me to death, doll."

"We definitely don't want that." I shook my head and gave him a devious smile. "How does near-death sound instead?"

"I could probably handle that." He was still inside me. Hard and insatiable. Pulsing and ready to move back into action. His palms skimmed over my waist. "Now where were we?"

"We were trying to get you to come."

"Oh, that's right. Well, let's get to it then."

We spent our entire Saturday having sex, eating expensive food, and watching reruns of *Friends*. Apparently, it was Frank's favorite TV show. *What do you know? He was human.*

I called Ashton twice to make sure my apartment hadn't been ruined in my absence. Once in the morning and again in the late afternoon. The loud music in the background threw me off. Of course, my initial thought was the asshole had invited his friends over.

"Red Hot Chili Peppers research, duh?" my brother said when I asked him what was going on. "'Walkabout.'"

"*One Hot Minute*." I plugged in the name of the album.

"Yep. Not digging it, though. Kinda boring."

"It'll grow on you, buddy. Just keep going. That's the price you pay for being a *Rewired* intern."

I heard Frank's laughter drifting over from across the room. He stood in front of the window overlooking the snowy mountain range, stretching. His shoulder was still aching after my airplane assault.

"You don't have to check on him every three hours, Cassy," he said as soon as I hung up.

"Trust me, I do." I was tempted to skim through my emails while my phone was in my hands, but Frank was very vocal about electronic devices. Unless they were sex toys, they were forbidden during our retreat.

"He's a good kid."

"He's not. Do you have any idea how hard it was for me to get him to stop playing video games? I pretty much bribed my brother with a fake internship and a promise of meeting celebrities to get him to give up his stupid Xbox obsession."

"And look who he's already met." Frank wiggled his brows.

"Pray he keeps his mouth shut," I joked.

"He will. Or he'll get his backstage pass revoked."

"Aren't you an evil breaker of teenage dreams."

Ashton had asked me about the Hall Affinity show at least three dozen times in the past week. He was on cloud nine when I confirmed that we were indeed going.

Frank crossed the living room. "Comes with the territory."

My gaze slid down his shirtless chest. Neither my laptop I'd brought with me, just in case, nor my phone seemed of importance anymore.

Frank wasn't what you could call a large-framed man, but he took good care of what Mother Nature had given him. Long limbed, thin-waisted, and toned to perfection, he had an impressive upper body. One look at his physique turned me into a wet mess.

I was a pathetic woman who'd discovered what great sex really meant.

According to my calculations, since the moment we got on the plane last night, he'd made me come more times than all the other men combined, when they managed, in my entire life. Both demanding yet attentive, Frank was a thorough lover.

"Any chance some chiro comes with that territory?" I stretched my legs in front of me and put my phone down.

"I can arrange it." He moved closer and settled on the couch next to me. His hand skimmed over my calf, tracing the outline of my very first tat.

I loved this. Talking. Relaxing. Sitting in front of the fireplace. *Feeling him near.*

To avoid being accidentally seen or outed by some greedy hotel employee, Frank had rented a private property, a two-story cottage twenty minutes away from downtown Aspen. I felt like a princess and that this entire trip was an adult version of my fairytale.

"You're going to spoil me rotten," I confessed as Frank began to massage my ankles.

"I plan to." His eyes traveled over my face. "And I'm just getting started."

My heart did a happy dance. No man had ever done anything of this sort for me. Sure, they'd asked me to dinner at Katsuya or taken me out for drinks at BJ's. But a trip to one of the most expensive ski resorts in the world on a private jet wasn't even on my bucket list.

My phone, which was sitting on the couch between us, vibrated.

Frank's brow arched in question. "Do I need to worry about"—he glanced down at the screen—"Jax?" His fingers rubbed lazy circles on my calf.

My mind stalled. It'd been, what? Weeks since I last spoke to Jax? I vaguely remember sending him an apologetic text for being a flake. However, the message was a courtesy, not an invitation to chat.

"No." I shook my head and reached for my phone. The preview of the message from my tattoo artist featured a broken heart emoji. Great.

Frank's hands froze. He leaned back and stared at me for a while, his eyes scrutinizing my every breath. "I'm not sleeping with anyone else," he said at last, tone serious. "I expect the same in return."

My blood thickened with shock. "Oh my God!" I couldn't believe it. "Are you fucking jealous of some dude whose heart I apparently broke because I'm seeing someone else?"

"I only wanted to make it clear, Cassy." The frost in his voice was evident.

"That *someone else* I'm seeing is you, by the way." Upset, I tossed my phone back on the couch and crossed my arms on my chest defensively.

"Did you *tell* him you're seeing someone else?"

"Not in so many words. Besides, I don't owe him an explanation."

"So why is he texting you on a Saturday night?"

"Look." I took a deep breath. "He drove me home once, then he asked me out. I never responded. End of story. You need to hold your horses."

Eyes dark, Frank continued to stare at me intensely. I couldn't read his expression. It was a confusing mixture of all his stage faces and his real one, a fusion of different emotions. When he finally spoke, his voice was distant. "My wife cheated on me."

And just like that, he was telling me things I couldn't possibly find online. Private things. His words hung heavy in the air.

"Frank..." I had no idea what to say to that. "You married a *Playboy* model."

His jaw set, he looked up at the ceiling as if he were searching for an answer. "Do you always have to be so blunt, Cassy?" He was clearly irritated.

"Did I hurt your feelings?"

"No."

"Then why are you so upset?" I did feel bad for calling him out on his marriage fiasco, but it was too late to retract it. We all make mistakes. His just happened to be as grand as his gestures. *Rich people. What do you know?*

"I'm not upset. Seeing that another man was contacting you brought back memories."

Trying to inject something less heavy into our conversation, I joked, "You're the most insecure millionaire I've ever met." My freshly pedicured toes thrust into his rock-solid thigh.

"I'll do you one better." He smiled, but it wasn't a happy smile. "She cheated on me with my best friend."

The air left my lungs, and I swallowed past the stiffness in my throat. "Dante?" That was unexpected.

Frank nodded.

"You're not kidding?"

"No. I'm not."

"And you still talk to him?" I wasn't sure how else to word my question. The two appeared to get along just fine.

"Remember what I said about being in a band?"

"Yes. You depend on each other. Your careers too."

"Exactly. Getting rid of a wife who signed a prenup is much easier than getting rid of a wife who you signed a major record deal with."

I took a minute to process. All the seemingly useless info I'd been collecting on Hall Affinity all these years swarmed inside my head like a twister. I knew enough to have a good understanding of who was who in the band, but I'd never pegged Dante for someone who held this much control. He'd always struck me as showman number two, who cared about nothing but his outfits, riffs, and getting wasted. "You don't split royalties four ways?"

Frank broke our eye contact and looked out the window. His hands were still, his chest hardly moved, as if he was holding his breath. "No. We don't. I get forty. Dante gets forty. Johnny gets twenty. Carter is on retainer."

"That's...interesting." I was under the impression that Frank got the biggest cut. I was wrong.

"Dante and I do all the songwriting."

"Lyrics too?"

"Yes. He also writes some bass lines."

"Is that why you two had a falling out right before you recorded *Breathe Crimson?*" Musicians were a special breed of artists. Feuds in this business were nothing unusual. Probably even the norm. I always thought creative differences were the reason behind their disagreement.

There was a shift in the air. I felt it. Anxiety slowly crawled underneath my skin.

Frank's gaze returned to mine. "I walked in on them fucking in my bedroom. Dante was doing a lot of drugs back then. I'd wanted to end things—the band and the marriage—then and there, but he was so fucking high, I honestly don't know if I can truly hold him responsible for it, because he probably doesn't remember that night, or the entire decade, very well."

I understood where Frank was coming from, but I almost wondered if his brain had short-circuited somewhere between last night and now. He went from brilliant and confident to childish and hurt in less than twenty-four hours.

"So let me get this straight." I needed clarification. Or maybe an explanation for why the woman was to blame in this case. "Because he's your friend and because you're in a band together and write money-making hits, he gets a pass?"

"He doesn't get a pass. I still hate him, but I've learned to live with that hate."

"I don't have anything against Dante. As a matter of fact, I think he's one of the best guitar players hard rock has ever seen, but you're willing to work with him, even after you watched him fuck your wife?"

"Things are a bit more complicated than that when not only does your and your family's fame and fortune depend on this conglomerate you created with your friend years ago, but you also owe a bunch of albums to one of the biggest record labels in the world, Cassy." He sounded broken and condescending.

"It's very sexist. Just because he's a guy doesn't mean it wasn't his fault. He's to blame as much as she is."

"You're taking my cheating wife's side now?"

"No. But if you cut her loose, you should have cut him loose too. I would've."

"Oh, really? And what makes you an expert?"

I didn't like the tone of his voice and I didn't like where this conversation was going. From scorching hot sex to double standards in less than an hour. My pulse jumped. Angry, I slid from the couch. "You know what? No one made me an expert, but it sounds to me like you're putting all the blame on a woman merely because she's a woman."

"Cassy?" Frank shifted but didn't make an effort to get up. "You're reading too much into it."

"I believe I need a little break from your pity party."

My mind was a messy place to be as I rushed to the bathroom. I hadn't asked him for his life story. The man was so bitter and insecure, it depressed me.

Minutes passed while I sat on the edge of the hot tub and absently stared at the tiled wall.

"Cassy?" He said after a while. "Can you come out please?"

"I'm not done being mad." Although he couldn't see me, I rolled my eyes.

"Come on. This is silly."

"Exactly. It's silly for you to think I have someone else on the side when I'm ripping myself apart to satisfy your strange after-hour rides and dinner cravings."

There was a long pause. "I'm sorry I doubted you. Can you come out now?"

"I'm still mad."

I sulked a little longer to see if I could get another reaction from him, but he was quiet.

Deafening silence welcomed me as I stepped out of the bathroom.

"Frank?" I called on my way downstairs.

No response. He was gone.

I woke to the mattress dipping under the weight of Frank's body as he slipped under the blanket. His gentle breath stroked the back of my head, his cold hands ducked under my shirt. "I'm sorry, Cassy."

My heart felt restless and heavy in my chest. I wasn't sure whether to continue pretending to be asleep or to pick up where we'd left off earlier. The man's behavior bothered me. He'd taken off without a word and didn't care to, at the very least, grab his phone. I'd waited for him for hours until exhaustion finally knocked me down.

Frank pressed a kiss to my shoulder, his scent wrapping me into a bubble of strange need.

"You said you'd call or text if you had to leave." My voice sounded small. "You didn't."

"It won't happen again."

"You can't just disappear, Frank. Especially not in the middle of a fucking snowstorm." The snowstorm was an exaggeration obviously.

"You really like to blow things out of proportion, huh?" He

167

laughed against my shoulder blade and traced the lines of my butterfly with his tongue. Shivers zipped down my spine and I melted into his firm body. He was so easy to forgive.

"So do you, Frank."

"Doll"—he pulled me against him—"I've never been in a relationship with a woman who wasn't some kind of a high profile public figure. I don't know what the rules are."

His confession confused me even more. I wasn't sure how to react. "Is that what this is? A relationship?"

"Yes." His hand skimmed over my stomach, soft fingertips caressing my skin.

I took a deep breath. My heart pounded and my pulse raced. "You're telling me all these things about you no one else knows. Things about your health and your ex-wife. What makes you think I won't go and sell it when we're over? Or write a book? Why did you pick me?" Those were all the questions I'd asked him before, but the answers he'd given me weren't exactly honest. Or maybe not what I'd expected.

"You have my permission to write a book when I'm gone, Cassy."

I didn't like the sound of that. "What do you mean, *when you're gone?*" I spun to face him. Our noses and knees brushed. Shimmering streaks of moonlight fell over the side of Frank's face, and I saw worry in his eyes. I could see that the stress had been eating away at him slowly but surely.

"One day I'll be gone. We'll all be gone, doll. It's the way life works."

"Why are you being so depressing?"

"It's called being realistic, not depressing. A bunch of metal plates are keeping my corpse together and sometimes I feel like one wrong move and this house of cards is going to fall apart."

"Oh my God, Frank. Your *corpse?*" I palmed his cheek. "Don't say stuff like that."

He smiled. "I'm only human."

"I'm sorry I overreacted earlier. It really wasn't my place to tell you what you should have done or should be doing. I'm just a bystander and have no idea what's at stake when you're running a million-dollar empire."

"You're not a bystander, doll." He paused for a second. "Everyone who stuck around while I was recovering is in it because of money or the benefits the reunion promises. I don't have any real people left in my life except for Billy and Janet...and you. Don't change a thing. Don't bend for me."

"I have to be honest. I might be with you because of your money too, Frank. I don't date men who can't afford to take me to Aspen."

He laughed and his hand cupped my head. "Darn it. I guess I'm a really bad judge of character. I figured a girl who couldn't interrupt her yoga session to flirt with the biggest rock star on the planet was the right girl for me."

I giggled. "There might be one more thing, though." My fingers slipped under the waistband of his boxers. "It's a tie between your cock and your millions."

He brought his lips to mine and captured my mouth. I felt him getting hard under my palm, and his muscles tensed. In a matter of seconds, we turned into a panting mess—sucking, biting, and licking. It was dirty and wonderful.

"Do you mind being on top, doll?" Frank asked between kisses. His breath caught in his throat.

"Not at all." Frenzied, I straddled him. My sex slid against his length, back and forth, taunting him.

Then we fucked hard and raw until we passed out.

It was the anxiety in Frank's whisper that woke me hours later. He stood in front of the window, his silhouette lit by the morning son, with his phone against his ear, jaw set, hair a mess.

I watched him silently, waiting. Sudden tightness held my chest hostage. I knew something had happened, because he'd broken his own no electronic devices rule; he'd taken this call. His panic in the air was palpable.

"What's wrong?" I asked as soon as he finished the conversation.

"The album has been leaked."

"What?" I rose and rubbed my eyes. "The new Hall Affinity album?"

"Yes."

"But how?"

"I don't know. They were all demos. Unfinished." Frank paced the room, his face devoid of emotion.

"What are you going to do?"

"Try to take down whatever we can. Trace the source of the leak. Must have been someone on our team. Very few people had access to those demos. We recorded most of it at my home studio."

I got up from the bed and approached him carefully. He was a wall of stress. His color was starting to leave him.

"Frank." I wrapped my arms around his body and pressed my chin to his bare chest. A lump choked my throat. The thrum of his heartbeat against his ribcage was a wild race. "I'm sorry this happened. Is there anything I can do to make it better?"

His hands moved to my hair. "You're doing it right now."

We stood there silent and motionless for a while.

"Cassy, I hate to do this," he said finally. "But I have to leave soon. I also think I might have been spotted when I went out, so it's best we fly back to L.A. separately. I'll have my PA get you a ticket for an afternoon flight."

My heart sank. I didn't want him to go, but I understood.

Chapter Eleven

It was everywhere—the New Hall Affinity album that was slated for release in late February and didn't even have a title yet. *In its entirety.* Twitter, YouTube, Blabbermouth, Instagram, Facebook.

The world was at war. Social media hadn't seen a shitstorm of nasties this big in years. The band's fandom divided into two armies —hardcore supporters who boycotted leaked demos and reported everyone posting unauthorized material and overly enthusiastic, impatient fans who didn't give a fuck and shared the heck out of unfinished songs.

At first, I wasn't sure which camp I belonged to. Temptation was a real bitch, but I fought it hard. And my sense of right won. Besides, I'd already heard "Awake." I knew Frank was going to deliver vocally. I knew Dante was on top of his game. I knew, once finished, this would be another chart-topping record for Hall Affinity. The fact that someone had disrespected the hard work of dozens of people involved in the production of this album only confirmed my fears. Today's society no longer knew good from bad. Shock value over integrity. The world was full of people who sucked and it saddened me.

Our morning was hectic. Frank and Roman left shortly after the call and I stayed for another couple of hours to pack.

My phone was on fire. Emails. Press releases. Texts with links to leaked songs. There were two messages from Levi. He wanted to know when I was returning from Oregon, because something had come up for tonight and he needed help. Residual chaos consumed my life.

I couldn't even imagine what was going through Frank's head at the moment. I didn't want to.

A car picked me up at around eleven. Heavy clouds hid the mountaintops and snow had dusted the city. The drive was beautiful, and for the first time since Frank and I became a thing, I regretted that we couldn't be open about our relationship, that we couldn't just explore outside. I regretted he was Frankie Blade, the paparazzi's most desired man on the planet, and I regretted I was Cassy Evans, a music journalist on the brink of losing her professional integrity because she'd slept with an artist she'd interviewed. We were the next big scandal waiting to be uncovered, a ticking bomb threatening to go off.

At the airport, a business class ticket waited for me. The man kept his word. He was spoiling me rotten. Another ride had already been arranged when I landed at LAX.

On the way home, I skimmed through my social media apps to get an update on the leak. No source had been found. An official press release with a message from the band, the same one Jay Brodie PR had slipped into my *Rewired* inbox a few hours ago, was pinned to the top of Hall Affinity's Facebook page. There were no comments from any of the band members.

Twitter looked awfully angry. A lot of name-calling along with encouraging messages of support from fellow artists. Including Taylor Rinehart. I had no idea how the actress had slid into my feed. I didn't follow her anywhere on social media, but as I clicked on the post, I realized it was a retweet from the Hall Affinity fan account.

My heart skipped a beat. Was it jealousy? Frank had said it himself. She liked the band and she was a decoy.

The separation from him drove me nuts as my brain scrambled to return to reality. Getting the man out of my system was nearly impossible. I wanted to hear his voice badly, and this sudden need scared me more than anything in the world. But I understood he probably didn't need another distraction right now. And I would be exactly that. A distraction. Like he'd become for me.

At the apartment, Ashton greeted me with a concerned face. "Your boyfriend just hit BuzzFeed's front page."

My initial response was almost, *he's not my boyfriend,* but before I could say it out loud, something stopped me—Frank's words. We were in a relationship. He'd put a label on it first.

The early morning and the travel had exhausted me. I only had enough strength to drag my bags to the middle of the living room, and that's where I left them. My feet hurt, and so did my back, although the latter was due to the non-stop sex.

My brother sat on the couch with his feet on the coffee table and stared into his laptop. He was getting too comfortable in my apartment and I didn't like it. His eighteenth birthday was approaching fast and I didn't intend to lease him my living room indefinitely. But this was a conversation for another time.

"Could you please not do that?" I motioned at his feet and peeked at the laptop screen.

He complied, grimacing. "Someone's not happy."

I grimaced back at him.

A picture of Frank took up a good portion of BuzzFeed's home page. It was a still of a newly uploaded video. He'd been caught on camera at the airport right after landing. Apparently, when things got interesting, even charter planes were of no use. If paparazzi wanted to find someone, they always did.

Ashton hit the play button. A jumble of voices filled the room.

"Frankie, do you have anything to say about the leak?"

"Over here, Frankie!"

"Any idea who may have leaked the music, Frankie?"

I watched Frank walking through the throng of shaking microphones. Frustration lined his face. He looked tired. I wanted to reach through the screen and hug him. Roman was one step ahead, making way for him. Corey mingled somewhere in the background. The questions kept pouring.

"You can't listen to those demos," I warned.

"Why not?" Ashton pouted.

"Because they're demos," I explained. "Because those songs aren't finished and aren't meant to be heard."

"What difference does it make since it's already online?"

"It makes a huge difference. Respecting the artist, for starters." I was too wound up to go on with my explanation, but I was mainly just upset. The leak had cut my vacation short.

"But people dig it."

"You're not listening to those demos, Ashton. End of discussion."

"Buzz killer."

"You're not listening to the demos," I repeated myself, dragging my bags to my room one by one. "Or I'll tell Frank and he'll revoke your backstage pass."

"That's blackmail." The slam of my door cut off Ashton's complaints. I didn't want to socialize with my brother. Or anyone, for that matter. I needed sleep and I needed to clear my head.

The muffled rattle of my phone somewhere between my sheets woke me up hours later. Frank's name lit up my screen.

"You have this stupid habit of calling me when I'm asleep," I said groggily.

"I can call again tomorrow," he offered, his voice a sweet murmur on the line, sending pleasant shivers down my spine.

And just like that, I was a bundle of nerves full of sizzling want. I was wide awake. "No. Right now is perfect."

"I'm sorry if I woke you up."

"You'll have to find a way to make it up to me next time we see each other."

"I will." His tone heated.

I was hot and bothered and it was my own damn fault. I needed to defuse this conversation a little before he drove me to the point of no return. I didn't want to end up masturbating myself back to sleep with Ashton in the living room. I changed the subject. "Did you figure out where the leak's coming from?"

"Not yet, but we have a couple of leads."

"Will you be able to take the songs down?"

"Probably. But not all of them. Even if we do, someone will upload the material later again. It is what it is at this point."

"Are you okay?"

"I'm fine now." He paused. I felt his anxiety and his fears. Things weren't going according to plan. Then came the words. "Do you want to stay at my place for a couple of days?"

The question startled me, shook me to the core. This *was* moving fast. We were like an express train that was going nowhere. "You mean like a sleepover?" I tried to sound light, but my mind was heavy with racing thoughts.

"Yes, a sleepover. It'll just be the two of us, naked, and I'll make sure I have tons of soy-free and gluten-free ice cream and crackers." His tone was suggestive, sexy. Desperate. He wasn't asking. He was begging.

"I don't want to be in the way." The Forum shows were only a few weeks away. He probably didn't have a lot of free time.

"And all seven seasons of Game of Thrones."

"Eight."

"Wait, there are eight?"

"Looks like I have to get you up to speed."

"I'd love that."

"Me too." I didn't know why I was agreeing so fast. I'd never spent a night at his place. I hadn't even seen his bedroom. This was unexpected. "Frank, I do have a lot of work. Levi and I are putting together a documentary for an artist."

"You can use my office when you need privacy. I don't plan on screwing you twenty-four seven."

Blood rushed to my cheeks. I loved when he shared his naughty ideas. "How many hours a day do you plan on screwing me then?"

"How does fourteen sound?"

"What a random number. Do you have enough stamina?"

"Don't you worry about my stamina, doll." He chuckled. "I'm gearing up for a tour, so that won't be an issue."

"That's disappointing, Frank. I thought you were an eighty percent guy. I'm only getting fifty. Looks like there are some issues with my membership. I might need me a new rock star."

"We'll just need to upgrade your membership. Your rock star is fine."

We laughed and my chest filled with happiness. Frank Wallace was sweet, funny, and...mine.

"Okay. I have to think about it. I don't want paparazzi to track me to your house. And I'll need to be in and out a lot."

"They won't. It's a private road."

"I heard they sometimes camp out."

"It's a mile-long private road, Cassy. There are two more properties down the hill."

"Who are your neighbors?"

"I believe they're both in the movie business."

"You don't know who you share a mountain with?"

"I'm a loner."

"So if someone snaps photos of me, I'll be rumored to possibly be sleeping with one of the three millionaires who live on that road?"

"No one's going to snap any photos of you. Not in Malibu."

He sounded so convincing that it all made complete sense. We were in a relationship. He wanted me at his place, I wanted to be with him, and we could still have our privacy. Simple.

"I guess we're doing this," I drawled, staring up at the ceiling. My room suddenly seemed small and stuffy.

"Pick you up tomorrow evening?"

"I have to have my car. And I'll get there late because Levi and I are covering an event. Midnight?"

"Midnight sounds great. I'm a night owl if you haven't noticed."

"That, I have."

"See you tomorrow, doll."

Frank's figure lingered on the front terrace as I steered my Honda up his driveway. There was a large suitcase in my trunk and a brand new toothbrush in my purse. I felt strange. Exhausted after a busy evening with Levi, but also hyperemotional. And perhaps giddy, infatuated, and a bit confused.

A small fraction of me still couldn't understand why this man had essentially chosen to be with a mortal enemy—a journalist. But I willed myself not to think about it. Frank and I were past the point of no return.

You need to stop doubting what the two of you have, Cassy, my inner voice said to me as I killed the engine.

A thin fog cloaking the property gave the house an eerie vibe. I threw the door open and drew a deep breath, inhaling the salty air. It was cool, cooler than in the Valley. Fresh and humid too, as if I'd been transported to another universe.

Frank hopped down the stairs and moved through the haze with urgency. My heart thudded as I drank him in. He wore a pair of sweats and a white T-shirt and looked...awfully domesticated.

"Hi." His voice drifted at me, and his eyes dipped to meet my gaze.

"Hi."

"I've got the hot tub going." A smirk tweaked his mouth.

"Oh, that's nice. I could use a back massage."

"Are you hungry?" He extended his hand to help me out of the car.

"Did you cook too?"

"I wish." Warm laughter rumbled in his chest. "No, but there's dinner."

"Dinner, huh?" I stared up at him, soaking in his charm and sensuality.

Goosebumps covered my arms when Frank's lips neared mine. He gave me a kiss and rounded the Honda to grab my bag.

We walked into the house without speaking. I needed a second to process everything that was happening. Yes, I'd been here before, but not like this. Not with my toothbrush, my floss, and a stack of panties.

"I've never given you an official tour," Frank said, depositing my suitcase in the living room.

"No, you haven't."

Smiling, he took my hand and pulled me in the direction of the artwork-filled hallway that led to a separate wing where his bedroom was. The man didn't waste any time. He was letting me into his life with such ease, it horrified me. He kept on sharing. Kept on revealing. Kept on erasing the invisible barriers between us.

Elaborate elegance touched every detail. Every piece of furniture and every piece of art was well thought out. There were no unnecessary items, no fancy extras. Just the essentials.

The first thing that stuck out to me when we entered the bedroom was a floor-to-ceiling window overlooking the ocean. The shades were up, leaving the room completely exposed to anyone who might want to hire a helicopter and fly over to spy on Frank.

The view from here was slightly different than from the dining area. Below, beneath the canopy of evening fog, I saw the curve of the land.

"Wow," was all that came out of my mouth.

"You like?" Frank whispered against the back of my head, his body aligned with mine. His fingers fumbled with my jacket to help me get it off.

Anxiety tightened my chest. "Yes. Very much." I swallowed hard and continued to stare. My heart raced.

"Good." Warm hands skimmed through my hair. "We can give this bed a test run later. Let me show you the rest."

The house was huge with a gym downstairs and a studio in the west wing. Everything was clean and organized, as if he'd been preparing for my arrival all day.

After showing off the rest of the property, Frank ushered me to the back terrace. There, beneath the dark spread of the starless sky, stood a small table covered with food and candles. A large infinity pool with glowing water took up a good portion of the lawn. The hot tub bubbled.

"I'm don't know where to even start," I confessed as I walked over to the table to check out what was for dinner and saw a plate with fresh fruits, a bowl of whipped cream, a bottle of champagne on ice, and two flutes. Then I detected the soft scent of cinnamon and vanilla. It was romantic.

Frank pulled out a chair for me. "No gluten. No soy. No eggs."

I sat down. He took a spot across the table. We stared at each other, unsure of what to do next. Apparently, this was new, somewhat uncharted territory for the both of us.

"Champagne?" he finally asked, grabbing the bottle from the bucket.

I melted a little bit on the inside each time the sound of his deep voice rolled over the roar of the ocean. "What are we celebrating?"

"Nothing in particular. I'm just glad you're here."

He filled my glass with champagne and poured himself water.

"Is there any word on who may have leaked the album?"

"No." His expression hardened. "At this point, I don't think I care. These things happen."

I wasn't convinced he meant what he said, but tonight wasn't about business or music. Tonight was a gateway.

I plucked a strawberry from the plate, dipped it in the whipped cream, and took a bite. "I'm feeling like swimming."

"Oh yeah?" Frank leaned back in his chair and watched me finish my fruit. His gaze roamed my face, totally unashamed, as if he was looking for something. The soft breeze fluttered his sandy hair and the candlelight licked his stubbly cheeks.

He was rough and enchanting and my eyes loved him.

Feeling adventurous, I kicked off my shoes, rose up, and shed my top.

Frank was silent and still, but his eyes sparked with lust. Something between us clicked. A dizzying and shiver-inducing desire.

"Are you coming?" I asked playfully, making my way over to the pool. The soft, dewy grass caressed my feet and the cool air bit at my skin. The night was perfect, filled with the promise of wild sex. After I wrestled off the rest of my clothes, I dove into the blissfully warm water.

I swam closer to the edge that met the slope of the hill and took in the view. In the distance, the curve of the road carved its path down the mountain. The lights of another house shimmered behind the wall of fog. The trees hummed. The crickets buzzed.

It was peaceful.

Frank stood and followed my lead, then seconds later, we were both naked in the pool. Our bodies twirled in the water, our hands on each other, our mouths brushing.

"You're beautiful," he said, running his wet thumb over my lips.

"And you don't have any clothes on." I grinned, my palms resting on his inked shoulders.

"Neither do you, doll." His voice teased my senses.

"What are we going to do about that?"

Frank nudged me in the direction of the deck. "I have an idea." He was hard, his erection rubbing along my stomach. Drops of water fell down his hair and face, glittering on his skin. Knees bumping and chests heaving with sharp want, we shuffled across the pool, rippling its smooth surface as small puffs of steam whirled in the air surrounding us.

The tile against my back felt cold when Frank pinned me to the side. I burned between my thighs and my craving for release swept me under.

"Are we alone?" I didn't know why I asked, but I needed reassurance that no one else was on the property.

"We are," he purred, dragging his mouth down my cheek. His hand slipped to the edge of the deck for leverage.

I wrapped my legs around his hips and rubbed my sex against his length. Our bodies were light, like feathers, floating along with the water. We were so in sync, I could barely breathe or think. I was losing my mind.

Frank's lips drew a broken trail of swift kisses along the crook of my neck. "I want to try something," he mumbled, cradling my head. His lustful gaze returned to me.

"It's definitely too early to ask me about anal sex," I joked, biting back a gasp.

"You're getting ahead of yourself, doll." He smirked. "I'll make a note of it, but that's not what I was going to say."

"What were you going to say then?"

"How do you feel about going bare?"

Panic rushed through my stomach.

"You don't have to say yes if you're not comfortable, but I'm clean. I've been tested." He slid his index finger under my chin and tilted it up so that our eyes met.

I'd wondered how he'd feel inside me without a condom, but the fear had always been there, hiding beneath the longing. Frankie Blade, the superstar, the golden boy of hard rock, had probably gone through a lot of women.

His words rang in my ears, sweet, scary, and wonderful. "I promise you have nothing to worry about. I've wanted it with you without a piece of rubber between us ever since our first time, but if you're not ready—"

"Shhh." I hushed him by pressing my mouth to his. "Yes."

It was the strangest thing—the realization of how my decision took us to the next level. I'd never let a man into my body without protection before. There had been a string of short-lived affairs that I struggled to call relationships. There had never been anyone like Frank.

"You sure?" he double-checked, rocking against me slowly.

"Yes. I'm sure. I'm on birth control. It's fine." I was babbling. "I want it too." My shoulders shivered and my legs clamped around his slick body under the water. My mouth spread into a silly grin.

"You're excited about it, aren't you, doll? Me fucking you without a condom?"

"I'm excited about you fucking me. Period." I giggled, throwing my arms around his neck.

He entered me slowly, letting me savor each second of this excruciatingly exquisite torment. Water slapped against the stones as our bodies moved together to the sound of an invisible beat. It felt different. Raw. New. Uncompromising. Giving myself away to someone.

It felt real.

Frank had a whole army of people to service his needs. He merely hid them well. I'd already figured out that he was at the gym during some of those early hours when I didn't find him in bed with me. I figured out someone cleaned and cooked on a daily basis, because dirty dishes magically disappeared every night and freshly baked croissants appeared every morning. I figured out there was someone who ran errands and handled Frank's schedule, because he never missed a call or a meeting.

He hid other things as well—the full extent of his injuries and the lengths he'd gone to in order to maintain his health. He masked his headaches with wide smiles, but I'd seen all his pills hidden away in the bathroom cabinet and I'd also seen what kind of diet he had to follow. He wasn't invincible. This was probably why he feared his upcoming performances wouldn't match up to his past ones.

After being there for several days, I still found myself getting lost in the endless maze of sparsely furnished rooms and artwork-studded hallways. The paintings enthralled me the most with their bold abstract lines and generous brush strokes. They made me wonder why Frank had chosen them in the first place. Had it been the color? The composition? Or had it been an impulse? Although he didn't strike me as someone who bought things "just because." Everything inside the house seemed to have its purpose and its place.

His physical therapy sessions were held in the gym. I'd never met his therapist, Reese, but I knew he came in the afternoons and spent at least an hour or two with Frank. The home studio, which was off-limits, occupied the entire east wing and faced the mountains. I'd only gotten to take a peek once.

Frank hadn't lied about access to the office. Contrary to my fears, we weren't simply ignoring reality and having sex day and night. He kept quite busy. Brooklyn was here every day and their conversations and the conference calls always ran long. Other times, he was either gone or in the studio. We barely saw each other, which was actually an ideal arrangement. His absence gave me an opportunity to prepare for the documentary project and catch up on everything I'd had to move around to fit in our last-minute trip to Aspen.

Frank's life was as wild as the roller coaster rides at Six Flags, and for some reason, he wanted me near. He wanted me in his house. He wanted me in his bed at night so he could wrap his arms around me and tell me all the things he couldn't tell anyone else.

On Thursday, I was yanked out of sleep by a combination of voices, footsteps, and the distant buzzing of the lawnmower. Levi and I had covered an event in Hollywood the night before and I'd gotten in really late. Frank had probably forgotten to shut the door and bits and pieces of his conversation with the owner of a heavy Eastern European accent drifted into the bedroom through the small crack.

"You need to listen to the doctors," the woman said, her tone authoritative. "You're not an acrobat. People don't pay money to see you jump through rings of fire. People pay money to see you sing."

"People expect a full set, Hannah," Frank countered. "Trust me, they'll notice if I'm five songs short."

"Aye." The woman sounded distressed and I heard a heavy sigh. "Crazy. That's what you are, Mr. Frank."

He laughed.

"And I know you were riding this morning. The next time I see you on a motorcycle, I swear, I will call a tow truck and have that thing taken to a junkyard."

After that, they walked off and their voices traveled through the house until their words faded away.

Rattled by the mention of Frank riding alone, I reached for my phone and scrolled through my social media feed, my gaze stalling on Taylor Rhinehart's face. Her tweet had been picked up by the Hall Affinity official Twitter account and TMZ got wind of it. The tabloids were going for shock value again, because the headline twisted everything.

"How Long Are Taylor Rhinehart and Frankie Blade Going to Keep Their Relationship a Secret?"

After I skimmed through the poorly slapped together article, I closed the app. This was a good thing, right? A perfect decoy. Yet it felt like a cheap, dirty trick.

I heard footsteps. Moments later, Frank's silhouette filled the doorway. Our eyes met.

"I'm sorry. Did we wake you?"

"Not really." I shook my head and stretched. His bed was the size of my entire bedroom, sheets so soft, I could never tell if they were covering me. Waking up here, in this house, to an unobstructed view of the Pacific was surreal. Like a dream that was about to end.

Frank crossed the room, his trim body swallowing up the space around me. Sometimes I wasn't sure what I loved more, fucking him or watching him. He settled next to me and his hands found my hair and ruffled it.

"*Mr.* Frank?" Giggling, I rolled onto my stomach and rested my chin on his thigh.

"Hannah is a little...uh"—he paused to look for the correct word —"eccentric."

"Are you hiding me from her or vice versa?"

"I'm not hiding you, doll. She just prefers to stay out of the way whenever she can. She knows you're spending time here."

"Levi and I have a couple of meetings today and an event this evening. I probably won't be back until late."

"Okay." He slid across the pillow until our faces were on the same level. His fingers kept on playing with my hair.

This, us being together in his house, me telling him about my day and what time he should expect me back, was weird. I'd packed a small bag with five pairs of underwear and three pairs of jeans and come for a sleepover on Monday night and hadn't gone home since. Except for one time to grab a change of clothes and check on Ashton.

I didn't understand the nature of our relationship anymore. When we were alone together, we were everything. But out in public, we were nothing. We *couldn't* be more than nothing. *Or could we?*

I bit my lip and stared at him for a while, studying the fine lines in his face, the morning stubble shadowing his jaw, the tiny flecks of gray in the pools of blue in his eyes. "Can I ask you something?"

He nodded.

"Are you aware of your secret relationship with Taylor Rhinehart?"

"Ahh." He laughed softly. "I heard about that. The press loves a good secret relationship story."

My throat tightened. I didn't know why. My mind blanked and scrambled for the right line, but it didn't come.

"Are you jealous?" Frank probed, sensing my confusion.

I braved a smile. "No. She's a decoy." But I didn't feel so sure anymore. The headline bothered me. We sort of fell into this, but he still had a public image to maintain. I had no clue what he was doing when I wasn't around. Or what kind of meetings he had. The idea that he was riding his bike alone gave me chills. He only told me what he wanted me to know, and while it was a lot, it still wasn't all. *It wasn't enough.*

Being with Frank had started to feel complicated. Because I no longer wanted to see headlines with his name next to the names of other women. Even if they were strategically planned diversions to ensure no one was looking at me.

"What's on your mind, Cassy?" Frank's whisper skated across my cheeks.

"I just have a lot of stuff to do," I lied. "I need to go through several hours of video today."

"The documentary you're working on?"

I nodded. "Yes. Levi wants to submit the final cut to a couple of festivals. We might try to arrange a screening. It's all still up in the air. We haven't shot enough material yet to see what direction we want to take, but I think this can be more than simply the story of an artist trying to make it. This can be a reflection of what it's like to be in the music business today. The good, the bad, and the ugly."

Frank's gaze held mine as I spoke. He was listening carefully. I hadn't revealed any details to him except for the general ideas, because my rule of thumb was not to discuss things I worked on with people who weren't directly involved with the project. Besides, I couldn't mix work and my personal life. That's what I was doing with Frank. And look where it'd gotten me. Hiding out like a dirty little secret.

"The ultimate goal is to bring awareness to what's going on in the industry at the moment, specifically what exactly labels are looking for and why so much real talent gets overlooked."

"And what are the labels looking for?"

"Pretty things, Frank." My tone was firm. I paused to give him a chance to react, but he kept on listening. "The labels aren't looking for voices. They're looking for girls who can rock lingerie on stage and guys who can guarantee a crowd of girls with money to spend. They're looking for nice packages to sell, for something they can brand, for something that has sex appeal. Something outrageous.

Talent has become secondary. People with money don't care about it. They care about turning money into more money."

"Hasn't it always been like that?"

"Yes, but at some point, talent began to matter and people with money had the power to bring the talent to the masses. Today, our live music venues get sold and demolished to make way for more hotels and casinos."

"That's a pretty hypocritical statement for a woman who's been fucking a man *People Magazine* once called the sexiest man alive."

Our gazes burned a wild, like a scorching fire. He was challenging me and he was right. I was a hypocrite, but I also wasn't going to back down.

"You come from the pre-streaming, pre-Instagram, pre-cell phone era, Frank." Heated up by the debate, I rose up on the bed. My eyes never left his. "You caught the last wave of the final decade of true live music. Your fans want to hear what new Hall Affinity songs sound like as much as they want to experience nostalgia that old songs promise when you play them live. They're memories people will be reliving during your shows. For some, it will be their first kiss, for others it will be their first concert...or their best. Today's artists don't have any of that. They have Instagram, Facebook, Spotify, and a dozen of other platforms to break through with, and unless they can somehow shock the crowd with something no one has ever done, they're doomed to play gigs in local bars. It's the sad truth. It's the reality of today's world. That's why we have fourteen-year-old girls rapping about weed while their parents collect the royalty money and spend it on shit they don't need."

My heart was pounding by the end of my speech. I didn't notice the pitch in my voice and my hands flying all over until I stopped speaking.

I waited, my breath heavy. I waited for Frank to say something smart, something hurtful even. He was on the opposite side of this barricade. He was the one who'd made it.

Instead, he said, "That's why I like you, Cassy Evans." His hand reached out for me and slipped around my waist. "You don't bend for anyone. Not even me."

"Oh, I can bend for you, Mr. Frank," I purred. "Just say the word." My rendition of an Eastern European accent could have been better, but it did the job. He smiled and a soft laugh rumbled in his chest.

"We'll resume this in a bit." He slapped my ass and stood. "Reese is going to be here any second now."

"Then you better hurry. Because I do have to leave at five," I said, checking the time on my phone. "Remember I've got meetings too. You're not the only one with a glowing career."

His warmth lingered inside the room long after he'd left.

My mind slowly descended back to planet Earth and reminded me that work couldn't wait anymore.

Hannah was organizing the kitchen when I came out to get coffee. This was my first time actually meeting Frank's property manager and I had no idea what to expect.

"Ah, Miss Cassy?" She poked her head from behind the massive fridge door. Her heavy accent filled the room. "Mr. Frank said you're allergic to eggs. Would you like some toast?" She smiled and the lines in the corners of her eyes deepened.

I shook my head and walked over to the coffee maker. "No. Thank you. I'm not hungry yet."

"Let me know if you change your mind, Miss Cassy." Though she'd never met me, she knew my name and didn't hesitate to use it.

"Maybe in a little bit." Returning her smile, I grabbed a clean mug. "And please don't call me Miss Cassy."

"Oh... I'm sorry." She seemed surprised. "What would you like me to call you?"

"Just Cassy is fine." Hearing a woman my mother's age call me "Miss" was weird.

Hannah nodded and continued organizing as I poured myself a cup of coffee. Small-framed and tan, she wore a pair of black pants and a Hello Kitty shirt. Her dark brown hair was styled into a pin-up victory roll and I couldn't tell her age, because of the daring eyeliner and excessive blush, but if I were to guess, perhaps she was late forties or early fifties.

Something about what she'd mentioned earlier bothered me, and maybe it wasn't my place to bring it up, but I did anyway.

"Can I ask you something?"

"Of course." Hannah switched her attention to me.

"Does Frank ride a lot?"

"Oh." Fright and worry etched her features. "Every week. God forbid something happens again." She took a deep breath and crossed herself. Her voice dropped to a frail whisper. "He's not supposed to get on that thing because of his shoulder, but the man is stubborn. No matter what I tell him."

I understood why Frank had the need to ride. I'd felt it the night he took me to the canyons. It was the purest kind of adrenaline rush. It was just your essence, the wind, and the road, and it was wonderful, but it was also terrifying. The fragility of the balance was terrifying. And I wanted to know what he was chasing every time he got on that bike. Was he facing the fear of the unknown, or was it an attempt to relive the life he'd had before the accident?

Hannah noticed my concern. "Maybe you can talk to him, Miss Cassy," she offered.

"Me? I don't think he'll listen to me."

"He will. He's very..." She paused for a second, the lines on her face crinkled. "You keep him busy. He doesn't have time for nonsense when you're here."

I wasn't sure how to interpret Hannah's words, so I smiled and excused myself to the office, where my laptop and hours of footage had been waiting for me all morning.

Maria had given us everything she'd collected over the years. Every single show, including the ones from Isabella's elementary school. Some of the recordings were poor quality, shaky with crackling noises in the background, and I found myself smiling as I sorted through them. My mind got lost in the reminiscences, in the life of a young woman whose promising career had been cut short in such an unfair and brutal way.

Even as a child, Isabella had a very distinctive voice—deep, elegant, and raw. She deserved to be heard and I wanted to help her get there. I wanted to make this happen because it was the right thing to do.

Though the office was private, I preferred to listen with my headphones on and didn't hear the door, so the footsteps echoing on the parquet floor caught me off guard. I tore my gaze from the laptop screen and registered the person I expected to see there the least, Dante. My heart nearly flipped out of my chest.

He stood in the middle of the room, face smug, eyes curious, mandatory lollipop in the corner of his mouth. His lips moved, but the music still boomed in my ears and I couldn't make out what he said.

Stomach unsettled, I paused the video and drew a deep breath. "Excuse me?"

"So...you and Frankie-boy, huh?" Dante plucked the candy from his mouth and walked over to the chair on the opposite side of the room.

"Nice to see you too." I forced a smile.

"And here I was, betting my money on Taylor Rhinehart."

His joke was a sharp knife to my ribs, but I refrained from reacting. My feelings toward him were a mixed bag. Part of me almost wished Frank had never told me about him and Frank's wife. The confession had stained the image of Dante I'd carried in my head. Years of idolizing a person. And *pow*! Destroyed with one sentence. Even his talent seemed duller now, although deep down, I knew the fact that he'd fucked his friend's wife didn't make him a lesser guitar player. He was still one of the best, and I was being a hypocrite. Again.

Dante stuck his lollipop back in his mouth and settled in a chair, one leg slung over the other. He wasn't wearing his usual flashy attire or any of his jewelry, and the black T-shirt and loose jeans threw me off a little. The man looked almost normal. Except for the permanent cocky expression.

"So what are you doing?" he asked.

"Preparing for a project." I set my headphones aside. The beat of anxiety somewhere in my gut grew stronger. This wasn't backstage at The Regency, and I wasn't armed with a microphone and wearing business casual attire. I was out of my element in a tank top and yoga shorts. "What are you doing here?"

"Frank and I were going to work on some stuff."

"What stuff?"

"We write songs, you know." The corner of his mouth curled up. "We're in a band. Hall Affinity. Ever heard?" The smirk became a sneer. "Kind of a big deal around here."

I played along. "Nope. I'll google it later."

He laughed and it wasn't light like Frank's. It was moody and had a devious edge to it.

"What are you working on?"

"It's a nonprofit project." I couldn't tell if he was genuinely interested or if this was his idea of small talk. Plus, I was still shaken up over the fact he was actually free to come here whenever he wanted.

"I'm listening."

"We're in the very early stages. I'm going through some live material. Looking for footage to use."

"So what's the project?" He lowered his leg to the floor and leaned forward. His dark blazing eyes searched my face.

"I don't usually discuss my work-in-progress with people who aren't involved."

He rested both elbows on his thighs and continued to stare. "Why not?"

"Because..." I paused. My mind quieted. This was strange, sitting in a room with Dante. Unofficially. Off the clock. Knowing his history with Frank and the real reason behind their tension during the *Breathe Crimson* era. My journalist brain finally kicked in and a long string of questions I knew I'd never get a chance to ask began to fill my head. "Why are you interested?"

"Maybe I want to get involved." He shrugged.

"It's a documentary my partner and I are working on to help a young artist who was dropped from her label get some exposure. We also want to raise awareness and secure some sponsorships. We'd love for her to be able to record the album the label was supposed to finance."

"Really?" His voice jumped. "You produce documentaries too? You're a jack-of-all-trades, darlin'."

"We don't produce documentaries. This is just a one-off project. The artist we're featuring was dropped because of injuries she suffered in an accident, which, in my opinion, is extremely unfair. This is a good cause. *Rewired* is an official sponsor of several nonprofit organizations."

Levi's vision for our baby was always big. He'd dreamed of hosting our own annual live show someday. We knew enough people in the industry and, technically, we could have put something like this together before now, but Levi wanted to wait until the right venue and the right time came along. He was a perfectionist. Like me.

Dante rose to his feet and began his approach. He rounded the table and positioned himself next to me, gaze focused on my laptop.

"Let's see."

I disconnected the headphones and pressed play. We watched several minutes of Isabella's recent video.

Arms crossed on his chest, Dante listened to the song very carefully until it reached the solo. Then he said, "Shitty guitar work. The dude needs to pick a different instrument. His fingers are like fucking used rubber. The singer is awesome. She should audition for *American Idol* or some other show. That'll give her a jump-start. The other guys are meh. Need to practice more."

The man was brutally harsh.

"They're teenagers." I rolled my eyes. "Of course they need to practice more."

"No pain, no gain, darlin'." Dante dropped his arms to his sides and spun to look at me, his eyes flickering across my face. Only a couple of inches separated us and I caught the fresh scent of his cologne and heard him swallow. Everything about him—the plain outfit, the goddamn lollipop, the one-sided smile, the glimmer of sun in his dark hair—was a lie. A facade. Dante Martinez was a can of worms just waiting to be opened.

"If you're investing your time into something, you better be fucking sure it's worth it," he said, the candy rattling softly against his teeth. "You don't want to waste your effort on some talentless joke. The girl is good, though."

Despite all the nasties in his feedback, Dante's validation meant a lot to me. Shitty friend or not, he was still one of the most well-respected musicians in the world. People wanted to be next to him, to be with him, and some wanted to be him.

"She actually did a really great job on the cover of 'Ambivalent.' I might have it here." Overzealous, I exited the player and flipped through the files in the folder.

Dante propped his hands against the table and continued to suck on his lollipop, his head level with mine.

This was me breaking my own rules again. Mixing my work and my personal stuff. And, oh boy, my ambitious side secretly wished for Dante to be serious about getting involved. I'd always wanted someone of his caliber to be a part of this project. This could be a game-changer for Isabella.

Frank found us when we were in the middle of watching the cover video. I heard his footsteps and felt his presence before I saw him. He'd showered and changed. The tips of his hair, still damp, brushed his shoulders.

Dante invited himself to pause the video on my laptop and motioned for Frank to join us. "You should see this, Frankie-boy. Your little do-gooder found some hot talent."

This wasn't happening, was it?

I started the recording from the beginning. Frank's face tensed when the images began to move, but he watched the entire video.

"The girl can sing, huh?" Dante bumped his shoulder.

"Yeah," he agreed, then added, "I feel threatened. Kids can do my songs better than me." There was a sliver of amusement in his voice, yet there was also something else. Bitterness. His fingers, long, slender, firm, touched my neck. He was marking his territory in front of Dante.

Despite the generous blasts of AC, the room felt hot and the air became heavy. Disturbing tension hung between us. Or maybe it was between them and I happened to be in the middle of it, but it was there. Every cell in my body sensed the stress of their relationship. Confusion and subtle anger filtered through me.

Dante broke the silence first. "I'll be in the studio when you two are done screwing each other." He was on his way out but halted in the doorway, took his candy out of his mouth, and looked at Frank. "You're bringing her to the party, right?"

"What party?" I questioned.

"The album release party I'm putting together in a couple of months." Dante whipped his gaze to me. "Gonna be some sick shit, short stuff. You should come. See how we do it."

He stuck the lollipop back between his teeth and exited the room.

I sat behind the desk with my eyes on the paused images as Frank stood behind me, running his hands up and down my shoulders. He breathed out a sigh that sounded a lot like relief.

"Just so you know"—I quickly collected myself—"I'm not asking you to get involved. I would never do that."

"Why not?" Frank twined his fingers in my hair.

"Because I can't. You're someone I'm seeing. I don't like to mix my work with my personal life." That was only half of the truth. The other half was the complication of our relationship. We were a well-kept secret. Getting Frank involved could trigger the public's interest. *In me.*

"But you have, Cassy." His mouth neared my ear, hot and inviting on my skin. "I think what you're doing is very noble. I'd love to hear more."

The press of his lips against the back of my neck was an electrical current. My body stilled in the chair, my legs weakened, and my chest filled with kind warmth.

"I'll see you later," Frank whispered, and then he was gone.

Chapter Twelve

Three days after my strange encounter with Dante at Frank's place, Levi and I worked an art show in West Hollywood. It was a small get-together at a private gallery near Melrose. The evening featured expensive appetizers, drinks, a silent auction, and guests smoking weed in the back alley. I loved the vibe and having the ability to mingle and chat with some of the artists. Casual affairs like this were my favorite. It gave us an opportunity to connect with people.

The gallery owner designed jewelry and clothes for the rock 'n' roll elite. She was a fussy and loud woman who didn't miss a chance to hug every single person who approached her.

Most attendees were musicians from up-and-coming L.A. bands and their plus-ones. Though the event was invitation only, a small group of eager fans waited to grab a selfie outside. Merch and cell phones in hand, they crowded the main entrance.

We wrapped up at around ten, but the party was still going strong. Music blasted, people laughed, champagne bubbled. I wanted to stay a little longer and socialize, but Levi insisted we push tonight's coverage fast. He aimed for a full recap and a photo gallery before noon. What my partner didn't take into account was that I had an hour drive ahead of me and a needy man to cuddle with. Frank had been taking up a lot of my time, and the deadlines I'd been able to meet in the past now seemed unrealistic. Between my affair, *Rewired* commitments, and Ashton, there were very few hours left for sleep.

"I think we should bring Carlos to the rehearsal. We need some candid shots of the band and Isabella's mother," Levi shared his ideas with me as we crossed the parking lot.

"Candids would be great," I agreed.

"I also talked to a buddy of mine from NYFA about renting some extra gear."

The documentary was becoming a massive project. Levi was pulling resources from everywhere. Now we just needed to find sponsors, people who wanted to support our cause.

We were saying our goodbyes for the night when a pair of head-lights swept through the air. The car that pulled in was a limo, and for a moment, I thought it was Frank. My gut knotted. Levi was standing right next to me, and there were people hanging out near the rear entrance. Mind blank, I watched the vehicle roll through the parking lot until it reached us.

The door swung open. "Cassy? What a surprise to see you here," a voice that sounded a lot like Dante's called.

I swallowed past the lump in my throat and leaned forward. My guess was correct. It was Dante. He sat in the back, dressed in his usual flashy attire. Someone else's silhouette lingered in the shadows.

"Likewise. What are you doing here?" I responded and shot Levi a confused glance over my shoulder.

He gave me one of his whatever shrugs.

"Looking for trouble," Dante joked and waved at my partner to acknowledge his presence.

"Any luck?" I asked.

"Not yet. You have a second?" His chin jerked invitingly.

"Sure. What's up?"

He motioned for me to join him inside. All the red flags were there. A semi-stranger asking me to get in his car. No woman in her right mind would agree to this, but it was Dante. Frank's best friend, lollipop addict Dante, who'd written my favorite guitar riffs and had said he wanted to find out more about my project. So I did what he asked me to do. I said goodnight to Levi and slid into his limo.

My pulse quickened when I saw Corey. He sat across from me, next to Dante, all suited up with stress creasing his face. It made me wonder if he had any idea how comfortable a T-shirt could be. The vehicle moved. I scanned the interior, trying to look for some signs of why I'd been summoned here. The divider was up. No music played. This whole thing didn't feel right.

My fingers tightened around the strap of my bag. "What's going on?" I dove right in, my gaze snapped from Dante to Corey and back.

"I think you know what's going on, Cassy," Corey started.

My heart dropped to my stomach. "Did something happen to Frank? Is he okay?" I couldn't come up with any other reason why his manager and his friend would want to ambush me in a public place. It was either Frank had been in another accident or the tabloids had found out about our relationship. Neither scenario was good news.

Dante stretched his crossed legs, and his dark steely eyes pierced mine. He didn't seem like the friendly type today. His lollipop was missing. But the Rolex was present. "Yes, Cassy. Something happened to Frank. You. To be more specific."

I blinked at him rapidly. My blood pressure skyrocketed. The car rolled through one of the back streets and I felt trapped. "Can you elaborate, please?" My voice shook, but I kept my shoulders straight and my chin high.

He was abnormally calm. "We know you stole the demos."

Panic crashed my chest. For the first time in my life, I was at a loss for words. People had called me many names, but never a thief. "Excuse me?" I drawled, dejectedly staring at them as if they'd just told me they were from another planet.

"It'll be easier if you go ahead and confess, Cassy," Corey said. "Considering the nature of your relationship with Frank."

The man was insane and I wanted to ask him if he'd ever considered pulling the stick out of his ass for a change.

My pride finally kicked in. "Are you two out of your fucking minds?" I wasn't going to let two arrogant assholes blame me for something I hadn't done, because they were too dumb to find the person who'd actually stolen the demos. *Typical.*

"This can be settled without police involvement," Corey continued.

"Police?" My heart plummeted against my ribcage, rage filled my blood. "You two need to get your facts straight."

Frustration danced across Dante's face. Unlike his manager, he didn't care about keeping his cool. It wasn't his job anyway.

"You want facts?" His voice was a racket in my head. "You show up and the next day, the entire fucking album is out on the internet. You're the only person who I can't vouch for with access to the studio. Do you have any idea what it did to our entire campaign? What it did to Frank? He waited seven fucking years and you came and shitted on everything he's been working on for all this time."

"Oh yeah?" My anger was complex, a maddening stream of thoughts and words, it was doomed to explode. And it did. Because the accusations hurt me. "Says the man who fucked his best friend's wife."

Corey's left eye twitched, but he didn't speak up. His hands were locked together, resting on his lap. The limo kept driving.

Dante leaned forward, lips stretched into a smile, the meaning of which I couldn't read. It was a puzzling blend of various expressions. Like Frank, he was a man of many faces.

We stared at each other for a good minute until he finally said, "I guess Frankie-boy hit his head harder than I thought."

My stomach flipped. "You need to check yourself, Dante," I hissed.

"And you need to mind your own business, darlin'." His tone wasn't mean. He sounded...wounded. Jealous. As if I'd trespassed on their relationship. "You know absolutely nothing about Frank and

me, so I suggest you stop playing the role of his mental health coun-
selor and stick to doing what you do best. Fucking him."

The wrath hit me then. It pulsed through me like a savage beat. A
wave of disappointment, anger, hurt. A combination of emotions I
didn't want to feel.

"Stop the car," my tremulous voice ordered. My gaze darted over
to Corey. He didn't react.

"Stop the car," I pressed, returning my attention to Dante.

He cracked the divider and told the driver to stop.

I wasn't sure exactly where I was when I stepped out of the vehicle. Loud breaths raked my chest and blood rushed through my
temples. It took me a moment to regain my control and shake off the
unease. I stood near the curb, my eyes following the limo until it
turned the corner. Streetlights and condos lined both sides of the
quiet road and the distant noise of traffic told me I'd been dropped off
only a few blocks away from a busy neighborhood.

There was a text message from Levi on my phone when I drew it
out of my pocket to get an Uber.

Levi: R U good?

Yes, all good, I typed back and added a thumbs-up emoji. I knew I
needed to come up with some kind of story because he was going to
ask about this next time we spoke, but my mind was hollow and my
hands shook when I tried to navigate the Uber app.

I called Frank from my car.

"Ashton lost his key," I lied. "I'm going to have to drive to Burbank. I
think I'll just see you tomorrow." Part of me craved the calm of the intimacy with Frank and wanted to drive to Malibu, but the meeting with
Dante and Corey had left a bad aftertaste in my mouth. I needed a short
break from my secret life. Although it'd already started to mix with my
public one. The video of Isabella's "Ambivalent" cover had piqued
Frank's interest and he'd asked me for copies of her recent performances.

"Are you sure?" His voice was low and sad on the line and cut
through me like a knife through butter. It was sick how much I

missed him when he wasn't around. "I was going to get the hot tub going."

"Rain check?" The offer was very tempting.

"Do I have a choice?"

"The hot tub isn't going anywhere before tomorrow, right?"

"I don't think so."

After we said our goodbyes, I drove to Burbank to sleep in my bed for the first time in over a week.

***

The following day was busy. I woke up early and loaded myself with coffee to put together a recap of the art show. Levi and I met up with a couple of his college friends for lunch to discuss the documentary. Apparently, to get this project off the ground, we needed to involve the entire city.

After the meeting, we drove downtown to interview the drummer of Bleeding Faith, who'd recently gotten out of rehab. His publicist had been begging us to run an exclusive. We couldn't pass up the opportunity. As a matter of fact, reformed musicians who'd been through hell and back always got the most hits.

Levi kept asking about Dante and why the guitarist wanted to talk to me, and I wasn't sure if the story I told him held water, but I'd decided to play it safe and insisted it was a coincidence that he'd ended up in the gallery's parking lot. I had a bigger dilemma to face. The confrontation with Dante and Corey left me confused and rattled, and at some point, I needed to tell Frank.

Afternoon traffic was bad and I didn't make it to Malibu until eight.

I knew something had happened the moment I stepped inside. The house was quiet and cold and far from inviting. Frank sat in the dining room, facing the glass wall, and stared at the flickering spread of the ocean. His posture was stiff, shoulders corded with tension. A drink sat next to him on the table. This was how I knew the incident with Dante needed to wait.

I dropped my bags on the floor and started my approach. Light tremors rushed through my limbs.

"Frank?" I reached for his arm. He didn't move. "What's going on?"

The hard stillness of the welcome rattled me. I grabbed the glass and brought it to my face. The sharp smell of liquor crept up my nostrils. This was the second time since we'd met that I'd seen him consume alcohol. All pretense of normalcy that had lingered inside these walls was gone. Tonight he slipped, deviated from the path he'd been on to prepare for the upcoming shows. And I needed to find out what had pushed him into the abyss of ignorance.

Alarmed, I breathed out a heavy sigh and set the glass back on the table. "You know you can't drink, Frank."

He didn't say anything. His hand searched for mine and he pulled me closer. His cheek pressed to my stomach. There was something awfully fragile in his movements. Unsure of what to say, I ran my fingers through his thick sandy strands. They were silky and soft to the touch, like a tangle of feathers.

Frank finally spoke. "I need to go to Arizona for a couple of days." His voice was a quivering murmur.

"Okay." My fingertips reached the nape of his neck and brushed his skin. "When are you leaving?"

"Tomorrow afternoon."

I knew what, or who, was in Arizona and feared the answer to what I was thinking, yet I waited for more. I waited for an explanation. But he chose to keep me in the dark. No more words were spoken. Instead, he snaked his arms around my waist and drew me into the space between his thighs, burying his face into the soft fabric of my crop top.

We were in a strange embrace, a ball of conflicting emotions and ragged heartbeats. I didn't dare move. I was scared he'd lose the peace he'd found in this awkward hug. The hard feel of his jaw on my ribs and the soft tickle of his breath on my skin made me drunk with feelings and I was ready to hold him until the morning if that was what he wanted from me.

"Ever drive a Ferrari?" Frank finally broke the silence. His palm slid up my back and he looked up at me.

"No." I shook my head. Our gazes connected. His was unreadable.

"Do you want to go for a ride?"

"Can we take my car?"

He stood up and grabbed my hand, his height towering over mine. "It's really easy, Cassy."

"I don't think this is a good idea. I'm not familiar with manual."

"It's semi-automatic."

Hannah was right. The man was stubborn.

He led me across the room and outside to where the Ferrari was already waiting for us. Its bright red roof glittered under the stream of virgin moonlight. I heard crickets, tree frogs, and the fierce laps of the ocean down below, the sounds crashing at me all at once.

I'd stopped paying attention to Frank's cars a while back. There were too many to keep up with, but they made a nice backdrop because he hardly drove them. Most of the time, he was just a passenger. He wanted to be the passenger now too.

Fear paralyzed me as we climbed into the Ferrari. There wasn't enough room for my heart inside my chest. I felt panic everywhere. In my throat, in my joints, in my mind.

"Frank." Hands on the steering wheel, I turned to face him. "I don't want to wreck your car."

"You won't."

He adjusted his seat and began to explain the basics. His palm slid over mine carefully. Skin to skin, I followed his movements. The warmth of his touch soothed my roaring mind. There was something extremely sexy yet extremely patriarchal in the way he gave instructions. It wasn't my father who taught me how to drive. It was my mother. And I had no idea what it would be like to actually have a father who wasn't drunk in front of the TV, who took his time to show you the things parents were supposed to show their kids. And at this moment, I let myself pretend Frank wasn't my lover. I let myself pretend he was someone else. I had no idea why he'd never had kids, but I had no doubt he'd make a good father one day. He was attentive and caring with a pinch of crazy, and I loved that about him. I loved every little detail, every smirk, every inhale, every moan...

We went over everything twice, then I started the car. The engine vibrated through me. It was a sudden surge of power I had no choice but to take.

"You're doing great, doll," Frank said. I could hear encouragement and a hint of a smile.

We drove past the property gate and down the hill until the road hit a fork. My hands clutched the wheel so hard, my knuckles hurt. I'd never driven an eight-cylinder vehicle, let alone a vehicle that cost a small fortune. And this...this felt like an achievement.

Frank reached for my shoulder, his fingers slipping to the back of my neck. We sat in front of the lonely traffic light, waiting for green.

"Relax," he whispered. His voice hummed over the noise of the engine. It flowed through my chest, wrapping around my heart like a soft blanket. "You're overthinking. It's just a car."

I drew a shaky breath and wiggled in my seat. His touch was a pleasant distraction.

Up ahead, the light changed. My foot hit the gas. First came a rumble, then came a jerk

"Take a left and jump on PCH." Frank motioned at the signs that flew by.

My eyes never left the road, but I could sense the burn of his gaze on me. My cheeks flushed and my stomach turned over. Too nervous to speak, I stared at the stretch of highway we were running along.

"You're a natural." Frank laughed and rolled down the window.

Cool breeze hit the side of my face and ruffled my hair. "Is wanting to pee my pants considered natural too?" I yelled through the noise.

"The first time only."

He took his hand off my neck and fiddled with the stereo. Loud music blasted through the car seconds later. We were on PCH, heading north. All this—the clamor of the ocean, the wind biting my skin, the thunderous shrill of the engine—rolled through me and pushed blood through my veins with the intensity of a thousand watts. My body shook, but not because I was scared to wreck. It was a different kind of fear. A fear to never experience this rush again. A fear of boredom. A fear of life without adventure.

This was adrenaline. Pure. Sweet. Raw. Adrenaline.

I understood it then. Frank's need to get back on the bike again and the need to keep the set at ninety minutes. For him, it was all or nothing. No in-betweens.

We drove for a long time until the lights became very sparse and the road began to curve. This was Ventura County.

"Where are we going?" I asked.

"There's a place," Frank said mysteriously.

"Is it before or after Santa Barbara?" I joked.

He laughed. His hand rested on my thigh and I felt the heat of his palm against my skin, even through the denim. Soft flames of desire spread through me. My head spun from the overload of adrenaline.

"We need to get gas," Frank muttered, glancing at the dashboard.

"Okay." A flash of panic burst in my stomach. *What side was the gas tank on in this thing?* "Why didn't you give me a tutorial on that too?"

"You don't need one. It's probably best you stay in the car for this one." He rolled up the windows and motioned at the exit and gas station signs ahead. The lot was empty, and we were greeted by four lonely pumps and a small convenience store sitting against the dark ocean backdrop. I was surprised the station was open so late. Nothing in this part of SoCal operated after midnight. This wasn't L.A. People in Ventura County didn't go for random joyrides in the middle of the night in search of something they didn't even know until they saw it.

Only Frank did.

I cut the engine and looked around.

"Sit tight, doll," he said. His knuckles brushed my cheek and I shivered at the graze of his flesh against mine. I was a muddle of feelings. Anticipation of the unknown kept me near the edge.

I watched Frank round the car to read the instructions on the pump. A frown lined his forehead. I couldn't grasp the concept of him doing anything remotely human. He was a performer and a lover. Seeing him trying to figure out how to operate a gas pump was strange.

"Is it not working?" I squeaked from my spot after I cracked the window.

"Just hang on." He shook his head and walked over to the convenience store.

I waited inside the car for a few minutes. My cheek still burned where he'd touched me, but there was another feeling harbored somewhere in the pit of my stomach. Guilt. I'd promised Levi I'd finish the Bleeding Faith editorial before noon. That wasn't happening. Not unless more hours were added to the night.

Frank showed up with a pack of Twizzlers. He was like a teenager going on a rampage. First alcohol, now sweets. He grinned. "I haven't had these in years," he confessed, tossing them over to me.

"Are you serious? They're horrible." I scrunched my nose, scanning the oversized package. "These things taste like rubber." I hated Twizzlers. They were my least favorite candy.

Frank filled the tank and slid back into the passenger side. There was a shift in his mood again. He crumpled in his seat, his face dulled. The silence that stretched between us became unsettling.

"Is everything okay?" I asked carefully. The candy pack still sat on my lap.

He spun in his seat, his gaze meeting mine. Then I heard his whisper. "She died."

Heaviness pushed against my chest. My heart tripped and fell. "Your mother?"

"Yes."

"When?"

"Last night."

I felt the weight of his words on my shoulders. It pulled me to the ground. "I'm sorry."

"Don't be, Cassy." He shook his head, a sad smile gracing his lips. "I won't miss her. I never did."

But I didn't believe him. Maybe he wanted to think he didn't care, but deep down, he did. I knew it. I knew it for the both of us.

We fell back into silence. The air inside the car was thick with ache and grief.

"Do you want me to go with you?" I asked softly. I had no idea why I did. I just knew I didn't want him to be alone there. Alone with the broken memories.

His dark, piercing gaze roamed my face. "Yes."

"Okay. I'll make some adjustments in my schedule." I leaned into him, flung my arms around his neck, and drew him into a tight embrace. There was a moment of absolute stillness where we both stopped breathing, our chests pressed together, our cheeks brushing. This was an exchange of thoughts and feelings, the most intimate I'd ever been with him before. Sex didn't even come close. The pulse beating in his throat vibrated against my skin like a live wire. He was an agony of flesh and blood and I wanted to take some of his torment.

We returned to Malibu without music. His hand was on my thigh, his jaw set, his shoulders slumped. There were no words, just the rumble of the ocean and the whip of the wind.

It was later at home when we were in bed that Frank finally spoke.

"You don't have to go with me if you don't have the time, Cassy." He lay next to me on his back, his left arm tucked under my pillow. My body still buzzed and my fingertips tingled from driving the Ferrari.

"I want to go." I rolled over to my side and pressed my lips to his chest.

"I don't even know if she wanted to be buried or cremated." I heard a hard swallow. His Adam's apple rolled beneath his skin.

"Are there any other relatives?"

"I'm not sure."

"No one recognized you when you went to see her?"

"Hannah always made all the arrangements. My name can't come out." He drew a ragged breath, the rise of his chest against my cheek shaky.

"What about Billy and Janet? Do they know?"

"Yes, but they've never been fond of my idea to track my birth mother."

"Why not?"

"I think they felt threatened."

"How come?"

"I don't know." He paused. "Probably because they're very protective of me." I heard a soft chuckle. "You'll see. They're coming over to see the shows."

"You mean they're coming over here? To your house?"

"Yes. There are six bedrooms in the house." He laughed. "Should I put them in a hotel instead?"

"No. I mean..." I was at a loss for words. They were his parents and he talked about me meeting them as if it were as simple as buying a cup of coffee at Starbucks down the street from my place.

"Are you getting cold feet?" He shifted his body to face me. His lips found my forehead.

"No... I don't know. We're not exactly screaming about our relationship from the rooftops."

"Cassy"—he cupped the back of my head and pulled me closer —"I don't want the press to discuss me and you and what we have, but that doesn't mean it lessens your importance." His whisper caressed my face. "I love that you're a part of my life and that you make me smile and that you're understanding of my situation and don't ask for something I can't give you at the moment. I want us to keep going on. It won't be easy, but I do want it. I just have to concentrate on the tour and the album right now, and I don't need the tabloids stirring the pot while I'm trying not to ruin what's left of my career."

This was the strangest confession I'd ever heard from him. "Of course. I'm fine with what we have and I'm fine with keeping it discreet."

Are you really fine with people thinking the man you're sleeping with is dating a rich, hot actress, Cassy? Are you?

"You're still meeting my parents," he reassured. "And I still want to be involved in your project. I watched the videos and I loved them. We simply have to figure out a way to keep the press off your back."

I let out a breath and shook off the worry. A feeling a lot like excitement swirled in my insides. "Really? You'll do that? You'll help us?"

"Yes, I'd love to meet Isabella."

"There's a rehearsal next week. You can come."

"I'll see what my schedule looks like and talk to my PA."

I wasn't sure what made me happier, his confession that he wanted me in his life indefinitely or his desire to help me with Isabella's documentary. But at that moment, a small part of me loved him. Deeply and madly. Not the image of him. The real him.

Chapter Thirteen

Deep down, I knew it would happen sooner or later. Juggling my secret relationship with Frank and trying to keep up with deadlines and the documentary wasn't an easy task. My sudden trip to Arizona pissed off Levi. Of course, I didn't tell him where exactly I was going. I simply said I needed a break. He guessed that the reason behind my last minute change of plans was my ongoing affair that, according to him, had turned me into a zombie. Levi was very direct. He asked me if I was still seeing the mystery man and if I was ever going to introduce him. I told the truth. Well, half of it, anyway. I confirmed that I was still seeing someone. I just didn't tell him that someone was Frankie Blade.

Then Levi asked me if I'd seen a retweet of Isabella's video. Too busy speed-packing, I hadn't had have time to check my social media. Apparently, Hall Affinity's official Twitter account picked up one of the YouTube links with Isabella's cover of "Ambivalent." The recording had been trending all morning and had raked up over seventy thousand views.

I knew it then. Frank was going to come to the rehearsal.

Arizona was hotter than hell in the daytime and colder than

Antarctica during the night. We stayed in Paradise Valley, where Frank had apparently bought a house right after he'd tracked down his mother. It was a large gated property that sat on ten acres of desert land. The Mediterranean-inspired estate came with a guesthouse, a pool, a two-story gym, and a wine cellar.

Frank didn't need it, but he couldn't risk staying at a hotel. The property was just another hideout, a safe place where he could be left alone. The deed was in Hannah's name and there was little chance someone would make a connection between international rock star Frankie Blade and deceased Arizona woman Lilly Rickett.

The funeral was depressing. The only attendees were the four of us—Frank, Hannah, Roman, and me, plus the priest. I was a little surprised Brooklyn didn't come, but something told me she'd stayed in L.A. for a reason. There was an empire to run. Because Lilly hadn't left any will or wishes on how she'd like to be buried, Frank had made the decision to cremate her body.

We spent a total of three days in Arizona, surrounded by endless miles of rough desert. No phones, no emails, no social media. Just Frank and me. In a sick way, I liked it because I didn't have to divide my time.

I could give it all to him, which I did.

I held his hand when he sought me out during the funeral. I hugged his hard body at night when we were lying in bed together. I kissed away the ache in his scars hidden beneath the layer of ink. I listened to stories about what he could remember of his early years with Lilly. They were a string of obscure images of a boy who'd lived in dozens of different places and didn't know where he'd come from.

Frank's sadness wasn't the sadness of a person whose close relative had died. It was bleak. He seemed lost rather than upset. He could go on for hours without uttering a single word, but his eyes said it all.

He was scared.

Roman drove us to L.A. in his black Escalade. Hannah had taken a flight earlier. We sat in the back, silent, thighs brushing, hands locked together. It was going to be a long trip, but something told me Frank needed it. He needed to clear his head and this was the way to do it. Nothing but the road and time.

We reached the California border in the late afternoon and that's when it started happening. Reality. It was my own mistake. I looked at my phone because, after hours of dead zone, messages and email alerts that began to litter my screen begged to be checked.

Jaw set, Frank stared out the window. His hand clutched mine tightly, and he seemed far away. Removed. I couldn't tell what was going on in his head. He'd been mostly quiet these past few days, except for the occasional trips down memory lane. The hum of the engine and the hard blast of the AC were the only sources of noise inside the car.

My gaze swept over my email previews. Most texts I ignored, but the ones from Levi and Ashton held my attention longer than necessary. The itch was too strong. I was a child of the millennia, an information junkie. I had to get my fix. Not being online made me feel disconnected. My brother's messages normally contained useless semi-spam or pocket money requests, so I caved in and clicked on Levi's text first.

Ambivalent cover went viral. Got word from Maria last night. Someone from camp Blade reached out to her!

My pulse caught. In a way, this had been expected, but seeing the proof that Frank was going through with his plan made me a little nervous. And excited. It was well thought out and was aimed at keeping me out of the picture. It was perfect. I needed Levi to stop asking about Dante and my non-existent mystery man. The new development in Isabella's project would ensure my partner's mind was preoccupied.

Holding my breath, I re-read the message and checked the time-stamp. It'd come hours ago when we were still in Paradise Valley.

Though withdrawn, Frank sensed the change in me. His fingers squeezed mine into a bubble of rough warmth.

I closed Levi's text and went to Ashton's. It was a TMZ link and I felt the car melting around me. Everything disappeared. Everything but the stupid headline glaring at me from the tiny screen of my phone.

"Move Over, Taylor Rhinehart! It's Official: Frankie Blade is Taken!"

There were photos of us from the gas station in Ventura County that looked a lot like cell phone snapshots of the security camera footage. They were grainy, but only a person who'd never seen Frankie Blade wouldn't be able to recognize his sandy hair and the fine outline of his sinfully perfect body. No matter what you put on the man—a T-shirt, a tuxedo, or a winter jacket, he was like a tiki torch on the beach at four in the morning in the middle of January.

Agitated, I zoomed in on the photos of us inside the car and studied the images. Asking me to stay put had been the right call. From the camera's angle, my face was a blur behind the windshield of the Ferrari. Just the dark tangle of my wind-beaten hair stood out.

"Frank?" I called his name and handed him the phone.

He skimmed through the article, his brows knitted. "Your name isn't mentioned here."

"Do you think there are more photos?" I was nervous.

"I doubt it. Did you stay in the car when I went inside?"

I nodded.

"We're fine." He shifted to face me and smiled, but it didn't reach his eyes. They were bloodshot and tired. "We'll just have to be more careful."

The question was, how? Especially after this.

The rest of the drive was silent. We held hands again, but Frank had drifted off. His confusion and the weight of his stress drilled through my bones.

It was nearly dinnertime when the Escalade finally pulled up to the house. My back ached from the long ride. I was beat. Hannah had already returned and the faint smell of rosemary chicken floated through the house when we walked in. Roman carried our bags.

The sun was setting right above the steely surface of the shimmering ocean and I took a second to savor the view. I stood in front of the dining room glass wall and stared at the splash of yellow and orange bleeding into the grays and blues.

Behind me, Frank's voice boomed through the living room. There was a short exchange with Roman, followed by a long phone call to Corey. He didn't mention his mother once during that conversation. At least, not during the part I heard before moving to the bedroom.

I wasn't sure Frank had accepted what happened in Arizona. His withdrawal seemed more like denial, not grief.

My phone buzzed.

Brother: did U C what I sent you??? Y'all gonna get caught.

Yes, I saw it.

Brother: can I borrow another 20? please pretty pleaseeeeeeeeee

A silly grin stretched across my lips. Ashton was finally catching on. Words were a very powerful weapon and he'd figured out "borrow" sounded better than "give me."

I'll be there in a couple of hours.

Tossing my phone on the nightstand, I kicked off my shoes and peeked into the top drawer of my dresser. Yes, I had my own dresser at Frank's house. I didn't keep a lot of stuff here. Just some basic clothes, towels, cosmetics, and a toothbrush, but he'd made sure I had everything a woman who'd permanently moved into a man's place would normally need.

However, I couldn't call this arrangement a permanent move. Maybe constant migration. My life here was calm luxury. My life out there, in the city, was a wild race. And sometimes, especially lately, I felt as if I was falling behind. My gut told me I'd soon need to reevaluate my priorities, and my gut had never been wrong.

Approaching footsteps pounded in my head as Frank neared me. His broad chest against my back, he ran his hands along the curves of my shoulders while I fumbled through the modest contents of my drawer.

His lips pressed against my neck. My heartbeat leapt to my throat. I didn't know why after so many not-so-innocent encounters that his every touch still made me come alive. He was a spark to my fuse. A detonator to my dynamite. The way our bodies reacted to each other reminded me of dirty magic.

Frank pulled his mouth away from my skin and stilled. Warm waves of his breath rolled across my neck and fell down the line of my spine.

Finally, he spoke, "I have something for you."

My stomach fluttered. The timing was strange. The gesture was even stranger.

His right hand left my shoulder. I registered the rustle of his jacket and the subtle movements of his body, then I saw a long black velvet box on the dresser in front of me.

The air stuck somewhere between my lungs and my mouth.

"Open it," Frank whispered in my ear, his fingers curled around the base of my neck.

I did as requested. My hands shook. Inside the box, lay a necklace. I was so taken aback by the sparkle of the diamond solitaire pendant, I didn't notice the Tiffany & Co. logo at first.

"Do you like it?" Frank asked.

I nodded because I was at a loss for words. His lips touched the tip of my ear. "Would you like to try it on?"

"Yes," I choked out and lifted my gaze to the mirror above the dresser, where our eyes connected.

"It looks very expensive, Frank," I confessed. "What if I lose it?"

"Your man is giving you a present and you're scared you'll lose it?" A smirk tugged the corner of his mouth. "How about you let me see it on you?"

"You know what I do for a living." I tried to rationalize my thoughts, but they were a mess. I was a mess. A hot one, actually. A wet one too. No one had ever given me anything this shiny, this exquisite, and this...intimate. "What if I accidentally drop it in a mosh pit?"

"I don't think interviewing in a mosh pit is something I would attempt if I were you."

"You know what I mean." But even I had no idea what I meant. I was rambling. My chest heaved.

"Cassy." Frank rubbed his stubble against my cheek. "You're allowed to lose it. It's just a necklace." His voice was a fiery hum in my temples. His palms collared my neck and my legs quivered.

"Thank you," I murmured. My eyes roamed over our reflections —the outline of his solid shoulders arched above mine, the shades of the evening falling across his sharp face, the sun-kissed blaze of his hair spilling into my blue-black strands.

My pulse raced against the press of his hands like a mad drumbeat. I was drowning in the hardness of his embrace and the inferno heat of his body.

"Allow me," his voice said. Cool air tickled my skin as his hands helped me move my hair aside and up. He carefully took the chain from the box and placed it around my neck.

"What do you think?"

I let my hair fall down my back and studied the necklace in the mirror for a few seconds while his lips went to my shoulder blade to kiss the tip of my butterfly tat. "I love it." I didn't know what else to say. My mind was full of thick clouds and filthy thoughts. His erection, now evident, bulged against my ass.

He ran his fingers over the pendant and nuzzled the crook of my neck, pushing me against the dresser. The drawer closed under the weight of our bodies. I shivered. My heartbeat was tripping. When my gaze dropped to the empty box, Frank's lips traced a wet trail along the edge of my shoulder. This was a delicious kind of torture. His hands, hot and greedy, inspected my curves. They teased between my thighs through the denim until I couldn't stand anymore. I needed to come and I needed to come fast.

Satisfied with the outcome of his little game, he reached for my jeans and panties and pulled them down. His breaths were ragged as he unzipped his pants, the fabric of his shirt slipping across my ass as he freed himself.

"Look at me." He grabbed my jaw, lifting my chin to meet his eyes in the mirror.

I saw the reflection of his silhouette outlined in the backdrop of dark sky behind the glass wall. A pulse of desire shot to my center. He was a delicious torment. The epitome of seductive devastation. My cheeks burned and my clit thrummed from a single glimpse.

With one hand still wrapped under my jaw, holding me in place, Frank slipped the other one between my thighs and found my pulsing entrance. He dipped two fingers inside and pressed them against my sweet spot, drawing a loud and desperate moan from me. My toes curled. I was no longer in control of my body and was losing my balance. The tip of his cock brushed my center. Flesh to flesh, we exchanged lingering gasps, and I gripped the edge of the dresser as his knees bumped into the back of mine. A surge of anticipation vibrated through me.

"You're always so wet for me, doll." He slid his lips over my cheek and rearranged my body. His desperate breaths pricked my skin. His cock, hard and thick, pushed into me roughly, bringing me almost to the edge. A soft whimper left my throat as pleasure swirled in my stomach. My knees shook. My chest fluttered.

I felt him whole, every raw inch buried deep inside me, his strokes long and angry, filling me to the hilt. I cried out and my body fell forward. His palms hovered above my knuckles, our ink touching. Then he tangled our fingers together and they moved across the expensive wood finish of the dresser as it rattled against the wall.

He owned me completely and entirely. My every heartbeat and my every scream. He was a wave of agonizing bliss that simmered across my skin.

Manic, he slid his hands to my hips, thrusting harder. I caught a glimpse of his elegantly muscled arms flexing beneath the thin fabric of his shirt. My vision went hazy. I couldn't keep my gaze still anymore. I wanted to crawl into him, into his every cell, be a drop of his blood, a hair on his head. Be a part of him. Forever and always.

His groans grew louder and blended with mine. The room spun.

Frank's palm slipped across my waist and up my stomach to pull me against him. His stubbly chin grazed the side of my face. The sweat that coated his forehead dripped over my breasts and shoulder. We were a lawless and tragic entity, swept away by the maddening heat. The slick grind of our bodies turned me inside out. Then his index finger went to my needy clit and my breath caught in my lungs, my heart drumming a fierce rhythm.

"Come for me," he ordered, pumping faster. His skin rubbed against my skin, his hair tangled with mine. The rush was incredible as he tore my climax out of me.

Eager, I fell apart for him. My limbs trembled and my mind screamed as our orgasms mingled. This was intense and dirty and for a second, I forgot who or where I was.

We stood limp in front of the dresser. His cock was still inside me and his shaking arms encircled my body. Our breaths were labored, our chests rising and falling at each inhale and exhale.

He pressed his lips to my temple. "Thank you for taking the time to go with me to Arizona." His voice was a shudder. A collection of broken pieces.

"Of course." I swallowed and tossed my head back to rest against him. "I think we might need a shower."

"I think so too," he agreed, and after he slowly pulled out of me, I still felt him between my legs, dripping down my skin, burning my thighs.

We moved to the bathroom and shed our clothes. As we stood under the stream of warm water, I watched the glimmering rivulets flow down his broad chest to his scar-littered sides and his hard stomach. He was a beautiful wall of ink and fine, lean muscle, and I wanted to stay in this shower cabin with him forever, to take in the view and the feel of him.

After, we sat in the dining room and destroyed Hannah's chicken while an episode of *Friends* played in the background. I was wearing Frank's shirt and he had on a pair of sweats. It was a casual, half-naked dinner I didn't want to end, but the little voice in my head reminded me about my responsibilities and begged me to check on my brother.

"Are you going to get mad if I stay at my place tonight?" I asked, pushing my plate aside.

He shook his head. "I can't be mad at you. I'll be lonely, though."

"I want to make sure Ashton hasn't sold my stuff on eBay while I've been gone," I joked.

"Okay." He laughed softly.

Then came a long pause.

"Frank?" I reached for his hand. "I'll be back tomorrow."

"I know." He smiled, and this time, the smile reached his eyes and also reached my heart.

Roman took me to Burbank right after the dinner. The closer we got to my apartment, the greater my fear of a paparazzi ambush grew. Frank didn't insist on my staying in Malibu. He understood I had a life and I had a family that needed some sort of attention.

My seventeen-year-old brother pretty much lived on his own and had very little supervision. I suspected he'd found the Xbox and played video games in secret, but Levi and I had figured out a way to keep him busy. Every week, we'd given him a new assignment. Turned out, my brother wasn't half bad at sorting music. His best-to-worst list of all the Korn albums had become his first official *Rewired* post. Of course, the article had gone through some heavy editorial revisions, but it was real. It was available for people to read and Ashton's name proudly sat below the entry.

I heard voices from the staircase. My heart flipped in my chest as I hauled my bag to the door.

In the living room, Levi and Ashton sat cross-legged on the floor and sorted through Levi's gear.

"What's going on?" I marched past the bags and tripods and

peeked into the kitchen, where a sink full of dirty dishes and a stack of pizza boxes greeted me.

"Welcome back, sis!" Ashton grinned. "How was Oregon?"

"Boring." I shot him a warning glance and assessed the geek central convention taking place in the middle of the apartment. "What are you two doing?"

"Getting ready for the big day," Levi explained. "Showing your little bro some basics." He patted Ashton's back.

My mind was blank. "What big day?"

"Didn't you get my message?"

"Yes. The 'Ambivalent' cover went viral."

"Frankie Blade wants to meet Isabella."

I knew that too. I sort of made it happen.

Gaze bouncing between Levi and me, Ashton bit his lip. He was itching to tell my partner he'd met Frankie. I knew that smug expression on my brother's face like the back of my hand.

"Can you please wash all those dishes?" I waved in the direction of the kitchen and picked up my bag to take it to my bedroom.

"A little busy at the moment," Ashton countered and held up one of Levi's battery packs.

"Right now. Please." I was beginning to regret my decision to spend the night at home. Come to think of it, I didn't even know where home was anymore. The total number of days I'd slept in my own bed over the course of the past two weeks was awfully close to zero.

Levi rose from the floor and followed me. I heard running water and the clanking plates. Ashton was cleaning up his mess.

"Are you sure this is a good idea to bring him along?" I whispered, shutting the door to my bedroom.

"Why not?" Baffled by my skepticism, Levi gave me a perplexed look. "You wanted to keep him busy. This *will* keep him busy. I can teach him how to log footage."

I took off my jacket and walked over to my closet. "I'm sorry, I'm just tired," I confessed, sifting through a pile of T-shirts on one of the shelves. This, the constant back and forth, exhausted me.

"Is this serious?" Levi probed, his tone discrete. "The thing you have going on with this dude we're never going to meet?"

"I don't know." I grabbed the first tee that stood out and spun to face him. Muffled noises drifted into my room from the kitchen. Ashton was singing a Korn song. Of course, he was light years from Jonathan Davis, but the sound of his pitchy voice still filled my chest with a happy flutter. It'd been a long time since my little brother was so engrossed in music, and as much as I didn't want him hanging around Frankie during his meeting with Isabella, he needed this gig more than anyone. The fake internship that had turned into a real one was the only thing that kept him from wasting his time on the devious Xbox.

"We got an okay from Linda for all three nights. One photo, two passes," Levi said matter-of-factly.

Anxiety rushed to my gut. With everything going on, I'd forgotten about the most important detail. *Rewired* had sent in a request to cover the Forum shows and I would be the one to write the reviews. I would also be the one to escort Ashton backstage. Brooklyn had already arranged our passes, per Frank's request. Explaining to Levi why I couldn't review any Hall Affinity shows promised to be a real clusterfuck.

Sooner or later, I was going to get caught in a lie.

The lump in my throat grew bigger. "I actually wanted to talk to you about that." My heart raced. "I bought VIP tickets to the first night."

Levi blinked at me rapidly, his brow furrowed.

"I'm taking Ashton."

"Okay." Hands on his hips, he nodded.

"I think we should ask someone else to review it."

Confusion creased his face. "Why? You're going to be there anyway."

Because I'm sleeping with the singer. Because my review will be an ode to his hot body and his beautiful soul, and the entire world will realize I've fallen for him.

But I couldn't tell Levi that. Just like I couldn't be impartial in my review. I had to distance myself from my work for the duration of the show, and letting someone else cover the event was only fair.

I was in too deep.

"I'm sorry, Levi." A heavy sigh dashed out of me.

He stood in front of my closet, startled, while I paced the room. My body shook. I didn't have a better explanation. Ashton was still belching Korn lyrics, his singing traveling through the apartment. I heard the rustling of the carton and plastic followed by the slam of the door. Hell must have finally frozen over, because this was my brother taking out the trash.

"Since when are you a Dodgers fan?" Levi finally asked, voice brittle.

I turned around and saw him pick up Frank's baseball hat from the shelf. It had been sitting there since the night of our very first late-night dinner at Tommy's. Honestly, I'd forgotten about it.

Something shifted inside my room. Something shifted between us.

I stopped pacing.

"This is going to sound really crazy." Levi moved closer and slid the hat over my head. "But I'm going to take a wild guess here." His eyes raked over my body, inspecting me. "That mysterious chick Frankie Blade got caught with a couple of times looks a lot like you."

I snorted out a laugh, or at least I tried to. What came out sounded more like a pathetic squeal.

"I'm actually pretty sure it's you," Levi added.

The visor hid the top half of his face and I tilted my chin up to see him better. A combination of emotions lined his features. Shock. Disappointment. Disbelief. Frustration.

Deny everything, I told myself, but I was too wound up after the trip. Yesterday, I'd watched a man I cared about bury his birth mother. The words danced on the tip of my tongue, threatening to come out.

I sank my teeth into my bottom lip to keep them from spilling.

"I've never seen you in two-thousand-dollar jewelry before either." Levi motioned at my neck and I realized I was still wearing Frank's present. My breath hitched. I wasn't sure whether it was because of the price or because my partner had figured us out.

We stared at each other for a good minute. I pulled the hat off and said, "You can't tell anyone."

"Fuck." Groaning, Levi threw his arms in the air and locked both hands behind his neck. "Fuck, Cass."

"Promise me?" I pressed.

He squeezed his eyes shut for a second as if he needed to reset his brain. "You're sleeping with Frankie Blade. Well, fuck me." I heard him mutter.

The statement was crass. We weren't just sleeping together. We did it all together—slept, ate, laughed, talked. There was more to us than mindless sex. Levi's words seemed to demean what Frank and I had, and part of me wanted to ask my partner to take his last statement back.

Instead, I insisted he promise me to keep it between us.

"Who am I going to tell? Your brother?"

"He already knows."

"And he hasn't posted it on his Facebook yet?" Sarcasm laced his voice.

"Very funny."

There was an awkward pause.

"So...the tweet?" Levi scratched his head.

"Frank...Frankie saw some of the videos and wanted to meet Isabella in person. It just can't come back to me."

"You don't think people will eventually figure it out, Cass?"

"We're careful."

"Doesn't look like it. The gas station photos are pretty damn intimate."

"It could be any woman with black hair."

"It'd be great if Taylor Rhinehart had black hair. Problem solved."

"Jesus!" I cried out. "You've known for a minute and you're already making jokes about it."

"You're jealous."

"Am not."

"What are the chances that one of these days, someone will actually take a really good photo of you two?"

"Like I said, we're careful."

Silence took over the room. This was a lot to process.

"Is that why the video interview didn't get the green light?" Levi finally asked the question I feared the most.

I nodded.

There was a low mutter. "Fuck."

"I'm sorry."

"That video could have gotten us ten times more hits."

I didn't know what to say, so I gave him a shrug. *Rewired* meant a lot to me. But Frank meant more.

Isabella was a storm of emotions the day of the rehearsal. She wore a Hall Affinity T-shirt that matched Ashton's and her blue hair was teased and styled to perfection. Maria hovered. Everyone could barely hold their excitement. The sweet bliss of anticipation filled the tiny, equipment-clad rehearsal room.

The studio itself, a warehouse-like building with eight sound-proof spaces for rent, was located in the heart of Hollywood. Brooklyn had contacted the owner a few days ago and requested extra security. She'd also requested they not post anything about Frank's visit anywhere on social media.

This was dubbed as his personal project and for now, he wanted to keep his involvement out of the media. It conflicted with the Hall Affinity PR campaign. Although the album leak and rumors surrounding his private life, including all possible romantic interests, were a much bigger hit with the crowd.

Eager fans and paparazzi camping out in front of the building were the last thing Frank needed ahead of the upcoming shows. Especially since I was on the premises too. One shot of us together and we'd be screwed.

The space was booked for a full day. The band had a few shows lined up around L.A. and needed plenty of time to work on their new material. Levi was hyped. He'd gotten his hands on a sick Steadicam and could finally feed his creative muse.

Ever since his discovery, he'd been trying to drag Frank and our affair into all of our conversations, but I successfully shot his attempts down.

Ashton fully embraced his role as Levi's camera assistant.

The room was small. I assumed the larger one cost more, and money wasn't something Isabella's family had to throw around. A drum riser stood in front of the exposed brick wall. The AC was cranked all the way up. Snacks and drinks sat on a table in the corner.

I chose coffee and energy bars to keep me sharp and awake throughout the day.

Frank and I had spent the entire night having sex. He'd needed to leave early to meet with the label rep and I woke up in an empty bed, sheets still damp with sweat. With him, it was never enough. I could go on for hours. Suck him, lick him, ride him, inhale him. He was the sweetest poison, and I wasn't sure how I was going to be in one room with him all day with his scent still on my skin and pretend we were strangers.

He showed up in the afternoon. At around four. The band had already gone through their full catalogue and all the new material twice. There were a few covers they wanted to try; two of them were Hall Affinity songs.

Levi was on a roll, and I wondered if he was secretly aiming for an Oscar nomination. He majored in film in college. Another reason for the tension between him and his parents. Sadly, things just never took off for him and after a few unsuccessful attempts to break into the movie industry, Levi decided to follow his other passion, music, and created *Rewired*. The rest was history. Or perhaps *history in the making* worked better here.

We took five. Maria needed to make a phone call and Isabella needed to rest her voice. She'd been pushing it really hard all morning.

Story, the guitarist whom Dante had trashed a few weeks ago, sat on a stool and plucked at the strings of his Jackson. He was a nice kid, shy too. He wore a Led Zeppelin T-shirt and a pair of skinny jeans and looked nothing like Kit, the drummer, and Isabella. Although they were all somehow related. Kit was a couple of years older. He had olive skin and thick black hair, like Isabella and her mother. Their new bassist, Andy, was an odd duck. While he was the same age as the rest of the guys, he looked older. His calm demeanor suggested he'd been playing live shows since he was a kid and meeting celebrities wasn't unusual for him.

He was showing Ashton some basic bass lines.

I sat in the corner with my iPad and watched the band. To me, though just a few years younger than I was, they were still kids. Green and hopeful. They all had bright eyes and trusting faces and they were about to meet a man who'd won two Grammys and written a whole lot of chart-topping songs that were now considered classics of modern rock.

I gave myself a mental pat on the back. I wasn't scared to take the credit for making this meeting happen. I was damn proud of it too, and I wanted Levi to also be proud of me.

There was a knock on the door. The studio associate, a twenty-something girl with a Jamaican accent and a permanent grin, poked her braided head through the crack. "He's here."

She didn't say anything else. The door slid closed leaving us all in silence.

"*Dios mio.*" I heard Maria whisper in Spanish, which was highly unusual. Nervous, she clutched her hands in front of her chest, phone between her palms, eyes wide.

"Mom," Isabella hissed.

Story and Kit exchanged long excited stares. Andy hugged his instrument but stayed calm.

Despite the AC, the air inside the room became hot. A mix of horror and adoration danced across everyone's face. Voice and footsteps filled the hallway. I sat in my chair with my legs crossed and trembled like a leaf. I was anxious. Not because I was going to see Frank in his natural habitat, but because these guys were going to meet someone they idolized. A paranoid part of me also wondered if these people would be able to tell Frank and I were intimately involved, but my common sense told me that was an impossible scenario. We were great actors. We could fool everyone.

The door swung open and Brooklyn marched into the room. She surveyed us with a professional smile and approached Maria and Isabella to shake hands.

"Hi. I'm Brooklyn, Frankie's assistant. We corresponded via email."

More noises came from the outside. I heard laughter. Frank's laughter. He was talking to the studio associate. My pulse jumped.

Once all the introductions were finished, Brooklyn moved to the middle of the room. Her heels clacked against the floor. She wore her usual, a bright-colored blazer and a pair of black dress pants, and looked very impressive.

This woman made shit happen.

"Please, no cell phones, no cameras, no GoPros, or any other recording devices." Her piercing gaze darted over to Levi and Ashton as she explained the rules of conduct. They obliged and put away all the gear. "If Frankie decides he wants to take photos, he'll let you know. Any questions?" She topped her speech off with a wide, teeth-glittering smile.

After a short pause, everyone nodded. Then hysteria laced their voices as they started blabbering.

Seconds later, Frank stepped into the room. He wasn't the biggest person here, but it felt as if his frame took up the entire space and he swallowed up all the air. Breaths were held and eyes stopped blinking.

I noticed Roman and Corey out in the hallway, but they didn't come in.

"Hey, all." Frank smiled and marched toward Isabella. She met him halfway. The wheelchair didn't stop her from being her usual feisty self. They shook hands and exchanged a few words before he moved on to greet Maria and the other kids in the band. I watched him with fascination. My eyes scanned the length of his body, drinking in his jean-clad thighs and the outline of his shoulders. He wore a T-shirt and a leather jacket, and his face was relaxed while he spoke.

Then he made his way over to Levi and me.

"Cassy and Levi with *Rewired* are producing the documentary," Brooklyn said as her cool eyes caught mine. She was one hell of an actress; the woman didn't even flinch. She could probably give Taylor Rhinehart a run for her money.

"We meet again." Frank tipped his chin and held out his hand for a shake. I took it. Our palms connected and our fingers locked. Electricity surged through my arm just like it did at El Capitan. Inches of space separated us, yet we were one. We were a bubble of body heat and pheromones and my skin burned raw where our hands were linked.

We broke the handshake and Frank switched his attention to Levi. Then once all the introductions were done, he settled on the couch in the corner and watched Isabella and the guys perform a couple of original songs. Brooklyn fetched him a bottle of water. Maria stood nearby and answered some of his questions.

The atmosphere inside the room was casual. Levi and Ashton sipped on their Red Bulls and everyone chilled.

After finishing up their newest song, the band took another break and Isabella told Frank about her accident. The conversation took on an intimate tone and watching the two together made my heart melt a little.

I was a fucking softie.

In the end, they shared a joke about broken bones. This was the first time Frank actually revealed that he had metal rods in both legs to someone who wasn't a part of his entourage. I wondered if Isabella had signed some sort of a confidentiality agreement or if Frank was finally coming to terms with the challenges he'd been facing since the crash.

Brooklyn was the one who brought up the tweet and the cover of "Ambivalent." The official story was that she'd seen the video and she was the one who'd shown it to Frank.

Oh, the power of mighty Twitter.

My heart began to sprint at the mention of the song.

"I'll be very honest with you," Frank told Isabella. "You do a way better job than me." She didn't. She couldn't. "Ambivalent" *was* Frankie Blade, but she made it her own and he wanted her to hear the praise. He didn't just throw the words out. He knew they would mean a lot to this nineteen-year-old girl. Even years after today's meeting.

Story ran through the chords to warm up. Kit returned to his drums. Then Andy joined in. They took a moment to give each other encouraging glances and dived into the song. The familiar melody spread through the room.

My body froze, my hands curled into fists. My veins filled with smoldering heat.

Isabella adjusted the microphone and began her climb through the lyrics. She was as generous with her voice as Frank. She gave it her every breath and her every heartbeat. Eyes closed, hands in the air, she powered into the first chorus.

I looked at Frank. He leaned back, one palm rested on the arm of the couch, another one on his thigh. There was something new in his eyes. Something I hadn't seen before. Surprise. Admiration. Respect. All of those things twisted together into a shock of revelation. He felt it. He felt the immense power of her voice. It spoke to him, his own creation in a way he didn't know it could.

During the guitar solo, he turned his head, and when his gaze captured mine, we stared at each other covertly while Story tried to measure up to Dante's playing. He couldn't, but we didn't care. It was thirty seconds of just him and me in the room. Thirty seconds of music. Thirty seconds of strange orgasmic connection.

When the song finally ended, there was a collection of gasps and claps.

I needed a minute. My mind raced and my heart was pounding its way out of my chest. It wanted to crawl into Frank's instead, cuddle his heart, and bleed tender words to it.

Frank wrapped up his visit by posing for a couple of photos with the band. Brooklyn used Maria's cell phone to snap the pictures. Then she went through all the shots and deleted the ones that didn't seem to appeal to her, although I didn't think Frank had a bad angle. He was perfect and these kids adored him.

He shook everyone's hands again and complimented each band member. He leaned over and hugged Isabella while Brooklyn explained to Maria that Frankie wanted to remain an anonymous donor for now and definitely was interested in meeting again in the near future.

They were on their way out. The room felt chaotic. Every single person plunged toward the door.

"I'll try to find time and see one of your shows." Frank gave the kids a wide smile and glanced at me. "Would you walk me out, Cassy?"

I heard Levi grunt and shot him a glare. He responded with a smug grin.

Play along! I shouted to him inside my head.

"Absolutely." I nodded and followed him out. Brooklyn stayed behind. My guess was that she did so to keep everyone occupied—i.e., to keep everyone off our backs. The thud of the door cut off the elated voices. We stood in the empty hallway. Roman hung nearby. Corey was nowhere to be seen, but I heard his pitch drifting from the vicinity of the reception. He was on the phone.

"What do you think?" I asked Frank, looking up at him.

"She's a great kid." He stared at me intensely before his eyes dropped to my lips and then to my cleavage. Today, I didn't wear my usual rock 'n' roll attire. I was in a pair of slim-fitting dress pants, a flowy top, and high-heeled shoes. Neat and professional.

The music still coursed through me. "She is. I'm glad you came." I had the hardest time keeping it together with him standing two inches away. My hands itched to touch him. He was like hard rock's own Santa Claus. He'd just made four teenagers' lives, gifting them hope and promise.

Multiple doors and framed photographs lined each side of the hallway, which was now empty. Frank hooked his arm through mine and pulled me aside. His movements were very subtle, but very risky. Anyone could come out and see us together, and that, the feeling of danger, only fueled my adrenaline.

"Do you have a second, Cassy?" he asked, his voice low. Bedroom, playful, and sexy.

"I do."

Frank drew me toward the door on the left and pushed it open. Inside was dark. Not a sound. No people. I caught the shimmer of the glass wall and a mixing board. My pulse quickened to a sprint. My mouth went dry and my panties, the opposite.

He ushered me in and shut the door. I heard the click of the lock and felt his greedy hands on my waist. His breaths were loud pants.

"Frank!" I squealed, fisting the sleeves of his leather jacket. "What if someone walks in?"

"It's paid for." He pushed me against the wall. Not rough, but not gentle either. The right amount of pressure to light my body on fire. "I rented it." His mouth moved against mine as he spoke. His kiss was hungry.

"What?" I mumbled in disbelief before returning hard, deliberate strokes of his tongue.

He lowered his face to my breasts and pulled down the cups of my bra to free my nipples, which begged for attention.

His lips were merciless. Like a true tease, he ripped my moans out of me one by one. His palms slid down the curve of my waist and to my thighs to pull me closer. I was hot and bothered, and every flick of his tongue drove me deeper into an abyss of sexual frenzy. My entire body ached. This was insane.

"Do you have any idea how much you turn me on when you're like this?" Frank rasped against my neck.

"Like what?"

His erection pressed to my middle. "When you're all business."

"Is it the shoes?"

"It's definitely the shoes."

We moved against each other, my back brushing up and down the cold wall as our hips grinded together. I slipped my hand into his jeans and cupped his length. He was big and solid. I wanted to be dirty for him.

"Doll"—a heavy sigh escaped from his lungs—"you're asking for trouble."

"Didn't you know? I *am* trouble." I laughed softly, squeezing my palm around him.

"Fuck." He kissed me on the lips. His heated whisper vibrated inside my mouth. "You better finish what you started."

"I always do." My fingers worked him slowly. Long, firm strokes.

Our gazes lingered on each other in the dark. I could see the lines of his beautiful face and the curve of his strong shoulders. Brows pulled together, lips parted, he was nearing the edge. His chest rose and fell. Expensive leather rubbed against my bare nipples, sending pleasant shivers down my spine. We had no shame whatsoever. Apparently, charity work turned us both on.

"I won't be able to go out there right now if you don't finish, doll," Frank pleaded.

I drew my hand out of his jeans and steered him to the wall. His breathing grew loud, each inhale almost a ragged moan. I dropped to my knees and pulled down his zipper. Filthy euphoria filled me with reckless want. Want to make him feel good. Want to take him to that edge he needed to cross.

His fingers twined in my hair, palms pressed to the back of my head, pushing it forward. I wrapped my hand around the base of his cock and took him in my mouth as much as I could. He was too big and the tip hit my throat. I relaxed it and gripped his hard thigh. We'd done this many times before. Just not with dozens of people on the other side of the wall. It was such a delicious rush.

A long, pleasured groan soared through the dark room. It bounced off the walls and the glass and infused the air with the scent of our desire.

I worked him fast and hard. With my lips, my tongue, my throat, my hands. His cock fucked my mouth without any reservations and I loved it. I loved that I was the one to give him this gift. I loved that he couldn't get enough. He was addicted to me as much as I was to him, and I wondered if this mutual addiction was going to destroy us one day. I had no idea why these thoughts crossed my mind while I sucked him, but I pushed them aside and took him where he needed to go. Precum coated my mouth as he tossed his head back and his hands released me. I heard the slap of his palms against the wall and his moans as they escaped one by one. He pulled out before he came, and hot fluid hit my cheek and dripped down my chin and chest. My bra was down, but my shirt was still buttoned up and my common sense nudged me into the real world again.

There were other people in the building and I couldn't walk around like this, with Frank's come on my clothes. My fingers fought the stubborn fabric.

Then came a flick and the lights went on. Shedding my top and bra to save it from the traces of our sex action, I looked up at Frank. He was still buzzing. His hand near the switch on the wall, his eyes closed, eyelashes fluttering, every muscle tight.

I loved the view.

Seconds passed, then he cupped my head and gently pulled me

against his leg, my cheek pressed to his thigh. Long fingers grazed the side of my face and raked my hair. It was the strangest feeling. One minute he was fucking my mouth to the point of choking, the next he was softer than the softest plush.

We stood like this, him propped against the wall and me on my knees, topless, until our breaths subsided. It felt both wrong and right.

"You're so fucking good, doll," Frank finally said, running his knuckles over my jaw. "You're going to ruin me."

Not if you ruin me first.

He helped me up from the floor, and we scanned the room for paper towels and cleaned up. I put my bra and my shirt back on. Outside in the hallway, approaching voices boomed. This was his cue to leave.

"I'll see you at home," he whispered, kissing me on my forehead, then marching over to the door.

"Okay." I bit my lip and I moved to the side to make sure no one saw me. My body still burned with ache.

"I'll take care of you later." A smirk tilted his lips and I felt it between my thighs, the thirst for release.

Frank called it *home*. The place where I thought I was only a guest. The idea gave me chills.

When he stepped out, I locked the door and fell against the wall. My mind was adrift and I needed a few minutes to calm down. Returning to the studio looking like I'd just been mouth-fucked wasn't a good idea. Although I *had* been mouth-fucked and I liked it, and my sex couldn't wait until tonight.

Squeezing my eyes shut, I slipped my hand under the thin fabric of my panties and found my pulsing clit.

You're nuts, woman, my inner voice said. *You're masturbating in someone's place of business with a bunch of teenagers in the next room.*

I shook my head and sent the righteous thoughts to the back of my brain. *I need it. I need to finish the job.* My hand worked fast and I imagined Frank. I imagined he was the one stroking my clit and I imagined he was the one shoving his fingers inside me. My climax was close. Then it rolled through me, wave after wave, curling my toes. I was undone. Absolutely, irrevocably undone.

"I'm going to punish you for this so bad, Frank." I said through my strained moan as I came on my hand.

Chapter Fourteen

Inglewood hadn't seen a gridlock hell like the one that filled its streets this afternoon in ages. The first Hall Affinity show night caused a mile-long traffic backup and it took us almost two hours to get to the venue.

Frank needed to be alone on the day of the show, which I understood. Billy and Janet had flown in from Arizona last week and the house seemed crowded. Every morning, I'd woken up to the rattle of Brooklyn's voice in the living room. Sometimes Dante's. He'd been a frequent guest and I knew that at some point, I needed to tell Frank about what'd happened between us, but I couldn't bring myself to do it. Not with the shows approaching.

Frank's anxiety was infectious. It plagued every corner, every crack, and every crevice inside the house. But I felt his dread in my veins too. He wasn't nervous because he hadn't performed in a long time. He was nervous because he hadn't performed the way he was going to perform tonight. With restraint and caution. No jumping, no running, no lifting anything. Yet he still needed to make sure he delivered. His fans had expectations that needed to be met.

For someone whose entire career had been built on busting

moves and doing insane acrobatics on stage, this was a challenge. Deep down, I knew people would be ecstatic no matter what Frank did, but he wasn't the kind of performer who half-assed it. He gave it his all. One hundred and fifty percent. Because anything less would be cheating the fans. Would be cheating the people who'd put him on that pedestal of perfection he'd been on for nearly two decades.

A car came to pick me and my brother up from Burbank around three. Ashton was hoping to catch the soundcheck, but we didn't make it on time.

The freeway was bumper-to-bumper maddening. The streets of Inglewood were even worse. A honking limbo of cars of all makes and colors, the shimmer of their roofs spread out as far as the eye could see. We circled the venue for endless minutes until Brooklyn finally called security and instructed them to let us pass. Mouth agape, Ashton stared at the organized chaos that surrounded the building as we rolled through the armada of busses and trucks. People were running around, their faces screwed up in concentration, and the parking lot was like one big traffic jam.

Dressed to impress, Brooklyn was waiting for us outside. Her bright red blazer swam into my line of vision as the car approached the loading dock.

The back of the building reminded me of a beehive. Forklifts roared. People scurried. Walkie-talkies droned.

"You're right on time." The woman gave me a once-over and handed us our passes. "They just finished the soundcheck. He has a couple of minutes."

Brooklyn knew about the nature of my relationship with Frank. I didn't know how exactly she felt about it, but even if she didn't like me, she hid her feelings well. As a matter of fact, I wasn't sure she had any feelings. It was impossible to say what she was thinking. It was also impossible to say what she looked like without three layers of makeup.

What I knew was that the woman was indispensable. Frank needed her like he needed water.

We followed her through the maze of hallways filled with crew and security. The upstairs area was packed, and Ashton dove into the middle of it. He knew that if anyone asked about his pass, it was a gift from a radio station.

Giddy, I snapped a photo of my brother in front of the standing Hall Affinity banner and texted it to my partner.

Levi had a mezzanine ticket and he'd brought Shayne Mason. She was my replacement for all three nights, and although I almost hated him for picking her, I knew it was for the best. It would be wrong to review the set of the band whose singer I'd been sleeping with. Although Frank was a bad influence and my morals were pretty much in the gutter when it came to unhinged sex, I still managed to retain some level of professionalism, and my integrity told me to sit this one out.

"I'll be back in a little bit," I told Ashton, surveying the crowd inside the lounge. "Wait here."

He wore the T-shirt Frank had signed for him and looked all grown up. Now I just needed to make sure he didn't flunk his SATs on the second try. Lately, I'd been wondering if I actually was a bad sister. Instead of pushing my little brother to do better, I dragged him to a show on a school night.

Brooklyn had left and I had to find the way to the dressing room on my own. The twists and turns of the backstage hallways reminded me of a maze. The air almost crackled with electricity. Be it the rock 'n' roll elite or working crew members, their anticipation was palpable. My heart hammered and my heels clicked on the hard floor as I rushed through the brightly lit curve of the walkway in search of the dressing room. It wasn't difficult to spot. Roman guarded the door. His emotionless face hardly moved when our gazes met, but he let me in without question.

Inside, Frank sat in front of the large bulb-studded vanity mirror. Brooklyn stood next to him with her iPad. Corey took the spot next to Billy on the couch. Janet and Frank's private doctor stood in the corner with them, talking quietly. I couldn't hear what they were saying, but my stomach tightened, nonetheless. I wasn't certain if it was because of the fact that Frank needed to have a medical professional on standby here tonight or the concerned look on Janet's face.

Mrs. Wallace was sugary and eccentric. A product of the wild '70s with its early beat of true rock 'n' roll, she dressed and looked the part. Minimum makeup, flowy dress. She still wore her silver-colored hair loose and long and gave really cheesy pet names to everyone she came across. Including me.

We hadn't gotten to spend too much time together, but I liked her, and my sixth sense told me the feeling was mutual. She'd called me "child."

I froze for a second, unsure of what to say or do. This was new. The man I'd been in a relationship with was at work and I didn't know whether I fit in here, whether I fit into this part of his life.

Frank's voice carrying over the hum of the dressing room snapped me out of my daze. "Hey, doll," he said. His gunmetal eyes found mine in the mirror. Our reflections connected.

Yes, you fit in, his gaze said. *You have as much right to be here tonight as everyone else.*

I crossed the room and reached out to him. His hand snatched mine and he pressed his lips to my knuckles, ignoring the hairbrush and blow dryer being used on his hair.

"Was the traffic bad?" he asked, releasing his grasp.

"Are you seriously asking me this question?" I laughed a little and leaned over to whisper in his ear, "Didn't you hear? Hall Affinity is playing their first show after a-seven-year break."

A smile flashed at me from the mirror.

"Where's Ashton?"

"In the lounge."

"Did Brooklyn show you where your seats are?"

"I'll do it in a bit," she cut in and shoved her iPad at Frank. I caught a glimpse of tonight's setlist. Fifteen songs. A mix of older material and two new singles, with "Awake" and "Ambivalent" being the encore.

"You can watch from side stage too," Frank explained. "But I recommend a seat for the full experience."

Brooklyn dropped two pills in his palm and handed him a bottle of water.

The stylist needed to finish her job and I moved out of the way. The eerie tension hanging inside the dressing room grew stronger. Stress riled Frank's face and frame. With his leather-clad thighs and a black T-shirt stretched across his taut body, he was a seductive package. Man candy wrapped in layers of expensive stage clothes, boots, and jewelry. A man who'd been sliced open and sewn together more times than he could remember.

His hair was a deliberate sandy mess, soft waves falling down strong shoulders. I'd never seen him wear earrings until tonight. They were small studs, one in each ear and a string of hoops in his left one. Watching him getting ready was like watching an episode of Fixer Upper on HGTV. Not that there was anything wrong with his off-stage persona. But his stage one was something else. Delicious, lickable, fuckable something else.

You need to stop drooling, my inner voice said, *at least while his parents are here.* Although I wasn't going to be the only one. Tonight, thousands of women were going to drool over Frank too, some probably would go home and get themselves off after the show. Some might try it during the show. It was rock 'n' roll, after all. Sex was its faithful companion.

Once the stylist finished her job, Frank asked to be left alone. Billy and Janet ushered everyone out. Brooklyn took advantage of the short break from her boss and took Ashton and me to our seats. It was a box for two with a table, leather chairs, and a clear view of the stage.

I tried to text Levi to see if he wanted to meet up in the lobby, but the messages stopped going through. Reception had gone to shit. The venue was full, every seat taken.

"I'm going to get a drink," I told Ashton. "Do you want something?"

"Beer?" He grinned.

"Non-alcoholic." I rolled my eyes.

"Come on," he whined. "Just one."

"No, Ashton. That's not going to happen for another three years."

"Can you get some nachos then?"

"Sure."

The lines in the general admission lobby were insanely long, and I decided to get Ashton his food backstage, which was probably a mistake.

There, in the VIP lounge, surrounded by a wall of bodyguards and other celebrities, stood Taylor Rhinehart. The Emmy-nominated red-haired goddess whose full-lipped angelic face was slapped across every billboard on Sunset Boulevard this summer. The floors underneath me began to shift. For a moment, I forgot why I'd come here.

She was refined. Thin, tall. Short leather dress. A string of diamonds glittered around her neck. I had to remind myself to breathe. Confusing emotions rolled from the hollow of my chest to the pit of my stomach.

"Why am I not surprised to see you here?" A voice drawled behind me, bringing me back to life. I spun and came face-to-face with Dante. My heart flipped for some unknown reason. While he'd come over to Frank's often, we hadn't really spoken about what'd happened between us, because the opportunity had never presented itself. I'd almost let it go. The leak still hadn't been traced and the band's PR team had come to the conclusion the incident wasn't worth their time and effort anymore. The upcoming tour was more important.

I caught the faint smell of alcohol and cherry on Dante's breath. He was buzzed, lollipop in his mouth, drink in his hand. His outfit consisted of his usual loose silk shirt, tight jeans, boots, a hat, and a truckload of accessories and jewelry. Dante Martinez looked the part of a rock star. He was bad, he was sleazy, and his guitar skills were going to break thousands of hearts in less than an hour.

"Hi," I said, straightening. Though he was taller than Frank, his height didn't intimidate me. At this moment, I was more upset over the fact Taylor Rhinehart was in this building. Out of all the places to be tonight, she'd chosen to see the Hall Affinity show.

She's a fan of the band, I reminded myself, plastering a smile over my lips.

"How's Frankie-boy doing?" Dante asked, taking a swallow from his glass.

"How are *you* doing?" I dodged his question.

"I'm ready to rock 'n' roll, darlin'." He shot me a dazzling devil-may-care smile. "Are you excited to see the show?"

"Yes, I am."

This was frustrating. Dante behaved like nothing had happened, as if he wasn't the one who'd accused me of stealing demos, and the tension between us bothered me. I wasn't the kind of woman to swallow down offenses.

"I think we need to clear the air," I began.

He inhaled loudly through his nose. "The air feels pretty clear to me." A smirk made an appearance. "Now, after the show, this will all be sweat, puke, and weed. Nasty shit."

"Dante." My hand rested on his shoulder to get his attention. "You owe me an apology."

His eyes widened. "Excuse me, darlin'?"

"Here's how it is. I care about Frank and what we have, and I believe it's safe to say you were wrong. I didn't steal the demos. I would never do that. So I want you to accept the fact you attacked me for no reason."

"Are you high, Cassy Evans?" He leaned over and smelled my hair, his nose scrunched up.

I wasn't sure whether to laugh, cry, or punch some sense into him. I did the latter. I slapped his shoulder. The man was sniffing me in public. In front of Taylor Rhinehart. Crazy wasn't even the right word for his behavior.

"Ouch!" He backed away. "Did Frankie-boy teach you this kink? Just so you know, not all men like to be dominated."

I rolled my eyes and took a deep breath. Dante was impossible to talk to. He turned my every word into a joke or an innuendo. I didn't mind innuendos when they came from a person I was going to fuck later. I didn't want them from a person who had a very unhealthy interest in my and his best friend's sex life. It wasn't a turn-on. Not in the slightest.

"Oh, hey!" Dante plucked his candy from his mouth. "I heard Frankie-boy is going to pitch in to promote your documentary." Talk about short attention span.

"He's financing the production of Isabella's debut album," I explained. The documentary was still my and Levi's undertaking. Frank had brought up money once, but I declined. I wanted this project to stay nonprofit for a number of reasons.

We never got to finish the talk. Javier came up and whisked Dante away to get ready for the set. The lounge continued to buzz, but some of the guests began to leave right after Carter made a quick appearance. A photographer, most likely hired by Jay Brodie PR, took photos of Taylor Rhinehart and other celebs. I knew Carlos would probably kill to be in his place, but these gigs were exclusive. You needed to know people who knew people who could vouch for your talent.

I headed over to the snack bar and joined the end of a short line to buy nachos for Ashton and get a drink for myself, but my insecurities were crawling out of their hiding places. *Why was Taylor Rhinehart here?* I couldn't just sit in the booth and wait for the set to kick off while watching my brother destroy his smelly junk food.

Truth be told, Ashton didn't need me to be there in order for him to enjoy the show. I suspected I was holding him back from being a total goof, so I delivered his nachos and returned to the VIP to join Janet and Billy side stage.

From my spot, the venue looked like a net of shimmer. Awaiting murmurs soared through the crowd. The lights dimmed and I heard a cluster of gasps. My gut twisted in nervous excitement.

Dante stood to my right. Eyes hooded, candy stick between his lips, he rolled his shoulders and took a deep breath. His tech strapped a black Stratocaster around his neck. Carter was stretching. He flung his arms in the air several times and grinned at Johnny. Johnny returned the gesture. They were anxious to get this show started. Bruce, the band's manager, looked all kinds of stressed.

Frank wasn't present.

Sparse clouds of sparkling fog licked the stage. The lights went off, and darkness swallowed up all twenty thousand people who were gathered on the floor. They were chanting the band's name. Almost like a prayer. I felt it then. The rush and the agony of anticipation. It was adrenaline pumping inside my veins.

Murmurs took over the backstage area. I turned toward the noise and saw Roman marching through the barrage of VIPs and crew members. Frank was right behind him. Face hard, lips shut, he strode past the guests without looking at them. When he met up with Dante, Carter and Johnny joined in and they formed a group. Or more like a group hug. I watched them pat each other's backs and talk for a few minutes. Then they exchanged fist bumps. At that moment, whatever history they all had and whatever bad blood had been spilled between them didn't matter. They were about to make magic and all the problems needed to be swept aside for the duration of their ninety-minute set.

Then I understood it—Frank's decision to keep playing with Dante. To keep the band going. Thousands of frantic people that waited on the opposite side of the stage were proof he'd made the right choice. Sometimes hard choices bred better results. It just wasn't an easy road. It wasn't a road for everyone either.

Frank checked his monitor and shook his arms. He closed his eyes. He was in the zone. Concentrated entirely on the task he was set out to tackle tonight—deliver a heart-stopping performance without overdoing it.

The crowd began to roar. Thousands of feet stomped along to the funky beat of the show intro. Carter went first. He grinned and settled behind his kit. The screams amplified. Johnny marched up next. The audience was relentless.

Dante tossed his candy into the trashcan one of the guys held out for him and walked out on stage. When he finally entered the spotlight, all hell broke loose. He waved and ran through a chord. The crowd responded with a thunderous scream of adoration. My heart rode an intense roller coaster inside my body. It leapt to my throat, then dropped to my feet. I didn't consider myself a religious person, but I still said a prayer when Frank moved toward the microphone. I saw his hand rise to greet the fans. I saw his smile light up his face. I saw his eyes taking in the crowd. All the stress he'd been carrying around disappeared. He belonged there. He belonged to those people, the people who made him.

And at that moment, I knew he was going to make every single person who'd come here tonight happy. Including me.

I'd forgotten how seductive Frankie Blade could be on stage. Every word that came from his lips pushed me deeper into a state of dark sexual glee. The sound was a chaotic rattle from where I stood, and even though I couldn't fully enjoy the songs the way the crowd did, I was stupefied. The chemistry between the band members alone made my head spin from the overload of sensations.

I was a teenage girl again, lost in a time warp, high on music, high on the memories of my first crush and my first heartbreak. My body swayed to the beat and my chest was full. This was the worst kind of ecstasy. The most dangerous one, but oh so good.

My hungry eyes followed Frank's every move. He was magnificent. Commanding, sexy, charming. The fans were going crazy. The line of security inside the pit had a busy night. Hall Affinity wasn't exactly a wild band, but people were too excited not to crowd surf. Bodies sailed above other bodies. Hands clapped.

If there was a way to chase an orgasm without having actual intercourse, this—watching Frankie Blade, my lover, unravel twenty thousand people—was it.

He wasn't part of the show. He *was* the show.

Three songs into the set, Taylor Rhinehart emerged in my peripheral. She had a drink with a colored umbrella and her body-guard lingered in the background. I knew I had no reason to be scared of this woman. Frank belonged to me. But a pinch of jealousy twisted my stomach. Not because I feared she'd steal my man, but because she had the freedom to be herself with him while I didn't. I was the secret only a handful of people knew about. Today, he didn't speak to me outside the dressing room. He didn't hold my hand like Johnny held his girlfriend's while they hung out in the lounge.

He didn't want anyone to see us together.

And I'd been okay with that from the beginning. Or I thought I was. I kept telling myself that keeping my name out of tabloids by hiding our relationship was for the best, but my heart stopped believing it tonight. And I hated my heart for it.

My heart was stupid.

I couldn't tell when exactly things went wrong. There was an inaudible exchange between Dante and Frankie during the "Hollow Heart Dream" guitar solo. To me, this looked like any other perfor-mance. They were having a moment. Musicians communicated on stage all the time. But the second Frank turned to face the backstage area, I knew he wasn't okay. His silhouette moved slowly through the wall of colored fog that spilled on stage. All but a single spotlight dimmed. Dante was now the center of everyone's attention. He ripped through the chords on his Stratocaster. It was a mean progres-sion that rose until it hit its screeching top. The crowd responded with a delighted shriek. The comedown was just as elegant, note after note, the solo descended. Drunk or high, Dante knew how to play guitar. He wasn't on the list of 100 Greatest Rock Guitarists of All Time for his smoldering looks.

Heart clenched, my eyes followed Frank as he stumbled off stage and into the middle of a human mess. Mayhem was everywhere. I saw Billy, Janet, and Brooklyn rushing over to him. Corey's face was whiter than the first snow. People yelled into their walkie-talkies. Bruce was running around in panic and giving out orders.

Dante kept playing.

The blend of the intricate riff and the screams of the crowd crashed into me really hard. My stomach lurched. The noise was a raging pulse in my ears and I didn't understand what was happening. Then I saw it. The paramedics. The crowd dispersed to make way and I pushed through. A flashlight pierced the darkness

"Take a step back, please!" Roman's voice ordered.

He waved his arms and signaled for people to move away. Frank was sitting down, face abnormally pale, hair damp. A layer of sweat glistened across his forehead and chest. The doctor leaned over to hand him an oxygen mask. Frank shook his head but took it. He breathed hard and I could tell his lungs were struggling. My mind scrambled through all the scenarios I'd overheard during his meetings with Reese and his doctor. He needed to watch how much pressure he put on his right shoulder and he needed to make sure he didn't overdo it with the acrobatics. He was great during the rehearsal. He went through the setlist with ease. Whatever was going on with him wasn't what the doctor had feared most.

I stepped closer and caught Janet's arm. She glanced at me over her shoulder, her eyes filled with genuine terror.

"What's going on?" I mouthed.

"I think it's his blood pressure." That was all she said.

On stage, Dante was entertaining the audience. Carter joined him on drums, and now this was a two-man show and people who'd bought tickets had no idea the singer was in no condition to walk. When were they going to catch on? How long was too long for a guitar solo? Five minutes? Ten minutes? Twenty?

I got closer to the front of the circle surrounding Frank. The paramedics were taking his vitals. His physician hovered.

"We need you to lie down, sir," someone said.

"Large bore fully open," another voice boomed. "Get the line started."

An IV needle was stuck in Frank's arm. Oxygen mask back in place.

This felt a lot like witnessing the end of the world. Worst part was, I couldn't do a damn thing about it.

The onstage shebang was just Carter now. The spotlight shifted over to the drum kit, where he was pounding out a wicked beat.

Ignoring the medics, Dante nosed his way in and leaned over to Frank. They were cheek to cheek, and he hovered there for a few seconds. The contrast of their skin tones, cream gold versus bronze olive, was striking. Frank's eyes were lost and unfocused as he breathed through his breakdown with a needle in his vein, and Dante's shoulders were tense with worry as his lips moved. He whispered something to Frank, then glanced at the doctor. They talked. Bruce ducked in. Their voices meshed with the cymbal-filled drum sequence that rattled on stage.

Uncertainty clutched my mind.

"You sure?" I caught Dante's words.

Frank nodded and drew the mask away from his face. The medics were still administering fluids.

"Cut the set!" I heard Bruce yelling over his walkie-talkie. "Going straight to the encore."

Technicians began to sprint. On stage, Johnny and Carter were doing a trade-off. The crowd was eating it up.

Gaze trained on Frank, I inched closer and he saw me. His eyes captured mine when Dante swiveled around to give everyone instructions. His face had no color and his hand shook when he flipped it over and opened his palm. Terror clenched my chest.

"We'll do 'Awake' first, then 'Fire and Blood.'" Dante's voice roared against my eardrums. He turned to Frank, head dipping. "You sure you're up for it, Frankie-boy?"

"Are you out of your mind?" Janet protested.

"Mom, it's fine."

"You can't even stand!"

"I just need a minute."

It was decided. They were skipping the rest of the set, all five songs, and going straight for the encore.

The backstage was chaos and dread. People swarmed around Frank with water and towels, and I was helpless to stand there, watching him struggling with whatever his body had been going through. His palm was still lying open on the stretcher next to his body.

Then it happened. Glancing over to me, he raised his hand and reached out. In front of everyone. The entire team, his parents, Dante, Taylor Rhinehart. It was a covert movement of despair and I clutched to him like a confused child to an adult in the middle of a busy mall during the Christmas season. Only, the roles were reversed right now. He was the child. He needed someone to tell him everything was okay.

A wavering smile lurked on his lips and I slid my small palm into his, large and familiar. Bruce and Dante were working out the set change logistics. Frank's fingers squeezed my wrist. They were cold and sweaty and he was a wreck, but he was going through with this. He was going back out there because twenty thousand people had paid a lot of money to see the band. Twenty thousand people had been waiting for this moment for seven years and he wasn't going to let them down.

Minutes passed. Johnny took over the microphone and made a small speech. The audience had no idea what was going on. To them, the bassist getting sentimental was part of the show.

"You good, Frankie-boy?" Dante dropped his face to Frank's ear again.

"Yeah."

"I'll hold you if you need me to hold ya, brother. Right?" He braved a smile, but I knew it wasn't a real one. It was a mask, an attempt to give everyone, and perhaps himself, a shot of false security. I could tell Dante was scared by the glint in his dark, pensive eyes.

He marched off to help Johnny. They kept the fans occupied for a little while longer. Frank sat up on the stretcher. Janet wiped the sweat off his face and chest.

"You don't have to do this, sweetheart," she mumbled.

"I'll be fine, Mom." He gave her a small smile and slid to the floor. His hand deserted mine.

Roman pushed everyone away to make room for Frank to stretch. He rolled his shoulders and breathed in and out. A small line above the bridge of his nose twisted with concentration.

"Okay, let's fucking do this!" his voice rumbled over the noise. "Let's give these people what they want."

Corey and Brooklyn walked with him until the safety line and then he disappeared into the fog.

Panic rose at the back of my throat as I stared at the blurry shape of a lonely microphone erect in the middle. My heart hammered against my ribs. The spotlight dipped and Frank's silhouette finally emerged from the shimmering thick clouds. A sigh of relief left my lungs. He raised his hand and waved at the crowd, mustering up a smile. Hungry for more music, all twenty thousand pairs of eyes zeroed in on him. A storm of deafening applause blasted through the arena.

Frank sang three songs, wrapping up the show with "Ambivalent" and walked off the stage before the final sequence of pyro was over.

Dante, Carter, and Johnny stayed behind. They tossed drumsticks and picks into the crowd. Security helped Dante into the pit and he gave high-fives to the entire front row. The man was brilliant. No one cared about Frankie at that moment.

My phone buzzed in my pocket. Then again and again. I wasn't sure if all the messages that hadn't been getting through decided to attack me all at once or if enough people had left for the reception to clear.

I didn't look, though. I waited for Frank at the bottom of the stairs leading up to the stage. When he finally approached me, he reached for my hand and I gave it to him. His entourage and the paramedics swallowed us. A cacophony of voices trailed after the group as Roman led everyone through the bright hallway. In the dressing room, Frank's physician checked his vitals again. The paramedics gave him more fluids.

I stepped aside and glanced at my phone.

Levi: Did they cut the set?

I didn't know how to respond to that. It wasn't my place to tell, but obviously, people were going to bitch about it tomorrow morning. No band would consciously ever choose to play for only an hour. Another text came.

Brother: Where are you?

Dressing room.

Brother: Be right there.

Not a good idea.

An eye-roll emoji popped up on the screen.

My mind raced. I didn't want my brother seeing this. I didn't trust him enough.

Corey paced. Brooklyn was on the phone, arranging for an overnight nurse. Janet and Billy stood over Frank, their faces tight with concern. I slid my phone to the back pocket of my jeans and began my approach. Here, no one but family and his regular team were present. Here, I didn't have to think twice about being myself. About whether to be there for him or not to be. Whatever he chose.

"Do you want to take a shower here or go home?" Janet asked, clutching his shoulder.

"Home." He shook his head and flicked his gaze over to me. "You don't mind me sweaty, do you, doll?" A playful glint sparkled in his eyes. Even with a tube in his vein and a tremor in his voice, he found the strength to joke.

"Not at all." I bent in front of him. We joined hands and our knees bumped. "Anything I can do?"

A soft smile curled his lips. "Stay with me tonight?" Exhaustion lined his face. He was splayed in a chair and one of the medics was trying to lay him down again.

"Sure."

"Brooklyn will get Ashton a car."

"Levi can take him home."

The air inside the dressing room smelled like fear, sweat, and... disease. There was a knock on the door. Roman marched over to check who it was. Dante stood in the hallway with my brother directly behind him. I noted a few more pairs of curious eyes, but security wasn't letting anyone in except for Dante.

"Give me a second." I patted Frank's arm and stepped out.

"What's going on?" Ashton peeked inside through the small crack, but I whooshed him away from the door.

"Levi will take you home, okay?"

"Sure." He drawled, shoving his hands into the front pockets of his jeans. "They skipped a bunch of songs from *Hollow Heart Dream*."

I dialed Levi's number and held a finger in front of Ashton's face. My shoe tapped nervously against the polished concrete.

"What the fuck, Cass? They cut the set?" Levi grumbled.

"Could you please take Ashton home?"

There was a pause on the line. The noise of the crowd filled the background.

"Please?" I begged. My voice cracked.

"Of course. Tell him to meet me outside. I'm parked near the club entrance. Lot K."

"Thank you. I owe you one."

"You do, Cass." There were more words. I could sense his anxiety as it bounced off mine, but we left it at that. My secret was driving a wedge between us and we both knew it. The question was whether something needed to be done or whether letting events take their course would be best.

I explained to Ashton where to find Levi and pulled him into an awkward hug. His flat chest bumped against mine, his hands never leaving his pockets. Our laminates tangled. He was startled by what was going on as much as I was.

"Be careful, okay?" I said, giving him a light pat on the arm.

"Yeah." He rolled his eyes as if I'd said something absurd like reminding him not to forget to breathe air.

"I'll text you tomorrow."

Golden curls on display, his lanky figure maneuvered through the backstage crowd until I couldn't see him behind the wall of people anymore.

Can you please text me when you drop off my brother? I shot a quick message to Levi.

Levi: Will do.

We drove to Malibu in an Escalade. Roman took the front. Janet and Billy sat with us in the back. Jaw set and eyes closed, Frank hardly spoke. His sweat-drenched clothes stuck to his body as if they were a second skin. Our clasped hands rested on his thigh and I could feel the weakness of his pulse and the drag of his labored breaths. Endless questions swirled in my head, but I had to let them simmer. I had to turn the inquisitive part of my mind off.

"I really think you need to reconsider," Janet began, her voice a plea.

Billy touched her arm. He was the calm one, but I knew, like with Dante's smiles earlier at the arena, this was just a facade.

"We're not discussing this anymore," Frank growled. His eyes remained closed, but his grip on my hand tightened. His body was slumped on the seat, legs stretched, head tossed back.

"You're going to hurt yourself," Janet wailed, a somber frown coiling her neatly thread brows.

"Mother"—Frank looked at her—"a lot of people paid a lot of money to see us play a show. I can't simply pull the plug because of my fucking blood pressure."

"You're not well," she countered in a half-pout.

"We'll make adjustments to the setlist. What I need right now is for you to stop nagging."

She didn't respond. Something unsaid teetered between them. I didn't know what. The heaviness of their standoff was like a lingering wrecking ball, wanting to swing into action.

I could tell Frank's determination to perform tomorrow weighed on Janet's shoulders.

Billy was the mediator between his wife and his son. "Boy's going to get some rest tonight and we'll decide in the morning, huh?" he said. His gaze darted from Frank to Janet.

She shook her head disagreeably but didn't reply.

Grim silence dragged on until we got to Malibu. Corey and Brooklyn arrived moments after us and before I knew it, the house had been turned into a war zone. Turbulent chatter filled the living room as I marched Frank to the bedroom. There was a nurse in the house, but he insisted on privacy.

Watching someone who'd just walked off the stage of the Forum trying to peel off his clothes was strange. Surreal. Domestic.

I made a feeble attempt to help him, but Frank managed without my assistance. He stepped into the shower and I sat on the edge of the hot tub, listening to the water beat against the frosted walls and marble as I watched his splotches of ink moving behind the steamy clouds inside the cabin.

Up until today, we'd only shared the bathroom if we were having sex in the shower. We didn't have a habit of brushing our teeth together like some couples. Our schedules didn't really allow it.

I dropped my gaze to my phone and opened my Twitter. My stomach turned over.

The world knew something was wrong and the world wasn't happy.

Hall Affinity cheated us! the tweets screamed.

The set was too short. The fans were divided again. Half were defending the band, the other half wanted their money back.

I scrolled through the feed and clicked on one of the *Rewired* posts. It was a short video snippet from the concert. The finale. There was so much pyro on stage, I could barely see any members. Hall Affinity had never gone all out with the fireworks in the past. Either management really wanted to make a splash or they wanted to distract the crowd due to the fact the front man wasn't up to the task. The journalist in me could speculate all night, but the woman who was in a relationship with said front man didn't want to, didn't need to.

A low thud came from inside the shower cabin. Freaked out, I hurried over and pulled the door open.

"Frank?" His name was a worried gasp on my lips.

Large swirls of steam hit my face.

"It's just a shampoo bottle," he mumbled.

I heard the crack in his voice and I saw the tension in his shoulders. He stood facing the wall with the controls, both palms flat against the marble, eyes on the floor.

"Do you want me to get the nurse?" I probed.

He shook his head, and the water droplets that had collected on the tips of his hair splashed across my cheek. "I'm fine."

He was the worst liar ever.

I set my phone on the counter and stepped into the shower. In my clothes and with my makeup still on. I didn't know why I did it, but my stupid heart demanded I hug him.

"What are you doing, doll?" Frank's whisper drifted at me through the noise of the beating stream as I wrapped my arms around his naked body. My cheek rested against his shoulder blade and my fingers traced the scars beneath his layers of ink. His chest expanded and shrunk as he breathed through the steam.

"I'm providing comfort," I said, kissing his back. Heat rushed to my lips. They didn't want to leave his skin.

The water was ruining my shirt and my jeans, but I didn't care. We were a wet bundle of nerves. An awkward embrace that lasted and lasted.

"Thank you," he said finally, his body abnormally still and sagging.

"For what?"

"For staying with me tonight."

"Do you really believe I'm only with you because of your good moves, Frank Wallace?" I whispered against his back. A ragged black rivulet of my mascara slid down his skin.

"Well..." He chuckled. "My real mother was a stripper, just so you know. The moves and the love of being in a spotlight are genetics."

My lips stretched into a smile against his taut muscles. "You were phenomenal tonight."

"You think?" His tone was cocky.

Despite being scared shitless, I tried to match the mood in his voice. Something told me he needed a pick-me-up. "For a guy who's half-titanium? Heck yeah."

"So...you're not with me for my good looks and money, Cassy Evans?" He laughed softly. "If my memory serves me right, you said something different a few weeks ago."

My palms ran up his abs and I pressed my body closer to his. *A few weeks...* It terrified me to realize how fast I was falling for him. They weren't years, they were a measly couple of months, yet he'd managed to crawl into my heart and stake his claim.

I needed to feel all of him—the solidity, the heat, the ache, the weakness, the strength—to say what I was about to say. To say what I should have said a long time ago. "Do you know why I'm with you, Frank?"

"Do tell." He drew one hand from the wall and laced his fingers with mine on his chest. The low thuds of his heart reverberated against the wet tangle of our hands.

"Because you make me laugh and because you make me happy." I brushed my chin against his back. My shirt clung to his skin. "And no one has made me happy in a very long time." *If ever.*

Music was the only constant in my life. Everyone else came and